Wild Call to Boulder Field

What Readers Are Saying About *Wild Call to Boulder Field*

"The dust of the trail, the kiss of the sun, a person who seeks his healing in the loyalty and fortitude of dogs and the penetrating magic of wild things—this novel has everything I myself resonate with. Most of all, it has love. A deep, heartfelt passion infuses these pages, sweeping us along in the hero's quest."
—Carl Safina, Author of *Becoming Wild and How Animal Cultures Raise Families, Create Beauty, and Achieve Peace*

"Here is a surprisingly good book by a dog and wild animal lover who stalks lost animals and the biggest cat on the continent in the boulder strewn maze of the Lower Sonoran Desert. The natural history is immaculate, but it is how Robert Ronning treads the edge of the sentient with animals both wild and domestic that got my attention: The author has an uncanny eye for this wild boundary, occasionally crossed by the huge cats and bears of our primordial dreams. There are great lessons of compassion in this book."
—Doug Peacock, Author, Naturalist, and Wilderness Warrior

"This is fiction that keeps on giving: It's a dangerous physical journey faced with courage and fierce determination, it's full of emotional connections, and it has a magical, mystical aura about it. It's a rare gem that leaves you daydreaming about what the characters will do next. It's about believing in and doing what is right and good! I can't think of one nature/animal lover who wouldn't adore this story."
—Jean P. Hankins, Writer and Artist *Tree of Life*

"A lively romp through the Arizona backcountry, in which the non-human characters are most fully alive."
—Richard Grant, *The Deepest South of All*

"Wild Call to Boulder Field is an utterly captivating read that seamlessly intertwines the characters (human, canine, wildlife, & nature/environmental) into a story that captures and holds the reader to the very end!"
—Debra Duncan, Canine Etiquette Behavior & Training Consultant

"In this romance where untamed nature itself seduces us, a man in search of his own peace encounters several other strays in the harsh canyons of Arizona--one of them is even a dog. Ronning is equally adept at moving the human heart and thrilling us with action. And did I mention the dog?"
—Becky Masterman, Author of *Rage Against the Dying*

"This is an original, heart-warming, and satisfying story for lovers of all creatures, great and small. I look forward to the sequel!"
—Jessica Groenendijk, Author of *The Giant Otter: Giants of the Amazon*

Wild Call

to

Boulder Field

An Arizona Trail Adventure

ROBERT RONNING

WILD CALL TO BOULDER FIELD

An Arizona Trail Adventure

Desert Paws Books (Tucson, Arizona)

RobertRonningAuthor.com

ISBN 979-8-9873338-0-8 (paperback)

ISBN 979-8-9873338-1-5 (digital)

Author's Note

A lawsuit-happy age compels the author to state that, although certain circumstances and characters in this story may bear resemblance to real people in the Southwest or elsewhere, all characters and incidents in this novel are purely the creation of the author's imagination. While the action takes place along the Arizona Trail, most of the referenced locations are fictional.

Subjects: Wildlife Adventure | Conservation Dogs | Hiking & National Parks

Purchase this book wherever books are sold.

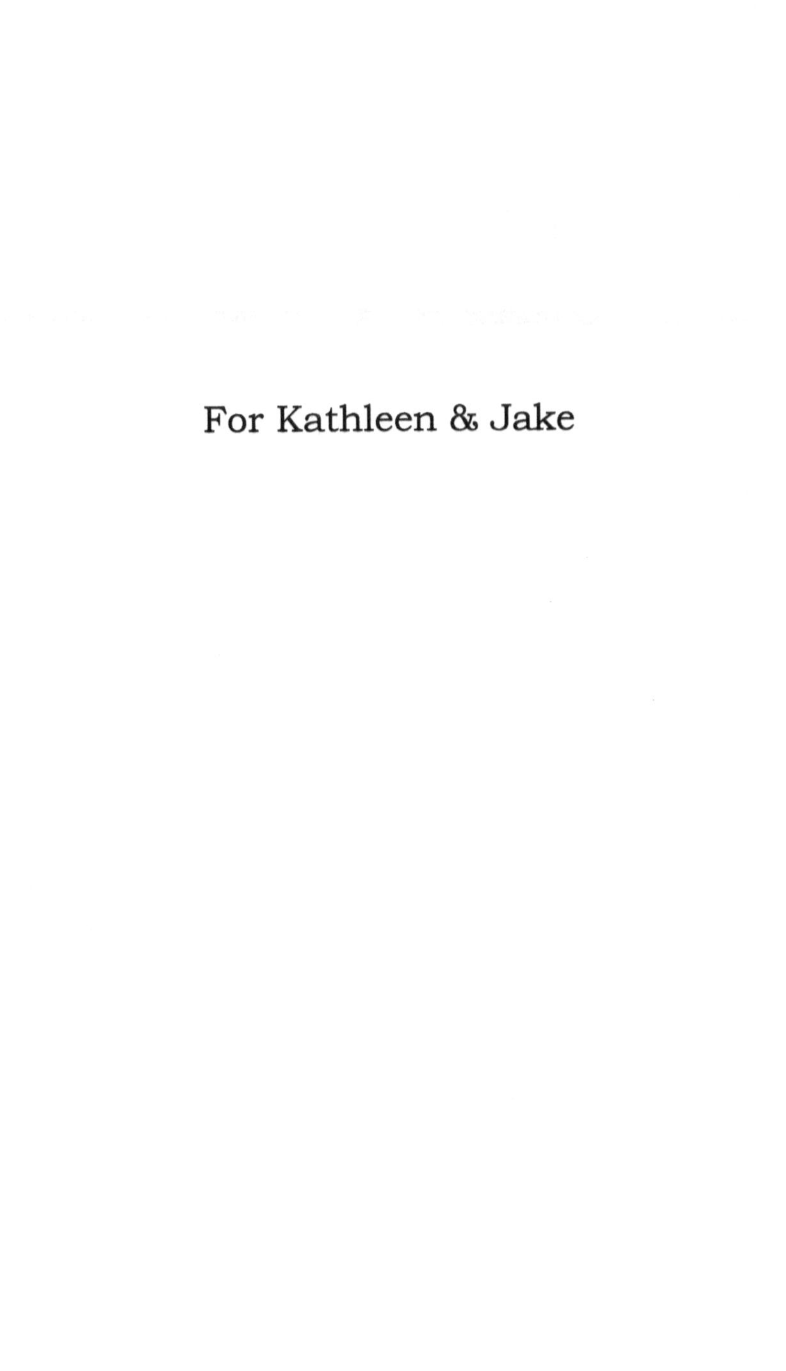

For Kathleen & Jake

Prologue

Spring, Southeastern Arizona

A large creature pads along a high desert ridge, its sleek body and long curling tail silhouetted against a magenta twilight. A granite-crowned mountain towers beyond, a dark canyon lies deep below, and boulders cluster in shadow—weird, eroded rock towers the desert people call "hoodoos." The animal's profile reflects a robust head and the powerful jaw of a top predator. It clutches an unknown prey and holds its head high to avoid dragging its kill along the rim trail. The game could be a young javelina, a coati, or a coyote—or is it smaller prey? The predator treads a crest toward a vast chasm to the south, a secret place familiar only to wildlife, natives, and a few animal biologists. The humans call it Jaguar Canyon, a wildlife path not far off the Arizona Trail, a rugged place where civilization meets the wild with surprising consequences.

1

"I'm a very loyal person. It's probably why I like dogs." —
Author Ann Patchett

Haggard and exhausted from another all-night search for his missing dog, Wade Conrad lay slumped in the cab of his pickup only a few miles from home. Whines and yelps coursed through his open window, but they did not rouse the park ranger.

A sudden agonized howl jerked Wade awake. "Abby!" he wailed. Disoriented, he rubbed his eyes against the bright sunlight flooding the cab of his Dodge RAM. He squinted at the tiny dust-pit of a town called Outpost, its main street a scanty mismatch of antique hawkers, outfitters, and junk purveyors. He peered across the road at a dying saguaro, its withered arms and head tipping back to desert ground. Yeah, ol' cactus, he moaned, I'm feelin' the same.

Sighing deeply, he started his truck. He'd moved no more than a hundred yards when he heard the full-throated, alarm-bark of a big dog.

His heart sank when he realized it wasn't Abby's bark at all.

Yet, a creature was in trouble and Wade, by nature, needed to investigate. He pulled up in front of the second-hand outfitter's store. As soon as he shut off the engine, he heard the whines. Commotion came from inside an old 4Runner, a metallic heap parked at a drunken angle, blocking the hitching rail in front of the general store.

Wade stomped to the truck. The sounds, heartbreaking yowls and groans from the rear of the vehicle, grew louder. Through a slobber-drenched window, he traded raw, pitiful looks with a large, black, short-haired dog crammed inside the hot cargo compartment.

He reached for the door, and the animal lunged, snarling raspy growls, slugging its huge front paws against the window. Wade faced a manic mix of LabShep, its snout oozing white drool down the glass, the entire vehicle shaking.

Wade tested the handle on the hatch door. Locked. Hell, it's pushing ninety and some shitheel's left his dog in this oven ... Baked Labrador on Sunday morning.

Wade muttered a litany of angry curses. His gut churned and twisted. He stared at the large black face and gaping brown eyes staring back at him, a window between him and the life of one fearful, foamy-mouthed creature, trapped and roasting.

"Damn," he griped. "Humans never did deserve dogs!"

He looked around—not a soul in sight. Did this no-count dust-pit of a place ever have a soul? Other than four-legged critters that count it home? He checked the sign on the outfitter's store—CLOSED. He darted down the street to the second-hand antique shop. Already, he felt himself losing it, something he would later admit in an anger-management session.

He spotted an old iron triangle hanging out front of the shop. He grabbed the striker and started banging the iron bars, sounding an alarm. Clang-clang-clang, clang-clang-clang. He rang the bars over and over, a harsh, annoying, tinny sound. He stopped abruptly and looked around.

Hell, that's gotta stir somebody or something! Nothin.'

So much for Plan A. Nothin' but sleepin' Jesus in a ghost town and tiny pockets of needy people barely hangin' on. Forget the "sleepy little village" crap. This place ain't sleepy. It's near-dead. Like this tortured dog close to heatstroke and a slow death because of some miserable Saturday-night loser. And nobody gives a rat's ass. Except maybe a kindred canine soul he could hear barking in a back alley off the main drag.

Wade launched Plan B, a woefully common solution in an animal emergency. From his pickup, he hauled out what he needed: a leash line, gloves, towel, and a hardwood mallet stowed behind his seat. At a water tank next to the hitching rail, he soaked the towel, squeezed it, and stomped back to the vehicle. He checked one last time for the dog's owner, then pulled on elbow-length gloves, left hand first. Before slipping on the second glove, Wade wiggled his fingers and shook his right hand as if trying to wake it up. Both gloves on, the leash in his left hand and the mallet in his right, he took aim away from the dog and shattered the cargo window.

A hot stench rushed out, like opening the door on a rancid, fiery oven. The deranged dog lashed out at once, lunging his bulky head toward his face. Wade bobbed to the side and took firm hold of the dog's collar, looping the leash at the top of the dog's neck for better control. A steady hand on the tight line kept the animal from struggling. Wade used a calm voice and touch to quiet him down. He pulled out some seventy pounds of panting male Lab—not much more than a runt by local standards—but way heftier than his Goldie, Abby.

Wade, six-foot and wiry, quickly had the dog wrapped in the wet towel. He carted him over to the water tank and let him lap up water. All in all, a good sign.

The whole time, Wade kept an angry eye on the deserted street. "Hey, there, big fella, where's that butthead that left you to suffer?" He had a soothing tone for the dog but itched for the owner to show his face. "You wouldn't mind if I ripped the bastard limb from limb, would you?"

The main entrance of the vet clinic was always locked on Sunday mornings. Wade carried the dog around to the side door and managed a rap on it.

He felt the animal's quick but steady heartbeat against his chest. When the door opened, a diminutive, sturdy-looking woman in her mid-forties, same as Wade, beamed up at him. Marie, the vet's assistant, lived in rooms at the back of the clinic. If anyone had a heart and soul in Outpost, it was sincere and sensible Marie.

"What'd you drag in this time, Wade?"

"Found this poor fella baking in a locked 4Runner. He's mighty overheated."

"Why, this unfortunate boy is Spike." Marie placed a hand on the dazed dog panting heavily in Wade's arms.

"You know the dolt that owns this animal?"

"Yeah, I'm sorry to say I do. He's a dirt-bag. I'd call him a real primate, but I guess that'd be an insult to monkeys." Wade followed her to the exam room and laid Spike gently on the stainless-steel table. Marie had a rectal thermometer inserted before the dog even noticed. "Let's get you stabilized and cooled down, boy." While examining him, she had Wade fetch another damp towel to wrap around Spike.

"Looks like you caught another one just in time, Wade. His temperature's elevated but not in the danger zone. Doc'll want some blood. We'll watch him closely."

She put a protective cone around Spike's neck, shaved his front leg and attached IV fluids. They moved him to a recovery kennel.

She made a weary face, "I swear, Wade, you attract critters like flies to cow pies. A coyote last time, right?"

"Long story."

He felt her usual penetrating gaze. "Hardly recognize you in the civvies." Everybody knew Wade by his park ranger uniform, not the Lee jeans or a blue-denim shirt, topped with a ball cap instead of the broad-brimmed, high-crowned ranger hat.

He shrugged, folding his arms across his chest. He set his square jaw. Marie noted new grey hairs sprouting, plus what Katy had called his "wounded eyes" these days. A sadness and restless anger he couldn't seem to shake—to those who cared to notice.

"I suppose Katy's got her nose in a book this morning. Doc Ruth's best student ever, you know." He nodded but avoided eye contact.

Marie tended to Spike while the ranger radiated angry waves over the lowlife that left Spike near heat stroke. He wandered into the waiting room where he stopped at the bulletin board and glanced at the notices. He zeroed in on the picture of his Abby. His face assumed a muddled mix of gloom and pain. He sensed Marie's steely eyes on his back.

"No leads on Abby yet?"

He started to speak but only shook his head.

Marie waited. Softly, she said, "She's sure to turn up. Don't give up hope."

Out the window, big Mt. Wrightson to the northwest held his attention.

"You're as lively as a fencepost these days," she said, trying to change his mood. "You know what they're going to put on your gravestone, don't you?" Marie paused, eyes wide, focused on Wade's back. "Here rests Wade Conrad, Park Ranger. He only cared for dogs and wild critters."

2

"Lane County Wildlife Homecare Network wishes that more motorists who hit animals would stop to see if they're actually dead. If they are, motorists ought to drag them off the road, so that other animals, whether offspring or scavengers, won't get hit as well … Death is not the worst thing. What's repugnant is the suffering. They have the same central nervous system as we have. They experience the same pain." —Kathy Kirsh, Wildlife Homecare Volunteer

Wade steered his beige RAM through a long curve south of Outpost until he came upon a tawny heap at the edge of Gray Wolf Loop. He pulled up close, his heart jack-hammering against his chest—was it Abby? His emergency flashers on, he got out and slowly approached the body.

Mountain lion, a still mass spread along the shoulder. Likely a fast, careless driver had left a big healthy tom for roadkill. Wade was sorry to see it, but couldn't help feeling relief that it wasn't his Goldie. As days had pushed into weeks, little else was on his mind. If he was awake, he was searching.

One of his ranger duties was to clear road kill from the byway. Mostly they were ground squirrels, skunks, and cottontails crossing the road to another part of their habitat. Rescuing house pets in hot vehicles didn't call for much special gear, but dealing with feral creatures hurt or dying was another thing. He traveled equipped to deal with them—a salmon net with a long handle, two sizes of pet carriers, disposable wipes for his hands, plastic bags, and those elbow-length leather gloves to ward off fangs and claws—with most of the gear stowed in the storage box of his pickup bed.

Wade examined the lion for any obvious trauma but suspected fatal internal injuries. He hoped the cat hadn't suffered long. Wildlife kill numbers were grim; one creature gone every 11.5 seconds nationally. Bobcats, coyotes, and other mammals and reptiles killed in his park every year—some 51,000 vertebrates dying just trying to navigate their own habitats, wiped out by distracted or self-involved motorists, some not even aware of running over a sentient creature. Damn idiots.

If the public at large thought of these animals at all, it was "roadkill." And it was the keystone species that caught their attention. While the power and charisma of these top predators could not be denied, most humans were unaware of the role these big predators and smaller vertebrates played in restoring and maintaining the balance between habitat and the environment.

He carefully pulled the cat off the blacktop, well clear of the shoulder, and called the ranger station so they could report the dead animal to the Native American Wildlife Society. There would be tribal interest in retrieving the carcass for religious and cultural purposes and to honor the dead animal. Back on the road, Wade remembered Big Girl, another lion hit and killed on the same stretch a few years back. More than a few mourned her passing. He approved of the locals nicknaming the wildlife. Naming cut against scientific protocol, but he figured if folks felt connected with the wild animals, that was all to the good. Even as a ranger, he reckoned he needed the naming bond to do his best caring work. "Give her a name, dammit, not a number," he grumbled.

Like truckers, Wade had a deer whistle attached to the front bumper of his pickup, alerting on-the-road wildlife as he passed through their habitats. But most park visitors remained clueless and easily distracted, thus the carnage. He took heart from locals who had a need to keep track of the wildlife. One old, eccentric resident culled area roads of dead animals, even giving them memorials, so the rumor went.

He turned onto an ancient trail at the edge of the National Forest. Long ago, it was a wildlife path, later a Native American walkway, eventually morphing into a broad, graveled Forest Service road for logging trucks and emergency fire and safety traffic supporting the timber industry. Now it was called Sierra Passage. He had another dusty five miles to get to his ranch house, desert scrub below him and a vast mountain landscape of rich conifer forest far above.

Wade usually took this gravel stretch slow and easy to keep the dust down, watching for the odd coyote or other faunae at daybreak or twilight. But wild sightings were of little interest lately and his relentless search for his lost Abby left him bone tired. After another all-night hunt, he was headed back home, worn, unshaven, stone-faced, more downcast and disheartened than ever.

Wade labored out of his pickup and headed toward the front porch. Halfway to the steps, he felt lightheaded, his legs weak and unsteady. He stopped and bent over for a moment, then managed to push on, barely reaching the porch before falling.

He heard a faraway coyote cry.

He tried to get to his feet but folded, collapsing sideways back onto the porch, gently coming to rest on the pine planks. Eyes drooping, the last thing he heard before going blank was the fading call of the coyote.

A beast with a big bushy tail passed by, a rabbit hanging from its mouth. It circled back and made a closer pass, no more than ten feet away. And no, it wasn't a rabbit but a small, pale-colored dog clutched in its jaws. The poor thing hung limp, pointy ears sagging, eyes hardly open, barely half-alive. The ranger lunged at the beast to rescue the dog but missed and stumbled forward. As the creature circled again, Wade took it to be a rare mix of coyote and dog—a coy-dog—a hybrid creature bigger than a coyote, more like a wolf.

As if from a distance, Wade saw himself lunge again, feeling rough fur at its neck but missing as it veered away. Angry and determined, he watched the animal circle twice, toying with him, then boldly moving in closer. With a last pool of strength, the ranger sprang forward and punched the beast squarely in the muzzle, fist smashing against hard bone. The strange coy-dog gave a yelp and leaped back, the dog slipping from its jaws and the beast dashing into the brush. The dog lay quietly on its side, amber eyes just open, watching ... waiting. The ranger dropped to his knees and reached out for the dog.

"Wade! Can you hear me? Wake up!"

Katy knelt next to him. Katy, the only lady friend he could abide around the place; the only one to put up with him, ever.

"You passed out right on the porch." She had a bottle of water and a wet towel in her hands. She propped his head in her lap and pressed the towel against his face.

He lay mute and woozy, his right hand in a tightfisted grip. He tried to focus on Katy—her dazzling green eyes wide open, her straight nose, strong chin, the perfect lips. Her short, dark-brown hair combed back neatly, the way he liked, the way she always looked when she left for classes.

She slowly got him to a sitting position on the steps. He tried relaxing his right fist, still closed. Katy massaged his hand, thick scars running from three fingers almost to the wrist.

"One of these nights you'll stumble onto some rancher's back porch. He'll mistake you for an intruder and take a potshot in the dark."

She looked bleak as he turned his head away. Most mornings now, Katy didn't ask about Abby. She didn't have to.

"I'm just leaving—are you going to sleep now?" She placed the bottle of water in his left hand.

He nodded and looked straight ahead, out toward the road. Her class schedule was tight. He didn't want to be a bother. She'd left teaching, now a part-time pet groomer and back in school to become a vet's assistant. Ultimately, she dreamed of becoming a nurse practitioner, for animals, perhaps for Doc Ruth.

He sensed Katy's eyes on him, his sorry state most likely. Both of them feeling helpless, like displaced souls with Abby gone. And the trouble at work was eating away at him. People telling him what a stranger he was in his civvies. He knew Katy truly hurt for him, on a required leave of absence, not allowed to do what he loved. He tried to reassure her not to worry. Still, these days he knew he was a bit of a riddle—or more like a pain in the ass.

"Why not take more time off?"

He knew she wasn't thinking of just him, that she was thinking of his effect on co-workers and park visitors as well. Who wanted to be around a human time bomb? He was used to reading their reactions—well, animals yes, people not so much. "Any day now, she'll turn up," Katy said. "And you'll need to be here." After several weeks, he noticed she no longer mentioned Abby by name.

Abby's disappearance was such a mystery—gone without a trace, no signs of where or how she had vanished. He plunged into a deep hurt, and his growing anger and grief had him wrapped into one miserable piece of work.

"There's always The Trail," she added, trying to be upbeat.

He did take to the Arizona Trail whenever his life got chaotic and stressed out. The trail helped clear his mind, limber his body, and cleanse his soul. It beat popping pills or boozing. Sometimes Katy had even come along with him and Abby.

"You know I've tried," he said.

"It really hasn't helped?"

"Hell no." A hike without Abby? He'd given up and turned back.

"If you do try again, don't be a bonehead. Promise you'll take your fancy GPS—and your cell." He gave a half-hearted nod.

He watched Katy, clutching a bundle of vet training manuals, hurry away for school in her old yellow Mazda 323. Drained from his dusk-till-dawn search, catching glimpses of wild-eyed creatures through the blackness, he sat staring up at the Santa Rita Mountains looming to the northwest. The bizarre dream about a hybrid creature and a dirty-white dog troubled him. An omen, a signal to move on? He hadn't the faintest idea, but for sure there was one thing Wade Conrad didn't know, and that was how to give up.

Get on with it—keep up the search.

When he heard another distant coyote call, he couldn't help wondering. Could they have taken Abby?

Fatigue was taking its toll.

3

"Anyone who spends time in the Santa Rita Mountains comes to appreciate the rich biodiversity that exists within the Sky Islands … If the theory holds that large mammals are excellent indicators for overall ecosystem health, the Santa Ritas make up a vibrant oasis in Southern Arizona."
—Matthew J. Nelson and the Arizona Trail Association

Wade headed for the Arizona Trail a few days later— after a firm nudge from Katy. He put his search for Abby on hold, and they drove along an old native pathway through Coronado National Forest. When they reached the trailhead, Katy got out too, but watched in silence as he pulled his backpack from the bed of the RAM. When he managed eye contact, she came forward and wrapped her arms around him, holding him for a time.

She offered to drop a resupply of food and water at the next trailhead. He'd have none of it. What he carried on his back would do just fine. He toted fewer supplies than rugged explorer John Colter, who left the Lewis and Clark party in 1807, boldly heading into the wild with only a thirty-pound backpack. Offering few words in parting, Wade turned toward the trail with only a glance back and a final wave.

Retreating from the human species, Wade hiked into the Santa Ritas. Not the lowland desert landscape that out-of-state folks associate with the Southwest, but higher, wilderness country most visitors never see—rugged slopes, lush forests, and diverse wildlife.

Wade was also avoiding his anger-management counselor who, during their first and only session, had said, "I understand you're experiencing explosive outbursts of anger."

He did not reply but gave her the once-over—short blonde hair, glasses, a bit young to him to be counseling adults.

"All right, Mr. Conrad, let's begin this way. How long have you felt troubled?"

"You mean, how long have I been a pissed-off park ranger?" Officially, he was on *forced* leave from his job rangering national parks in Arizona.

"What pisses you off, Mr. Conrad?"

"Just call me Wade, okay? It's fairly easy to remember if you imagine a job wading through the mounds of human garbage dumped on national parks."

"Well, why don't you tell me about that?"

He gave her a skeptical look and took a deep breath. "I don't think so. People don't much care to listen to work crap."

"It's my job, but we can come back to that. I've looked over your intake questionnaire, Wade. Clearly, you appear to be what I might call a cynophilist. Is that a fair observation?"

"If you mean I'm fond of animals, sure. They don't lie or cheat you. They just live and love."

"You certainly show real concern for animals. One question asked was, 'If a human and a dog were both drowning, who do you save first?' You answered, 'That depends.'" She raised an eyebrow.

"Well, it depends on the human. Though my dog, like most, would probably save herself."

"Well, that fits with what you wrote in the comments section." She tapped her iPad, reading a passage. "You said a friend once called you 'The Pied Piper of canines, coyotes, and critters.' Could you comment on that?"

"Well, it speaks for itself, doesn't it?" He went silent, but he could see she was waiting for more. "Marie, the vet's assistant," he gave up unwillingly. "She's sorta convinced I'm a regular magnet for wild beings. Maybe that's because I've pretty much given up on humans. If you'll excuse me," Wade said, standing. "I got a dog to see to."

Wade wouldn't be going back there, orders or not. He figured the Arizona Trail was better therapy than a green counselor any day. What finer rehab was there than a hike along any stretch of the 800 miles of Arizona trails crisscrossing the mountains and valleys, from Mexico all the way to Utah? And he'd tell this to anybody that asks when he gets back.

For most of the first day out, there was not one brush with another human. Of course, that couldn't last forever, not in the popular hiking month of May. The desert was on the cusp of a major weather change— ninety-degree temperatures already baking the lower elevations, all of life thirsty for the coming monsoon season.

Wade flinched when he heard a bark on the path ahead, but he instantly recognized the bark of a small dog—likely a day hiker out for a stretch with a mutt off leash. He pushed on and would say something about the leash rule if he ran into them.

Apart from the bark, there was another call creeping into his senses, a distant *drum-drum*, a sound he couldn't identify. At times it rumbled like faint thunder; at other times it sounded more mysterious—a deep groan of a nameless beast from some other wild place. He listened for dog barks, but now there was only silence.

Smoke. For sure, he smelled smoke. In wildfire season! His sense of smell was acute, especially for detecting smoldering campfires. It came from the slope below, a rogue camper. The odor set off his inner fire alarm; his adrenaline surged. About a quarter mile up the trail, a thin plume of smoke curled above the trees, barely visible to the naked eye, but his was a trained eye.

"No Campfire" signs had been posted earlier than usual on the mountain trails, with experts predicting early monsoons and heavy lightning storms. Ever since the Corral Gulch fire of '05, when he was among the hundreds supporting the firefighters, he made a solemn oath to smother all fires on his watch. The Gulch fire was the result of lightning, but each year the highest numbers were human-caused.

Wade was on it, his nose leading him forward, chasing the aroma of dried mesquite, piñon, and scrub in the air. He came to a small clearing and found the faint plume rising from an unquenched campfire, built underneath overhanging branches, no fire ring of rocks around the firepit for containment. "Not a Boy Scout or brain among 'em," he muttered, quickly dousing the ashes with water from his flask. After laying hands over the pit, certain it was smothered stone cold, he returned to the trail, ready to throttle the fire-starter—should they cross paths.

As if the fire wasn't enough, other messy, negative stuff invaded his mind. His leave of absence from the Park Service troubled him and he replayed past grievances in a continuous flashback-loop. There was the flap over the parking ticket he'd scrawled on toilet paper from a Port-a-Potty. A so-called "contractor" had rumbled up in a big, honking Land Cruiser, loaded with traps and weapons for "harvesting" coyotes and other wild "pests." To Wade, they were nothing but paid animal assassins hired by Wildlife Services. The ranger happened to stick the ticket on the window of the behemoth blocking the ranger shack just as the bounty hunter returned. When he realized what the ranger stuck to his windshield, a quarrel ensued, culminating in a shouting match between an angry park ranger and a contractor paid to kill wild animals.

Wade couldn't shake the memory of the quarrel. He tried picking up his pace, but sheer physical motion wasn't helping and the whole ugly outcome came flooding back. Unbidden, his brain reran the aftermath.

Blake, his park supervisor, summoned him to the ranger shack. "What were you thinking?" Blake began.

"Is that what you call a trick question?"

Blake—stout and getting on, his hiking days over— remained seated and silent, waiting.

"I reacted, that's all."

"Well, let me ask you this. What should you have said?"

"Let me see." Wade searched for an answer. He assumed a forced smile. "Hello there, sir. Welcome to Mayberry!"

"Oh, cut it, Wade. Get serious."

Wade couldn't decide how he felt about his latest tangle with Wildlife Services. Yes, he was consumed by Abby's disappearance, but national parks were transitioning to a cross between a zoo and a prison for the wildlife. How could he hang around to be a part of that?

"Well," he said with a straight face, "with your ranger shack blocked by an animal assassin, I suppose I should have suggested he take the toilet paper and shove—"

"That's enough!" Blake roared.

Wade headed for the door.

"I don't know, Wade." Blake shook his head, taking several deep breaths. "Time and again, you gotta do crazy things—showdowns with armed contractors, risky run-ins with those big predator friends of yours, and tangling with a badger." He glanced at Wade's scarred right hand. "Aren't you a little old for all this Grizzly Adams stuff?"

Wade didn't answer. He preferred thinking of his actions as 'good deeds gone a little haywire' at times, like the lost calf he carried a couple miles back to Cliff's ranch.

"Wait!" Blake called, waving him back to his desk. "For the time being, I want your badge."

Wade approached the desk, unpinning the badge from his pocket.

"Take the stinkin' thing!" He flipped it on the desk. "Who needs a stinkin' badge anyway!"

For the next few days, he had to ponder his fate—not for the first time. In the end, given his current grief, stress, and search for Abby, he was placed on temporary LOA. He also had to consent to enter a government-sponsored program for anger management and not to wear a park ranger uniform until a counselor determined he had better control of his temper. *Hell's bells!*

His pace quickened as his body tried to shed off a whole month of misery. A few dozen paces on, he heard the trickle of moving water, and quiet voices—not the raucous voices of urban crazies who leave hot campfire pits, but he reckoned he'd better confirm. Straight ahead, he spotted two small humans sitting on a large rock next to a creek, their backs toward him, attired in what appeared to be brand-spanking-new hiking outfits, topped by wide-brimmed canvas hats. Wade made a steady approach and stopped a polite distance from the two.

"You folks wouldn't own that campfire back on the path, off the trail?"

He noticed their tiny backpacks, colorful shades of pink in flowery designs, a dainty variety popular for strolling through shopping malls. "Campfires are no longer allowed," Wade went on, "definitely not on this slope in a no-fire season." He paused, waiting for them to turn around. "On top of that," he continued, "someone neglected to smother that fire out cold."

He waited for a response, but they seemed to be ignoring him. He took a deep, impatient breath and raised his voice. "Other than the risk of burning up the east slope of this mountain, I'm hoping the persons in question are keeping out of trouble." Again, he got no answer.

"Hello!" he shouted, stepping forward.

Startled, the two turned in unison and looked across at the ranger. They pulled earbuds from their ears and took off their sunglasses. Wade studied them, two elderly ladies smiling back at him. Could be twins. Twin grannies. How the devil did they ever make it up Corkscrew Climb?

"Sorry, young man. Did you say something?" from one.

"That campfire back down the trail?" He waved a thumb behind him. "You ladies didn't build a campfire, did you?"

"Oh no, sir," they replied as one.

"Because that would be a serious park offense."

"Bird watching," one said, waving her binoculars. "While we listen to hummingbird lectures," the other explained, raising an earbud.

Yup, couple of hummer junkies. Mountain's full of them this time of year. Why couldn't more mountain visitors be the same—innocent, harmless binocular bearing old birds?

He heard a buzz in the distance, an annoying sound he knew only too well. He fidgeted in place while he tried to get a mental fix on the location.

"Sir, are you a park ranger, by any chance?"

"Why? Do I look like a park ranger, ma'am?"

"Well, yes, you look just like one," they both chimed in, nodding at each other.

"Even without that cute park ranger hat."

"Or the uniform."

"Well, I am, ladies, but I'm out of uniform today."

The familiar whine grew louder. Frustration bubbled up.

The ladies paused, trading whispers. "Well, we think you look just like that Indiana Jones," one said.

The other added, "You know, the man who played him in the movie."

Wade jerked his head high in the air, a deer sensing danger. The awful drone came from off-road, all-terrain vehicles, a grinding noise of relentless chainsaws felling tree after tree. As the infuriating buzz grew louder and closer, the ranger homed in on its wails just below on Corkscrew Climb.

"No motorized vehicles allowed!" he shouted. "Not up in this stretch of wilderness. No ATVs—and no fires!" he shouted.

The grannies exchanged astonished looks.

Without another word, Wade charged off toward the vexing noise, breaking into a run, his backpack bouncing on his back. He pictured a gang of ATV-ers joyriding the trail. Joy for them, chaos for the wildlife. How many posted signs can a doofus ignore? When he reached a high point on the Corkscrew, Wade spotted the culprits twisting along the switchbacks below. Two of nature's assassins, so-called "innocent recreationists," running their crude toys along tight hairpin turns up a grade that truly tested seasoned hikers. He watched them carving ever wider turns, invading the brush beyond the hairpins, bulldozing new motor paths, destroying wildlife habitat as they went. Why can't a nation with over half a billion acres of national forests keep safe from these wheelie yahoos? But, no, Bundy Boys operate with their own bill of rights—we want a frickin' road or two of our own for our use. Public lands belong to us. Get outta our way.

Wade watched the marauders moving up the Corkscrew, doing their best to widen the hairpin turns for future ATV runs. In another couple years, the Corkscrew might resemble a downhill mogul run. Sure, why not let the news spread about a really cool ATV recreation site called Corkscrew Climb. Craploads of fun!

And there was Wade, no uniform, no badge.

I've seen it all, he reckoned. *Paths carved to nowhere, hikers taking wrong turns or worse— getting stranded at dead ends far from safe trailheads.*

When they were close to the top of the Corkscrew, Wade quickly moved in to greet them. Like angry lawnmowers, they roared around the last hairpin. Wade stood in the middle of the trail with his arm raised to signal a halt. They slid to a stop in front of him, both riders leather-fitted, head to toe. They looked surprised. They pulled their dark goggles off for a better look at Wade. Surprise turned to aggravation.

"What the hell's the celebration?" Wade called out. He thought of Katy and her warning for anyone who casually mentioned the words ATV or quad, 'Don't get Wade Conrad started!'

Wade was about to get started.

Both twenty-somethings—one had a biker look, the other a skinhead—glanced at each other, the question on their faces. "Celebration?"

The biker got out of his ATV. "Hey, man, what's up?"

"What's up?" Wade pointed toward the Corkscrew they'd just climbed. "You are. You're on a hiking trail— but you aren't hiking."

"So?" asked the skinhead, hopping out of his ATV.

"You need to turn those ATVs around and carefully vacate to the nearest trailhead."

"What makes you—"

"No ATVs allowed," Wade added, purposefully keeping his voice calm. He heard Katy's voice again in his head. 'Wade is no park ranger to tangle with when it comes to tearing up the national parks.'

"The signs are posted all along the trail."

"Hey, man, what business is it of yours?" the biker barked.

Wade remained silent.

"Not like yer a park ranger or nothin,'" the skinhead added.

"Yeah, let's see a badge," the biker challenged.

"Badge?" Wade felt that familiar gloom pass through him. "I don't need a stinkin' badge! No ATVs allowed, period!" He pulled out a pad and pencil, looked carefully at each of them, then slowly moved in position to jot down their vehicle license plate numbers.

Wade watched them consider their options. He calmly put away his pencil and pad with their plate numbers. He hovered in a place he'd been many times, waiting for an animal's next move, or, in this case, a challenge from a couple of possible thugs. But they retreated and got back in their ATVs.

They retraced their path back along the Corkscrew, waving farewell by flipping him the bird in a well-practiced, synchronized motion, with nary a look back. Gone, no doubt to terrorize another wildlife habitat. He shook his head. What's one more confrontation to a park ranger on leave? A chance to do a thing right, that's what.

Craving a quiet space, a trail far away from soulless dullards and the vile noise of their mind-numbing toys, Wade charged on, searching only for a place to breathe easier, with no humans!

4

"Large predators evolved with humans, and they learned,
that's one nasty predator." —Wildlife biologist William
Newmark

A strange feeling swept over Wade, an eerie sense of a phantom presence. Not the earlier distant drumming, but a thing alive—animal or human, he couldn't tell. But it was a being matching his pace, causing him to sweat. He slowed to a three-mile per hour pace, a crawl for him, listening for the slightest sound—a bark, a cry, another rumble. But he could not model a picture of the presence moving along with him. A strangeness lingered, a thing haunting him.

He chose to pitch camp in a small, bowl-shaped clearing against a slope of trees and boulders, with his back protected, the area before him open for observation. He wasn't packing a tent. It wasn't necessary for the mild desert nights of May in the Santa Ritas. He only had a lightweight sleeping bag and bivy netting to keep the bugs at bay. Ultralight he traveled; no camp stove and no hot meals, but a pack with plenty of snacks.

It's the best way to go, keep it simple.

He attached his tiny headlight to his cap and settled back to snack while he watched the orange twilight dissolve around the camp. To the west, a large dry wash stretched below him, awaiting the flood of water to come with the monsoons. He would keep an eye on that wash for whatever was out there.

He soon found relief in the serenading yip-yips of a prairie tenor. They persisted, signaling a coyote on the slope above his bivouac. Had the animal been tracking him? He thought it unlikely. He felt he knew them as he knew himself—and what a heart he had for these creatures! The eternal, literal underdogs of the wild, cussed and slaughtered by most livestock ranchers and sheep farmers, ever quick to demonize them as the chief consumers of their stock.

But do they eat enough? Wade wondered, echoing the words of irascible wilderness writer Ed Abbey. Even in his fretful, troubled state, Wade knew how absurd it was to blame coyotes for every livestock loss. Never once had he laid eyes on a fat coyote, in his own backyard or in the foothills close by. Mr. Coyote, dumped on for two hundred years, and still a top-survivor species. Despite the torturous traps, the poisons, and the relentless mass killings, the coyote would endure and remain free.

Whup-whup. Wade smiled in spite of a feeling of uneasiness.

Higher up on the mound behind him, Wade detected rustling—bushes shaking, rocks shifting. And unmistakable ticking sounds—animal paws and nails on the move. Tic-tic-tic-tic-tic. Nails tapping rock. Tic tic-tic-tic-tic, and huh-huh-huh of breath. An animal on the hunt.

A short yip was followed by prolonged breathiness and a deep, creepy groan. To Wade, the sound was foreign in these parts ... at least until the creature started dogging him.

Wade sensed a big predator in a foul temper with an aching belly. He strained hard to listen, anchored to his campsite. Everything disappeared but the breathiness, the quick in-and-out passage of air. Then a sudden barrage of alarming yip-yips, and the scene took a menacing turn. Heavier, grunting uh-uh-uh-uhs erupted among the higher mounds of boulders. He had a fairly keen ear, but they were moving fast and he couldn't pinpoint their exact location.

Was he hearing more than one set of four legs lurking around his camp? This was just too pushy and creepy. Ol' coyote was not alone. Paws padded closer, ten or fifteen yards away from him on the bank above. Big paws.

Inner alarms triggered. What were these animals? Were they setting up for a kill? And who would be the kill? Wade stood frozen—taking shallow, quick breaths—hyper-focused on the restless footfalls for a full minute.

At last, he exhaled and resumed a steady, quiet breath. Back and forth, he changed his mind. First it was a solo four-legged creature, then he figured it for two. It? They? Animals moved in a quiet, restive search for something—right above him.

Sunset squeezed a last orange flame on the horizon, and the campsite faded to dark brown. Think! A thing or things stalking, hunting up there. Time for a look behind those big boulders. Now, before this slope turns into a black shroud. Best not to delay and risk an ambush later. Wade switched his headlight on and moved slowly, quietly, one foothold to the next, with sporadic pauses to listen.

He stepped atop the ridge. There. Right there. He caught a glimpse of fur, but in shadows he was unable to tell what it was. His headlamp revealed a large form with two glowing, golden eyes reflecting back at him. Ranger and wild predator in a face-off? Wade took an abrupt step back, and the creature darted off under cover of dark and brush, leaving only the swish of bushes behind.

Coyote? It would be the biggest one he'd ever seen, if so. Whatever it was, it was gone. He light-footed it back to his sleeping bag. Darkness sank in; quiet resumed.

But, damn! Just as he settled in, he heard something up there again. A whimper? He focused. The whimper changed to a whine; one he'd heard earlier in the day. Something's under those boulders that needs knowing.

Wade took a long breath and slid out on the ground. His headlight guided him back up the rocks. He homed in on the whines, which came from an old oak standing between two huge boulders. He crept toward the sound and his light spotted a pocket hole at the root of the tree. A burrow. Coyote? Fox? Badger? He wanted no part of it.

But he bent to shine a beam on the spot and was jolted by whimpers. An animal crying out, hurt and scared. In rescue mode, Wade dropped to his hands and knees and peered cautiously into the burrow. Lo and behold, he faced what had to be a canine. Coyote pup? Nope—the eyes not wild enough; the pointy black nose was not the puggy snout coyote pups are born with.

However unlikely, he was betting the creature he faced was a stray dog.

Ignoring his gimpy right hand, he reached into the burrow with his left—foolishly, he realized, but went ahead anyway—and felt around in the hole for a body. It squirmed about, but he got hold of a firm, furry tail. He eased the creature free of the pocket and into his light.

Canine, for sure, fifteen pounds at least. More than a pup, small but not a toy dog, breed to be determined. The tangled mass of dirt, wet hair, and bones trembled and whimpered. No identity tags. A cursory check of the underpinnings indicated a neutered male. *Great. A house pet. Just great.*

Back at camp on bedding, the little stray cried and whined in Wade's lap.

What a fine mess. He shook his head. He tried to calm the dog, stroking his back in the vigorous way he did with Abby. From his pack, he poured water in a plastic mess kit, and the fella eagerly lapped it up.

But when offered a small piece of jerky, he would have none of it. Wade gave a reluctant sigh and took a dog biscuit from his pocket, an 'Abby treat' he always carried, just in case. Only one left. The runt already had it sniffed out. He had no choice but to break off a piece. The little beggar chewed ravenously, head bobbing up and down.

By headlight, Wade tugged a long string of cord from his backpack lining. He broke off the end braid and unwound the tough line into a long slim lead with a small loop tied at one end. He wrapped it around the dog's neck for a collar and tied the other end to a bivy string. Then he crawled back into his bag with the squatter snuggled next to him.

Another hour of blackness crept by. He had a fair idea what that yellow-eyed creature was hunting. The orphan pushed against him, having no problem sleeping through the whups of distant calls and songs.

But it was not so easy for the ranger. He recalled ancient stories of desert dwellers who claimed to recognize coyotes traveling through the dry river beds. As a boy, Wade imagined Indian warriors returning from the dead to call out in the night, through the bodies of coyotes. In his young innocence, he believed they sent native signals to faraway tribes through their unmistakable yips and vocal utterances. As a ranger, Wade had come to recognize their different voices, able to ID individual coyotes that hung around the ranch house. And now and again, he had observed behavior of whole families of coyotes in the nearby foothills.

But here in the dark, putting meaning and intention to these calls baffled him without direct observation of family interactions. Shorn of body language there on a mountain in pitch black, he could only guess about the number and relationships of these animals.

The calls faded, but he kept alert for the shadowy predator. Uneasy and wide awake, he asked himself questions. What the devil were those eerie sounds, those deep groans and grunting uh-uh-uhs? Was it some mysterious mammal calling out to its kin, all the while looking for a meal on its nightly prowl? Was this unknown creature still lurking? Wade made an involuntary shudder.

Somehow, it had fallen to him to protect this house pet from wild predators. A dog in tow and he had less than one dog biscuit for food. He thought of Katy needling him in his stormier moods. "To whom much is given, much is expected," she teased, but serious.

"Wonderful," he growled and drew a deep breath. "What a perfect, peaceful getaway."

5

"People react with fear because they have been led to believe that any wild animal bigger than a breadbox must be dangerous. Wild animals certainly deserve our respect. Despite their reputations, large wild animals are just not very dangerous. By far the most dangerous animals in North America, as measured in human fatalities, are bees, wasps and hornets … Coyotes are nowhere on the list." —Professor Peter Alagona

Jesse Hayduke could not get through another awful never-ending night, curled up in a fetal pose, shaking and sweating by a campfire long gone cold. Fear and panic gripped him through hours of cat shrieks and coyote calls from the wild darkness beyond.

In his blackest moments, Jesse was sure that if the creature didn't eat him, it would drive him crazy instead. He had to get his scrawny frame in motion, for sure before first light. He could only walk the bike, his headlight guiding him far from the camp, away from those eerie, endless sounds of menace.

His destinations seldom well planned, Jesse had foolishly assumed he could bike his way along the Arizona Trail, despite eco-volunteers warning him that riding was mostly not allowed—not even possible. He'd already learned that going lickety-split, he nearly ended up in a cactus or some other vicious plant. Now, after slow going—and several spills—he had to admit they were right.

They mentioned alternate trail routes for bicyclists, but those were far away. He could only hope that the closer he got to the trailhead, the better his chances of riding—and not having to resort to hike-a-biking, with his custom bike slung over his shoulder. Maybe he'd even reach the trailhead before noon. Stay calm, he kept telling himself. You can't push through day and night with no rest.

But the pace was so slow and spooky in the dark, with only his bike light to lead the way up and down the shadowy path. It veered left and right and he moved carefully, walking his bike without a thought of trying to hop on and pedal. The farther he got from the campsite and the terrible night, the more he hoped luck would carry him to daybreak. He sensed he was still not alone, that something lurked in the blotchy, black outlines of trees and bushes crowding his way. The beast seemed to be following, surrounding him, tracking his every step on the path. Would darkness never end and first light ever appear? Was he only hearing the sounds and stirrings of natural animals crawling and hopping about their turf, going about their own harmless lives? Or was he going crazy?

Another fear lingered in a crevice of his brain. Eco-volunteers had warned him about predator attacks against mountain bikers, in Arizona and all over the world. On his bike, they teased, he might end up prey to some ferocious animal. Best be on his guard! If they were joking, Jesse didn't consider it one bit funny.

Not that he would ever tell anybody about his personal demons. How could he ever talk about his painful secret, a deep-rooted fright of wild cats? His worst fear always haunted him, made more awful and real by his belief that a terrible predator cat stalked him as he pushed his bike through the wilderness—alone.

Another traveler had showed Jesse an attack captured on a GoPro camera. It was a popular clip from YouTube; showing a cyclist pedaling in African bush, when suddenly an antelope sprinted into view at his right flank, knocking the biker to the ground while the antelope continued on its way. The guy claimed there were scads of videos of wildlife accidents with bicyclists and offered to show him more.

Jesse believed watching just one was too much, considering how much time he rode his bike and that he was now being tracked deep in an unfamiliar wilderness. Besides, the last thing he ever wanted to see was a video of an "accident" with a big cat. When he hopped on and tried to ride, predators were never far from his thoughts ever since. He actually wondered if he and other mountain bikers should just keep clear of wilderness altogether. After this Arizona Trail, he was leaning in that direction.

Besides, he had left the volunteers who looked down their noses at him—like he was a lost kid needing help to find his way home. Sometimes, a stare said, 'Look at that poor, filthy teen drifter. Maybe we should take him to a pet-wash for a good bath.' Others mistook him for some crazy, homeless flake needing counseling. Eco-volunteering was no longer a blast—more a disaster. He was ready to vacate hike-a-biking Arizona after just a few days.

Jesse had enough daylight to see a good distance ahead. He stopped, checked the balance of his duffel bag on the bike rack, and clicked off the headlight. He decided to give it a try, took a deep breath, hopped on his bike, and slowly pedaled along the rough, rutted path that was almost flat in places. He tried to reach within himself for what his mother called "a calm that bordered on serenity," which he often hoped to achieve. But all he could find inside was anxiety bordering on the frantic. The noises outside last night's camp stayed with him as he escaped, much the same as the wild predators he once faced ... a shocking encounter, as it was then called and reported in the newspapers. A *trauma*, the doctor had called it. Later, Jesse learned he was suffering a phobia, a "cat phobia."

His mind backtracked to when he first struck out on his own, having run away from his family in Colorado. A desperate youth on the move, an outcast looking for something, for a cause to give heart and soul to—animal causes his first choice. That was when he found *Free the Wild*, the first eco-protest group he joined.

They had planned to stage a totally awesome protest against animals held in zoos. Their big challenge, they needed a daring demonstrator to perform the riskiest drama of the protest. Jesse, determined to confront his demons head-on, volunteered at once. Its group leaders, unaware of his past traumas, took Jesse for a natural, despite his never having performed any creative protest. Besides, no one had ever joined their group quoting passages from the classic, *Animal Liberation* by Peter Singer, the Australian moral philosopher and animal-rights advocate. But was the kid ready for a high-risk feat?

In a freak accident during the protest, Jesse fell from a faulty line rigged to swing back and forth over a big cat enclosure, partially open at the top. Caught in the cage, Jesse would never forget how he picked himself up and carried on with his memorized lecture from Professor Singer. "Speciesism—the word is not an attractive one, but I can think of no better term—is a prejudice or attitude of bias in favor of the interests of members of one's own species and against those of members of other species ... If possessing a higher degree of intelligence does not entitle one human to use another for his or her own ends, how can it entitle humans to exploit non-humans for the same purpose?"

Trapped in a cage with wild predators, Jesse remembered how everything changed for him, how his point of view instantly altered, standing there and looking out through the bars at another species—*homo sapiens*. Then and there, he truly believed he no longer belonged to a species so capable of control, cruelty, and destruction. He had gone into a state of shock and was later amazed to realize he had survived physically unharmed. He was thrown a safety harness and rescued and would always feel lucky those African lions took their naps after feeding time, hardly giving him any notice.

Still, that was when the anxiety attacks came back, and his first frightening protest often haunted and closed in on him. Two years later and dozens of protests with other groups both in and out of the country, and still Jesse could not force the cage encounter with lions out of his head.

Light streamed through the foliage onto the path and he pedaled a little faster. The slope came alive with birds and other beings awake in the trees and bushes. In his rush ahead, he caught sight of an overhanging thorny branch, felt a sudden, sharp tearing at his forehead. He stopped to check and felt his damp face and wetness running from his head—blood. He touched the bloody gash beneath the bandana he wore, pulled it off and used it to wipe the blood from his face and forehead. He got another one from his pack and tied it around his head. Fearing "company," he retrieved his GoPro, flicked it on, and strapped it over the bandana.

The wild presence seemed stronger, closer. He pedaled faster, but it kept pace with him. He pedaled and pushed himself to a higher speed with deeper breathing. Crunching bushes and cracking branches crowded the pathway. Trees seemed to close in on him.

Farther on, he hit the brakes, sliding to an abrupt stop. He listened intently for any live presence, hearing birds but nothing else. He patted his forehead. The rag was loose and slipping below the camera strap. Could the creature tailing him smell blood from his open wound? Anxious and unsteady and checking behind him, he pulled the camera off and fumbled to re-tighten the bandana. This time he re-strapped the camera so that it pointed behind him.

He needed water, but decided not to stop and search. Just off his path, he heard grunting sounds like pigs rooting around in the brush.

The path ahead became rough and steep and hard to pedal. He slowed, hopped off, and walked the bike uphill. He swore he heard the same deep throaty noise from last night. He tried to believe he imagined it, triggered by past traumas, and that he could force the sounds to go away. But they were real and very near.

Harder, faster he pushed his bike uphill. The sound grew louder, closer on the hilltop, where he stopped above a downhill that resembled a toboggan run. He jumped on his bike and without a thought, he sped down a slope that whipped and hammered him from side to side.

The big cat crisscrossed the paths following a strange prey, pausing only to pant and stay hidden when the prey moved back in her direction. With her speckled, multi-colored, earthy coat, the trees and brush offered ample cover as long as she remained still. Curious, the being and strange thing under him had her full attention. Sometimes they were one misshapen form and then entirely separated into two parts. This confused her.

When she moved in closer, padding lightly to avoid the crack and crunch of limbs and bush, she recognized its upright shape as a predator, not prey. But the way it raced ahead when the predator topped the beast was like nothing she'd ever seen.

The bottom of the path had troughs Jesse likened to moguls on a ski slope until it veered right to another downward run but twice as steep. Jesse slowed and heard the snap and crunch of brush. Was it possible the creature tailed him down the verticals at his wild speeds? Desperate to escape, he could only think to pedal faster and faster. Not daring a glance over his shoulder, whether from fear or risk of another crash, it didn't matter. Down the steepest grade he flew, chased by a phantom he sensed but could not see.

She slowed and put more distance between them, taking a position between the two slopes, camouflaged among trees and brush. Sprawled beneath a hefty alligator juniper, she held her ground, captivated by a predator riding a weird stick-creature in perfect unison. There she stayed, still and watchful of the creature's downward flight.

The vertical took another turn left until it swerved him right—and sent him airborne. Loud gasps turned into yelps as he hit ground, rolling and landing at the bottom of a switchback.

From cover above, the cat's head twitched as they hit the ground and separated in a strange uncoupling. Then something else up the path caught her senses, and she quietly turned away and loped softly on big paws back up the slope under cover of thick brush.

After liftoff and separation from his bike, Jesse took a hard dive and crashed into brush. He stayed very still, waiting for his numb body to speak to him. Rolling onto his back, he felt for his GoPro. It was still strapped to his head, so he pulled it loose and struggled to his feet. He shuffled forward in the bushes, fiddling with the camera. He lost his footing and started sliding down an embankment.

6

"Since dogs have been living with humans for thirty thousand years, dogs need us more than we need them, and they know it." —Elizabeth Marshall Thomas

Wade woke to a cool dawn breeze and a jolt of adrenaline—something soft and hairy sniffing at his face. He stared straight into two dark eyeballs, the color of topaz. The rascal peered back at him, his black nose touching his own. An obvious early riser, and he's hungry. The mutt drew back—mission accomplished— and snooped about the tiny camp, dragging his line behind him.

Wade rolled his eyes at the memory of finding the little fella, though grateful it wasn't a lion or bear in his face. He shook himself awake and began his usual, get-moving business—what he and Abby called "Hurry up" potty breaks. He imagined the day-trek ahead and how the dog would nose along male-marking the trail. It would be both messy and risky, more so with a male dog, its urine and poop an inviting scent-path for predators to track.

After a standing breakfast of snacks, which the dog scarfed up, they hit the trail. The ranger was surprised that the dog took to the rapid deployment like a soldier, but the cooperation didn't last.

From the get-go, this dog slowed, lingered, and stopped to sniff every twig, rock, and bush along the path. No matter what slope, elevation, or flora—cactus, oak, piñon pine, ocotillo, prickly pear—his nose was on it. There wasn't a plant, tree, or scat dropping the rugged little beast didn't stop to inspect. A cluster of dry oak caught his interest; a pungent scent around a large mesquite tree required special investigation.

Becoming ever more edgy and irritated, Wade watched the mutt with the prominent snout nudge every root, tuft of sand, and clump of dirt on the path. He eagle-eyed him circle another mesquite and immediately tangle his lead line around the trunk.

"Enough!" the ranger shouted, jerking the line impatiently. After an audible sigh, he untangled dog and line.

Wade glanced up the trunk of the tree. "Whoa!" He had caught sight of scratch marks—long, deep scrapes in the bark. He reckoned the scratches, a half inch deep, were from one hefty mountain lion. "What do we have here, little fella?"

The dog tilted his head as if listening and considering the question.

He tugged hard on his line, eager to move on to the next exotic aroma. The ranger pictured him as some hybrid species, not like the coy-dog or even its victim from his bizarre dream. More like a hairy turtle moving close to the ground and not much faster. Yup, Tur-Dog—that's the breed.

Tur-Dog swaggered ahead, sniffing out new terrain. Wade gave the line another annoyed jerk that pulled the dog up short. Wade tried leading him in a heeling position on a tighter line, but the dog cut across his path, veered to one side, then the other, wherever his probing nose led. Back and forth across the path they went, stumbling into each other.

"Hey!" Wade shouted. "Enough already!" The animal stopped and gave another bob of his head. "Well, hell, I can't keep calling you 'hey,' can I? How about Little Fella? That's what you are."

Wade tried moving out front, giving "Little Fella" as much line as possible, pulling him only if he lagged well behind. For a time, the dog gave up the nose-and-sniff routine, and he worked to keep up with the ranger's usual brisk pace.

Soon they were well beyond any sign of campsites. Wade felt a surge of relief; freed of campers and dopey questions, blunders and bungles, careless campfires, Little Fella dogs let loose along the trails, tents pitched close to food and garbage sources—all invitations to carnivores to come and share a meal, a pet, or a camper.

Unexpectedly, they came upon an "eco-project," and Wade's prospects for solace and reflection were lost.

"Wilderness volunteers," Wade muttered, "way out here." Do-gooders to the locals, laying tie-steps on a steep grade along the slope. A work crew of bright-eyed students on school break, supervised by a seasoned conservation instructor. Eco-volunteers took advantage of milder weather to finish projects before intense summer heat and the hoped-for rainy season set in. They were pushing it into May, he reckoned, with daily highs well into the nineties. In spite of the heat, they wore heavy work clothes, sturdy boots, most of them dusty and sweaty.

Wade often encountered idealistic young ones eager to get involved with wilderness and environmental projects, kids who believed in doing good deeds for wildlife and their habitats. The trail's a series of contradictions—just when you're ready to curl in on yourself, you find a dog to rescue and you run into a bunch of overeager kids. He braced himself as they waved hello. Three of them rushed forward to greet his four-legged buddy.

"Oh, isn't he adorable!" one girl said. Little Fella, clearly socialized, emitted instant charm with a dazzling effect.

"It's a Westie!" another exclaimed, pulling off her hard hat to reveal a swirl of dusty blonde hair. "Look at those dark button eyes and those pointy little ears—ooh, he's so cute."

"It's a Cesar dog," the third chimed in.

Wade looked confused.

"You know," she added, "like the dog food ad?"

"He's a West Highland White Terrier," corrected the blonde, bending and stroking Little Fella. "They're all white except some, like this guy, have that biscuit-colored patch running down the back." She ran her hand along his back to show a wide, pale-brown streak. "Ooh, his coat feels so soft."

"Westie, eh?" Wade murmured. "Terrier. That figures."

"They're amazing trackers," the blonde said and picked Little Fella up and hugged him. "I mean, what a sniffer this guy has, I kid you not. Our neighbors have a Westie. His name's Comet. They trained him in scent stalking. Comet tracked down a missing Lab from the scent of its collar. His nose led him right through our backyard, down the alley and around our block. Then they followed him all the way to the park—that's where Comet found the Lab playing with another dog in the baseball field. They said Comet did a flip-flop to celebrate." The girl beamed a big smile. "Can you believe it?"

Wade looked skeptical, while Little Fella enjoyed the hugs and kisses, especially from the girls.

Wade reckoned he might be lucky and find someone willing to take the dog off his hands. Or at least deliver him to a veterinarian in town where they could check for a microchip to contact his owner.

"Don't suppose somebody passed by, looking for a lost Westie?" he inquired.

"Oh, he's lost?" two girls said in unison.

"Afraid so. I'll be heading to the trailhead, if necessary, to look for his owner."

They bubbled on about Little Fella and lost dogs. Then they mentioned a herd of deer on the trail earlier that morning. "Mule deer on the move so near us," the blonde gushed, clearly thrilled by the close encounter with wild creatures. Wade half-listened, trying to show interest. But he perked up when they talked of some strange noises earlier that morning.

"What kind of noises?" he asked.

"Well, like real deep, muffled moans."

"You mean like a larger mammal lurking about?"

"Yeah, like a big grumpy bear after a very poor nap. Or a lion, maybe."

Back on the trail, Wade thought about their account. Overactive imaginations often went with young volunteers, but after the strange disturbances the previous day and the close contact the night before, this was all the more reason to keep his senses about him.

On the path where the deer had passed, Little Fella's nose went into overload, his muzzle close to the ground, sniffing along like a plow.

Fixated little rascal. The ranger shook his head. So here we are, he mused, a disgruntled park ranger and a stubborn, little tag-along Westie.

Wade was fast learning why people called terriers willful. Behind him, the nose moved at a slow, obsessive pace. It occurred to the ranger that with all his exposure to animals, he had no experience with this breed group. All he knew is they were bred for chasing vermin and pests. Katy mentioned a family terrier when she was a kid in the Pacific Northwest. From her stories, he took them to be wild, high-strung, and absorbed. Self-absorbed, for sure, with their noses.

He smiled and realized he was feeling easier and freer, in spite of being saddled with the Westie. He had to admit, it seemed right that he got that little push from Katy toward the trail. Even the temporary boot from work no longer felt like such a burden. And conditions were better with day hikers and wilderness backpackers avoiding the hotter, drier season. As he stepped along, Wade caught himself breathing a healthier rhythm.

With only twenty-seven pounds of bare essentials, he might only cover a few of the trail's passages north. Summer heat would soon make hiking a rough slog, with the terrain ahead changing to lower desert elevations between the mountains. Still, while a journey of uncertain duration, who knew where it might lead and what he might discover?

Downright strange, though, to find Little Fella on his first day out. His plans surely never included rescuing a dog—unless by some miracle he found Abby.

For a mile or more, they gained elevation along a narrow path thick with scrub oak and pine. Less distracted, the dog dragged the lead line along without trouble. But as soon as they dropped into a narrow valley of grassy vegetation, Little Fella got excited and abruptly charged ahead.

Rabbits ... prey grazing along a shallow hillside, offering a chance for a terrier to show his mettle and chase some quarry.

Sure enough, the race was on, white tails exploding every which way. Wade grounded his pack and kept up with the dragging line. This terrier was a master of the short sprint, charging after one rabbit, then changing paths for another. He zigged as white tails zagged and turned on a dime. With all these choices, would rabbit or Westie tire first? Wade gave up the chase—a spectator to a predator-prey contest.

At last, Little Fella came to a halt, plopped down on his stomach, legs splayed, pink tongue sagging from a panting mouth. Like all empathetic dog lovers, Wade tried to read something in Little Fella's expression, a look that said 'What a mighty hunter am I!'

But the hunter wasn't done, not yet. When Wade reached for the line, the Westie dashed off after another white tail heading for a thicket. A game can turn serious. Wade, far behind, cursed and called after him. Little Fella took a mighty leap, rolling and struggling, two bodies roughly the same color. When the dust cleared, Little Fella held a rabbit firmly by the scruff of the neck, shaking his prey back and forth in a quick neck-snapping motion, needing no lessons to apply the death shake.

Wade stood and marveled, stunned witness to a potent undersized predator. After a few dying spasms, the rabbit hung limp in the dog's strong jaws, and the ranger ventured forward. Bloody-faced, Little Fella gazed up at him proudly, dropping his dripping prey on the toe of his boot. Wade was both impressed and a bit shocked. Katy liked to say everybody deserves a chance. 'Specially sporty little terriers, for sure.

Wade heard a muffled roar from the thicket, like a distant thunderclap but without the warning flash of lightning. He flinched and a surge of adrenaline set him on high alert. A loud wheezing followed, the sound of danger lurking near. It was hard to say how near, though he had no doubt of its presence.

Rabbits were long gone—except for the dead one. Wade stomped hard on the dog's line, gathering in the slack. Instinct told him to leave the dead rabbit to the animals for recycling, but common sense told him that he had a hungry little carnivore in his charge. He stuffed the rabbit in a plastic bag he carried in a side pocket and knotted the bag. Swooping the dog up in his arms, he scrambled up the hill to retrieve his backpack. With an eye out for danger, he put the plastic bag of gamey rabbit in an outside pocket of his pack.

He watched for movement and listened for more cat roars. Nothing but an unnatural silence. In less than twenty-four hours on the trail, conditions had turned strange and menacing— improbable creatures in a marathon struggle somewhere in the brush, a small canine quivering in a burrow, and big predator scrawls marking a mesquite tree. Unsettling things, adding up to danger for a wee white dog.

Back on the trail, edgier than ever, Wade sensed something else amiss. A few minutes up the line, a most peculiar screeching noise shattered the unnatural quiet. Something came flying off the high bank above him. Wade dodged to his right as it whizzed past them, the dog in a fury of barking. The object careened over the pathway, coming to rest on the bank below. Man and dog peered down at what looked to be a mud-spattered mountain bike. It had an old, olive-drab colored Army duffel bag strapped behind the seat—but no rider.

From the higher ground, Wade heard dragging footfalls and rustling brush. He shifted to a defensive posture as a body slid off the bank. Starting with a low growl, Little Fella morphed into a fit of barking.

7

"Killing an animal is in itself a troubling act. It has been said that if we had to kill our own meat, we would all be vegetarians … most people prefer not to inquire into the killing of the animals they eat … Very few people ever visit a slaughterhouse." —Philosopher and animal rights advocate, Peter Singer

The body slid to a stop not far from Wade—a live body, a human in a sitting position.

A young man, maybe a teen, plopped down on the path clutching some sort of digital device, a cell phone or camera, shaking it as if trying to bring it to life. Wade shook his head. As with so many people these days, the youth appeared unaware of his physical surroundings.

When the boy looked up, his face was streaked with blood. He seemed startled by the ranger's presence but spoke right up.

"Hey, mister, sure glad to see ya!" he exclaimed. "You got some wild things out here."

"Yeah, we got plenty of wild things."

"Wild!"

Wade assumed he wasn't talking about the Westie and his barking. "You okay, kid? You landed pretty hard."

"I'm good," the boy replied with false bravado.

Little Fella's barking changed to a low growl—a terrier at the end of his tether and ready to spring. The ranger reached down with a calming stroke while he sized up the intruder. On a closer look, he could be a late teen or an adult pushing thirty—hard to tell. He was as scruffy and unwashed as anyone Wade had ever seen, even in the wild, with stubbly, patchy whiskers and long, straggly blonde hair. He wore only a t-shirt, dirty jeans, and a pair of worn sneakers, without backpack, though he had the big duffel bag for strapping to the bike.

"Bike accident?"

"Sorta, sir." He was back to examining his device.

Wade saw it wasn't a cell phone but a small camera he was messing with. "Plenty to shoot out here," he said.

"Shoot?" The kid, if indeed he was a kid, looked up again, worried.

Wade pointed. "Camera—photos?"

"Oh, yeah, lots to record, sir."

Wade pointed below the path where the bike lay. "Your bike took a crash, too." The ranger saw the young man needed medical attention. He pulled his pack off and reached for some basic medical supplies in a Ziploc. Once a ranger, always a ranger.

From somewhere north came muffled grunting noises. Startled, the three looked in different directions. Little Fella emitted a low growl, his body tense, his tail so rigidly pointed skyward that he looked ready for lift off.

The moans—deep, guttural puh-puh-puhs—came in waves floating in their direction. At first, Wade pictured an old steam engine chugging up a mountain slope, but the more he listened, the more he sensed a big mammal looking for a meal.

Little Fella, still wound as tight as a spring, seemed to focus on the sound waves, ready to pounce on some nearby prowler.

"Let me take a look at that cut." Wade tied the dog's line to the bottom of his backpack. "I'm a park ranger."

The boy quivered. "I don't like the sound of that noise, sir."

Wade shrugged, trying to ignore it for the moment. Large bandage in hand, he inspected a wide, ugly slice across the boy's forehead. "It's a fairly deep gash. You might need stitches."

"I hit a limb. Took some dives, too." He glanced over his shoulder, jittery and alert, a prey, ready for the unexpected to leap forth.

"What were you doing on that bike? Mojos, front-flips?"

"Oh, no. Nothing like that." In a whisper he continued. "Something dangerous out there." He turned an ear one way, then another, trying to locate the source of the sound. "Tailing me."

"Tailing you?"

"Yes, sir, I couldn't see it, but I knew ... I know it's out there."

"What'd you hear? Describe it."

"Like what we heard just now." His voice cracked a bit and he tried to point a finger but wasn't sure where.

Wade applied some disinfectant and tore open the bandage. The boy jerked his head this way and that, keeping tabs on a hovering threat.

"Oh, sorry." Wade applied the bandage, and the kid touched his forehead. "Thank you, sir."

Wade took a deep, patient breath. "Which way on the trail you headin'?"

"Oh, I'm outta here, mister."

"Better give it a break for a few minutes." He pointed him to a level spot overlooking his crashed bike. "Smell the pine—it'll calm you down."

"Much obliged, sir."

They sat at the side of the trail, the ranger pulling Little Fella in-between them.

"Awesome dog you got. What's his name?"

"Well, he's a lost little fella, so that's what I'm calling him—Little Fella. 'Til I find his owner." The dog sniffed at the kid, homing in on his worn sneakers and nosing the cuffs of his dirty jeans.

"Hey there, Little Fella." He petted the dog.

The ranger took the kid for a dog lover, in spite of his rough appearance. "So, what brings you to the Arizona Trail?"

"Oh, a mission, sir. Well, this time not so much a mission. I volunteered for an eco-work project. It didn't work out very well."

"Bad luck." Wade recalled the volunteers working down the line. "What didn't work out?"

"Well, there was this girl." The kid struggled while the ranger waited for a hard-luck story to spill out. "You know, she got pretty sweet on me, I guess. Before I adjusted to the project and everybody, she wanted to change me, like all inside and out."

"Do a real makeover, eh?"

"Yes, siree. Tidy me up and take me back to meet her parents in Phoenix. 'Whoa,' I said, 'you seem a real nice person, but we just met. And we're right in the middle of the project.' And, to be honest, sir, I don't think we'd have much in common—except we're both vegans."

"Vegans?"

"Vegans, sir, vegetarians, but we don't use dairy products." He seemed to be calming down as he rambled on. "Besides, how do you work with eco-wannabes, when they're mostly carnivores?"

"Go figure."

"And being Engelian, I didn't fit in at all."

"Engelian?"

"Engelian," he repeated. "Pardon me, mister, you haven't heard of Mylan Engel? Philosopher dude? Against eating animals and stuff?"

Wow, Wade considered, an enviro-vegan-bicyclist, out to save the world, and he's in a struggle to survive the Arizona Trail. "Well, maybe this Engel is onto something."

Wade was looking at a wasted, rattled kid, who'd hit the wall—in biker lingo, bonged out—and hadn't even the sense to wear a crash helmet.

"What's your name, kid?"

"Jesse, sir."

"Mine's Wade. Does your head hurt? Could you use some aspirin or ibuprofen, Jesse?"

"Guess I could."

"How about water?"

"Well, I am running a little low."

Wade pulled out a water bottle and some pills from his pack. The boy loosened up, taking the pills and water, while he prattled on about his many nature and eco-tours—"like religious missions, but not religious," he said. He claimed allegiance with various conservation and animal-rights causes, including a calling with Earth's Creatures, one of several groups the ranger had never heard of.

"Well, you couldn't find a whole lot better place than the Arizona Trail—for a mission or just a hike." Wade gazed at the piñon pine and rugged oak and the sublime mountain vistas stretching out to the Whetstone Mountains and beyond toward the Chiricahuas. "Real tranquil." Well, except for lost dogs, abandoned campfires, beat-up bicyclists, and deplorable biker-types running rough-shod with ATVs.

Little Fella managed another throaty growl and rose to attention. Wade noted his oddly deep growl for such a small dog, more the sound of a cantankerous grandpa disturbed from his morning nap.

Higher up the slope, the earlier train-chug had evolved into weird, huff-like groans, floating through pine-scented air. Much closer now.

"You sure about all that tranquil stuff, mister?" Jesse whispered. "Hey, whatever creature is out there, I'd rather be its friend." He got to his feet, took a long, deep breath, extended his lean arms high in the air, and shouted, "Come on, beautiful monster, I'm just a friendly enviro. I mean you no harm!" He made a forced chuckle and with a sigh of fatigue, folded back onto the path.

This kid really is bonged out, Wade decided. "Maybe you'd be more comfortable on one of those chase boats, tracking a Japanese whaling ship."

The ranger didn't wait for an answer. Predator signals increased. He stood and moved carefully up the path, checking their flanks as he went. "Saving whales or dolphins in the North Pacific, maybe?" he whispered to Jesse.

"Interceders—been at sea, done that." Jesse's voice squeaked and quavered. "Besides, they all eat meat and fish, same as the whalers and the other perpetrators."

The calls changed and echoed from the brush, duets from indefinite directions. The ranger tried to dissect the sounds. Little Fella, alert and tense, kept up a steady low growl, tugging at his line, ready to pounce. The ranger gave him some slack and followed along the path, while Jesse tagged behind, nervy and breathing hard.

That a blend of mammal calls echoed forth, Wade was certain. One of the voices he took for coyote, the other too hard to ID. He still leaned toward a big cat—but he hadn't heard screams or shrieks. He looked back at the jumpy kid.

Wade knew all sorts of animal activists and committed enviros, passionate about saving the planet and fervently protecting all God's creatures. But it was hard to know with this underfed scamp, just skin and bones. Whether calm or crazy as they worked their causes, Wade measured each activist by how firm their commitment was. Would they cave when they got hassled, when they faced the gritty realities of their "mission?" He recalled a comment by a famous old wildlife conservationist, "Once you're involved in protecting the planet and its wildlife, you can never stop." Only a hardcore enviro or a naturalist, he reckoned, would truly know such things.

"Are we safe, sir?"

"Probably." Wade pointed down the path. "Let's go back for your bike."

The wild calls died away, replaced by comforting bird songs. Wade heard an Acorn Woodpecker and a Flycatcher, a brown-crested, most likely. Little Fella slackened the line, and the ranger quickly led dog and boy back down the path. At the crash site, the bike looked crumpled into a mangled sandwich. The duffel bag lay next to it amongst the scrub.

"It doesn't look good, does it?" Jesse said, smiling. "It looks like a goner."

They extricated both the bike and the bag, and the kid inspected his so-called customized bike.

"Watch this, sir," Jesse said. He fiddled with a lever that held the two halves of the bike together. With minor twists and tinkers, he managed to fold and unfold his bike. He seemed satisfied it was as good as new.

"See. It's a custom bike for trails." He adjusted the lever on the bike's mid-frame, which enabled the front and rear wheels to fold or unfold. By adjusting the torque with a lever, he could fold the two wheels together like a wallet. He proudly demonstrated his very changeable bike by slinging it by a strap over his shoulder.

"Impressive." Wade had seen fold-up bikes but this one looked Rube Goldberg by comparison. Still, Jesse seemed proud of it and his didn't resemble a toddler's tricycle. "Where did you get it?" Wade asked.

"I barter for stuff with people I meet on the road. I did some work for a bike shop owner up near Seattle, and he designed and built it for me as payment. Carbon-fiber frame, light as a feather." To demonstrate, he unslung the bike, hoisted it up and down with one lean arm, and easily slid it back on one shoulder. As he stood on the path, bike slung over one shoulder and duffel bag over the other, the ranger wondered how this skinny, protein-depleted, carbon-fiber body—looking part vagabond, part sixties' folk singer—could ever carry such a load for more than a few hundred yards.

While Jesse readjusted the weight of the duffel bag, Wade explained a few dos and don'ts in hiking and biking the trail to the clueless kid.

"Be sure you pay close attention to the hike and bike signs on your way," he warned. "If you don't spot any, then you can assume no biking is allowed. There are plenty of stretches, like the one we're standing on, that are too confined and dangerous to handle both bikers and hikers."

"Yes, sir. I will stay alert all the way, and hike-a-bike it where necessary."

"You'd best get that cut attended to at once. In fact, I passed some volunteers working back a ways. They might even drop you off at a clinic." Jesse's face turned sheepish.

"Oh—" Wade nodded, "the girl's one of the volunteers."

He nodded back.

"Well, head up the line to the next trailhead, then. You're liable to find a ride out with trekkers by sundown."

Just as Jesse stepped toward that direction, huh-huh noises returned. This time they had a surreal surround-sound effect. Wade swore the earlier picture of the noisy steam engine now resembled a constipated MGM lion.

Jesse, loaded with bike and duffel bag, now antsy and unsure, made feeble moves to haul his scrawny butt up the path. Uncertain which way the monstrous moans came from, he turned and then froze in place.

What a bony, mixed-up kid, hardly desert bait, Wade reckoned. He's a good kid, though. Maybe someday—who knows? Might even amount to something if he doesn't wipe himself out crashing that customized bike.

Jesse appealed to the ranger and the dog. "I gotta tell you, mister, the things I do ain't nothin' as risky as facing whatever beast that's out here."

Wade was listening carefully to the hoarse rumble up the slope. "Is that the sound you heard?"

"Yes, sir—kinda a slow, muffled growl—like some old chain smoker trying to breathe. You got the weirdest-sounding creatures out here, don't ya?"

The ranger kept a close eye on the high bank to their left. "Yup, plenty of animals to protect in this neck of the woods."

"A lot of 'em don't seem to need protecting."

While he adjusted his backpack, Wade kept an ear tuned to distant noises and an eye on the kid. Little Fella took up another aggressive stance, and the ranger recognized two distinct sounds that seemed to be moving parallel to them. One, the sharp, plaintive whine of a coyote, and the other,

the rumbling undertone of another mammal—
then more silence.

When it came to feral mammals, Wade reckoned
he had good instincts. It seemed most strange that
a cagey coyote and a secretive big cat would be
sounding off so close together, and in the same
eerie combination he heard the night before when
he found Little Fella. Though he hadn't worked out
the animal interaction, the ranger imagined a wild
competition going on between two predators
dogging them, and it was an encounter not to be
ignored.

"Out here can be a risky place," Wade said. "But
rarely from the animals. We've got a few big
mammals, but they're good when left alone unless
they can't find food and water, or shelter."

Jesse, edgy and anxious as ever, didn't answer.
He listened for every peep and squeak, alert to the
next wild call, ready to make a run for it, worried
about becoming food for the creature stalking
them.

Wade saw the fear on Jesse's face and came to
a decision, one unthinkable only twenty hours
earlier.

"Well, Jesse, you could tag along with us if you
wish." He held his eye on the bank above. "I doubt
we'll be moving very fast. Though it looks like you
won't be breaking any speed records either."

"Oh, thank you, sir! That's mighty kind of you."
The kid had the look of a death-row inmate
granted a reprieve.

"If we prove too slow, you can always strike out on your own." Not likely, he knew, since there were no bike-friendly paths until at least the next trailhead, but he needed to say it.

"Mister, I've been mostly on one goat trail after another since I got here."

"Oh, one other thing we should get straight."

"What's that, sir?"

"Enough with the sirs and misters. Call me Wade, kid. Try and work on that as we go, okay?"

"Sure, Mr. Wade—sir."

8

"We love and cherish our dogs because they respond with loyalty and affection, and because they obey us. But the coyote, so much like the dog in appearance and even behavior, has refused to accept us as masters, has spurned us, and we can never forgive it." —Poet Richard Shelton

Wade kept a steady if cautious pace until a horrendous cacophony startled them—a gust of low, coarse huh-huh-huhs and screeching whup-whup-whups—bursting from thick brush above.

He raised a palm to halt their progress, riveted to the sounds, ready to muzzle the dog's slightest bark. The Westie stood frozen, though, his pointy ears at attention. Jesse opened his mouth, and the ranger stuck a hand in his face. The wave of caterwauls faded as abruptly as it started, and the ranger nodded a slow go-head to the kid.

Jesse looked all around. "I sure don't like that. What kinda animals you got out here, Mr. Wade?"

"We've got all kinds in the Sky Islands."

"Sky Islands?"

"That's what we call these mountains. They're like islands poking above the hot, dry valleys."

"Oh, I get it. They're like islands coming out of lakes and oceans."

"Yup. They offer a rich and diverse habitat for a great variety of wildlife."

"You mean really wild things, like wolves and bears even?"

"Sure." From over his shoulder Wade saw Jesse come to a halt, his bike and hefty duffel bag weighing him down like heavy armor. "But no wolves spotted in this area yet. The mountains are home to a variety of big cats."

"Even cougars?" Jesse asked, his voice shaking.

"Yeah, we call them mountain lions down here." For the umpteenth time, Little Fella lifted his leg on a spiky bush. The ranger shook his head as they slogged on.

"Mountain lions then," the boy repeated from behind. "These lions—kinda big ones?"

"Sure, but they keep mostly to themselves, especially when humans are around." Having a skittish kid tagging along, the ranger reckoned it better to reassure him.

He came to a standstill and turned to Jesse. At their current pace Wade knew the next trailhead was out of reach by day's end, so the kid would have to find a ride out the next day. With that dopey expression on his face, Wade judged there was no use in raising the subject for now. But maybe he'd talk less and cover more ground if he took the lead.

"Why don't you be point man for a while, Jesse? Focus on keeping us moving at a good speed."

"Sure. Thanks—Wade."

The point position made no difference. Jesse kept up his monologue, tossing comments back as he went. Whenever he had a stray thought he considered extra important, Jesse slowed until the ranger caught up, causing an even slower pace. Then Jesse nearly took a header from a tree root across the path.

Wade's hesitation about taking on this careless kid escalated to irritation. "Give it a break, kid! Listen to the bird calls and try to identify the source."

"Sorry, sir—I mean, Wade. I talk a lot when I get nervous."

"I've noticed."

After a few minutes of quiet, Jesse forgot about birdsongs and started up again—recalling a past mission tracking the numbers and health of wild horses along the western Nevada border.

Wade lagged farther behind and let Little Fella sniff the ground for a spell. With the snail's pace and a wider gap between them, Wade missed part of Jesse's real agenda: helping wild mustangs evade ranchers and government roundup agents in the Sierra Nevada foothills.

Jesse's voice grew fainter, so Wade shortened the gap again. He rounded the next bend at a good clip, but there was no sound of Jesse—and no Jesse, like he'd vanished.

Wade rushed on, with Little Fella jogging to keep up.

"Hey, Mr. Wade!"

They stopped. The dog pulled to the edge of the path. Wade and the Westie peered down a sharp embankment layered with rock scree.

"Hey there, Little Fella!" Jesse shouted.

Jesse was sprawled among prickly brush and rocks, his bike and bag nearby.

"Looks like a mission gone wrong," Wade voiced to the dog. "Come on back up here," Wade said and waved at Jesse. "No time for clowning around."

The kid grunted and strained, trying to free himself from a prickly bush. But he couldn't get free.

Something had one of his legs.

"What seems to be the problem?"

"Sorry, Mr. Wade. I got things clinging to me."

Little Fella gave a long, low growl. The ranger spotted the reason—a healthy-looking wild canine positioned just beyond where Jesse lay. Wade eyed the desert coyote maybe weighing ten pounds more than Little Fella but had legs about three times longer. The creature sat on a rock a safe distance beyond Jesse, watching the whole scene, panting heavily.

Jesse turned to follow their line of sight. "Hey, that's a coyote, isn't it?"

"Yup, checking out the stupidity of man—or boy."

"Wild!" Jesse stared at the coyote. "Never seen one up this close."

"You're looking at a Mearns coyote—our Southwest subspecies."

Wade kept an eye on the coyote and a tight rein on Little Fella as he calculated how to free the kid and keep Little Fella safe—and get back on the trail and resume hiking!

"Are you injured, Jesse? Any bones broken?"

"I don't think so." Jesse moved his leg and yelped. "I'm OK, but I'm caught." Jesse gave a little cry each time he tried to touch a sticker.

Wade scooped up the Westie and carefully stepped sideways down the rock scree. "Hold still—let me take a look."

He pulled up next to the kid and set the dog down to assess the damage. My, oh my. A mess of cholla—a prickly, troublesome cactus—ran along the length of the kid's leg. Wade gave the coyote a close eye. The animal had quit panting and stretched out, its muzzle on its front paws, apparently settling in to observe the rescue.

"Git, now!" The ranger waved an arm for the coyote to move along, but its only reaction was to raise and tilt its head, its long pointy ears trying to interpret strange commands. Odd that it won't move on, Wade wondered. Shy and wary as they are, that usually works. But he knew coyotes were smart, complex creatures—always vigilant, knowing when to leave things be.

He tied Little Fella's line to a juniper limb a few paces away, keeping himself between the dog and the coyote, and settled in to give Jesse a closer inspection.

"Jumpin' cholla!" the ranger exclaimed.

"What?" Jesse voiced in panic. "Is that like local cussing, Mr. Wade?"

"You're covered in jumping cholla, kid." He gestured at his leg. "Lucky you're wearing jeans, or the spines would've stuck to your skin. That would take hours, pluckin' you clean like a dead chicken."

"They're sticking to me!" the boy cried, expecting the worst.

"Well, of course they're sticking to you. They're stickers. When they contact skin, you have to scrape 'em off real careful, one at a time."

Jesse squirmed. "Hey, is this stuff alive—like, would it want to feed on me?"

"In a way, it does. They propagate by sticking on everything that touches them, dropping off another place to make new plants."

"Get 'em off me, please!"

"Nothin' to it. You've fine-plucked a bird, right?"

"No!"

Wade muttered to himself and eyed the coyote, still calmly watching the sideshow. The ranger glanced back at Little Fella resting on his belly under the shade of the juniper. The dog seemed alert for any movement from the strange canine on the rock.

"You wouldn't be carrying a comb?" Wade looked skeptical.

Jesse shook his head. The ranger pulled off his pack and reached in a side pocket.

"You getting a knife?" Jesse asked anxiously.

"Tweezers." He held them in front of Jesse's nose. He began scraping or plucking cholla off the kid's grit covered jeans, starting from the thigh and working toward the ankle. Wade tossed them well away, as familiar with them as he cared to be. "This'll take a while, so you keep your eye on that coyote and shout if the creature even thinks about making a move."

"It might attack us?"

"Not us—Little Fella." He handed him a rock. "Toss this in its direction, but only if the animal moves any closer, understand?"

"Wild!"

9

"America's deadliest government program, Wildlife Services, just released its latest death tally. The 2018 totals are heartbreaking. This rogue agency killed nearly 1.5 million native animals last year, among them 357 gray wolves, 338 black bears, 1,002 bobcats, 375 mountain lions, 3,349 foxes, 22,521 beavers and 68,186 coyotes — mostly at the behest of the agriculture industry." —The Center for Biological Diversity.

The watchful coyote hadn't moved an inch, except to turn its head and look behind it from time to time. Jesse couldn't take his eyes off the animal that, for him, was so much like a dog. The ranger nimbly pulled cholla stickers from the kid's leg.

"Up north, they kill 'em in shooting contests," Jesse said. "'How many KI-ohts can we shoot today?' Sick and evil is what they are!"

"One coyote killed about every ten minutes in the U.S.," Wade added. "And those killing games are so-called Derby contests, sometimes they last for several days."

"One every ten minutes? It's vicious killing, sir."

"Good ol' boys and their sick games."

"It's like killing dogs!" Jesse exclaimed, glancing at Little Fella, whose eyes were closed. Jesse had longed for a dog when he was young, now even more so, being alone on the road.

"That's not the half of it, Jesse. They play at being the mountain men of a couple hundred years ago, but without the skills or toughness."

Jesse nodded, studying the coyote. "This one sure looks well-fed. In top shape, isn't he?"

"How do you know it's a he?"

Jesse tilted his head to try for a better view of the sprawled-out coyote.

"Could be a female wandering about, looking for food and a mate," Wade said.

"Not in my world," Jesse muttered.

Wade chuckled. "Well, I seem to recall someone bragging about an offer from a Phoenix girl."

Jesse looked hangdog. "It never works out, sir. I end up turnin' tail."

"Some souls end up choosing to be loners. Left alone, that coyote will thrive just fine."

When the ranger got to Jesse's ankle, he found stickers on the kid's tanned skin—not so much suntanned but brown with layers of dirt. "Ouch!"

"You felt that one?" Wade tossed the last sticker free.

"Not much." Jesse turned his ankle and stopped. "I can feel that, though."

"What?"

"My ankle. It's a little sore, like I might have turned it or something."

Wade compared it to Jesse's other ankle. He couldn't see any redness or bruising through the grime, and the ankle wasn't swollen. "Let's see if you can stand on it." He got Jesse standing on his own. "How's it feel when you put weight on it?"

"It's OK. A little tender, but I can walk. I've had worse on many a mission."

They gathered up their gear; Jesse hopping like a gimpy old man at first. Wade monitored the kid's climb up the scree and noted he was moving much better. He followed him up the embankment, holding Little Fella in one arm and Jesse's bike in the other—having survived yet another crash.

"Maybe it's time to try a new mission," Wade said, deciding to take a different approach. "Are you game for a fresh cause?"

"I could be. Not so sure about this Arizona Trail, though."

"What do you know about Arizona, Jesse? Heard of our five C's?"

"Five C's?"

"Copper, Cattle, Cotton, Citrus, and Climate."

"I grew up in Colorado, Mr. Wade. That's the only 'C' I know."

"Well, we've got other C's in Arizona—Canines, Coyotes, and Critters, and Cores, Corridors, and Carnivores—which a lot of us consider really important."

"Oh, I think I get where you're heading, sir—I mean, Wade."

"That's good, Jesse."

"Hey, look, I think it's a female." Jesse, stooped over with his head at his knees, pointed toward the coyote, back up and on the move.

She took one last look at them and headed for nearby brush. Wade measured the familiar coyote lope, noting she was favoring a limb. He kept sight of her until something spooked her, and she turned and scampered off in another direction.

"Safe passage, Shóódé," Wade called out as she vanished.

Just two days on the trail and he'd already managed to take on the burden of a small dog and a confused kid. Marie was right; he was a magnet for dogs and outliers—of the human kind. I came out here to shed problems. Hell, I'm packing 'em on as I go, Wade stewed as they hiked, though "hiking" was a loose term at this point.

With Jesse it was slow and slower since he didn't own a brisk walk. Wade calculated that any normal walker or hiker could make Bedrock Springs trailhead before dusk. And there was still plenty of day left, but their slow journey seemed more like a caravan through the Arabian Desert than a timely hike through the Santa Ritas.

A deep, long howl rang out, then a strange muffled growl. They stopped.

"You sure there aren't wolves out here?" Jesse whispered.

"Forget about wolves. No wolf seen in these parts in a hundred years. If a wolf roamed this slope, some local would take a pot-shot quick enough. You're hearing coyote."

"Mr. Wade, what'd you call that coyote back there?"

"You mean Shóódé? It's Apache and means friend or coyote."

"You know Apache words? Wild!"

"Wild, huh? Everything's wild with you, kid."

"I feel like I kinda got to know Shóódé while I was stuck in the cholla. Are coyotes in trouble in Arizona?"

"Jesse, all wildlife is in trouble in this country."

"I mean, I was thinking about my next mission. You think maybe Arizona needs me? The coyotes need me?"

Jesse looked washed out. The dog was still holding his own, but for how long?

"Let's take a breather." Wade spotted a small, level gap ahead. "Little Fella's gotta be bushed."

They found a spot to rest their backs against a boulder, their packs padding them.

"For every wolf a livestock rancher might illegally kill these days," Wade began, "he's liable to kill a couple thousand coyotes—legally." The dog laid on his side, his eyes drooping closed. "Biologists tell us that the more coyotes taken, the more the females naturally breed—literally, it's in their biological nature. Some locals don't care to understand that."

Jesse shook his head sadly. "So, all this killing ends up making more coyotes to be killed?"

"Pretty much, but there are ranchers and farmers that just don't get that."

"Or won't get it," Jesse said. He squeezed his grimy hands against his head like a vise. "Everything is 'shoot and kill' out there!"

"The Department of Agriculture bankrolls their bloody work. And people don't complain about it or put enough pressure on their politicians."

"Of course, they don't!" Jesse slapped his forehead, startling Little Fella. "My mother says you don't cut off your nose to spite your own face."

Wade shrugged. "If you mean folks maintain a ravenous appetite for meat, which cattle and sheep ranchers provide, yes."

"They think they can't live without it. That's why we stage protests. Our main mission: Call attention to what's really going on, and shock people into taking action. Show them how awful the animals are treated— and how unhealthy a meat diet is for humans, to begin with."

Jesse went silent.

Wade noticed the dog staring him down. "Hey, Little Fella, I'll bet you're ready for water. Maybe you'll be good for another mile or two."

The Westie refueled, and they were back on the trail—Wade wondering if the kid was serious about staying in Arizona or even cut out for it.

Wade had his own long-term mission, but after

so many run-ins with Wildlife Services and its "specialists"—paid assassins, plain-speaking—it was more like a cross to bear. Frankly, he was surprised he still had a job. He figured the verdict on him was evenly split, for and against, among the locals. The bulk of ranchers and livestock producers suspected he held quirky ideas about the rights of wild animals. He was often accused of caring more about wildlife than humans, to which he gave a simple 'So-what's-your-point?' shrug.

"I could tell you things—like about what I do," Jesse yelled back. "About how I find creative ways to do public protests."

Exhibitionist tendencies, Wade judged. He was reluctant to respond, figuring another long rambling story would follow. Hard to picture how this wandering waif could ever manage a wildlife mission or environmental demonstration. A careless, feckless, maybe even reckless kid hardly able to be counted on in a crunch. How long would he be capable of focusing on any one mission?

Yet Jesse had refreshing traits for a youth. He didn't cuss, which would impress Katy, and he had an innate respect for his elders, though, like the ranger himself, he clearly didn't extend that to government and institutional authority. Jesse claimed he was raised in a strict household, a religious-conformist family—"my neo-puritan parents"—from a sect that had settled in the Colorado Rockies. Wade could see the kid had picked up some decent values.

A feline shriek startled them. Wade took it as a menacing signal. He looked ahead at Jesse; was a faster pace even possible? The kid looked like a zombie, lifting one plodding foot after another. Little Fella was going about the crucial business of keeping up with his adopted pack. He had a different, determined bearing that Wade took to mean, 'Let's get this hike to the next stop because I need a well-deserved nap—for about ten hours.'

Something brewed in the back of the ranger's mind—a protective attachment building for a dog that wasn't his. Could simple animal welfare evolve into a serious man-dog bond? Wade wouldn't let himself consider that—yet.

Wade could see there was no tossup in this race, the dog was out-walking the kid. When he called a halt for another rest stop, Jesse swiveled around and sighed deeply, pulled the duffel and bike off his shoulders, and dropped to the ground.

"You need a real backpack, you know, not that duffel bag from World War II."

Jesse studied his duffel bag, trying to see it differently. In the end, this confused him as he began searching through it.

Wade pulled a bowl and water from his pack, and the Westie went for a drink at once. The ranger sat down and took a swig from his bottle while he assessed the kid.

"We—Little Fella and I—will be making camp up ahead later. We'll finish the hike to the trailhead first thing in the morning." He waited for a reaction from Jesse, but he only nodded.

"If you want, you can hang around, camp the night if you like."

"That's real kind of you, Mr. Wade." He seemed to be thinking it over, as he poked around in his bag and pulled out a large bottle of water.

At least he's carrying some, Wade noticed. He wondered what else the bag contained in the way of basic survival supplies.

"What are you packing? Got the basics for camping?"

"Everything I ever need is in this bag, sir."

Jesse rummaged deep in the bag and pulled out an old rolled-up yoga mat. Then a plastic-wrapped bike cable and lock. The Westie sniffed each item. The boy dug way down deep and pulled out an inch-thick notebook. He opened it to a blank page and, with a stubby pencil pulled from the spiral binding, he began jotting.

"The USDA, you said, Mr. Wade?" He stopped writing and turned to him. "And Wildlife Services?"

"Yeah, yeah," the ranger nodded. "Wildlife is an arm, a strong arm, of the Ag Department. Every year some four million animals are shot, poisoned, snared, or trapped by Ag's Wildlife Services. Remember, one dead coyote about every ten minutes."

"I'll never forget, Mr. Wade."

Jesse scribbled away, shaking his head. "I keep notes for possible future missions." He finished and looked up. "It's so unbelievable that an animal so sacred to Native Americans could be slaughtered like that."

"You know the government doesn't care, right?"

Jesse nodded. "I know. They never have." He shook his head. "Mr. Wade, did you read the book about the dude who traveled all around the desert and other places. He actually met a talking coyote—it turned out the coyote spoke in Spanish! Wild!"

"A Spanish-speaking coyote. I think I know those books," Wade replied. He wasn't sure his admiration for coyotes could stretch to imagine them speaking a human language. It would depend on what they had to say, he judged.

"My parents didn't wanna talk about the book. They said it was a bunch of nonsense and I shouldn't believe a word of it. Sorta disappointed in them."

Another harsh shriek ripped the silence, then a heartrending whine, like a creature in pain. The dog levitated, all four paws leaving the ground simultaneously, followed by his piercing barks. The ranger spooled him in and pulled him to his chest. They listened closely, not sure which direction the blood-curdlers came from.

"Let's get a move on," Wade said quietly. "Look for a level camp spot and hunker down."

"I'm with you guys, Mr. Wade." Jesse frantically stuffed his possessions back in the bag.

As the wild shrieks faded, the area cloaked in an unnatural silence. While the trail beckoned them on, Wade accepted a simple ground truth. They were being stalked.

10

"Westies have remained strongly connected with their most basic instincts—hunting large and small vermin. In critter mode, Westies are incapable of hearing human words or commands—they are not ignoring you; they just cannot respond to anything but their overwhelming critter instincts."—Deb Duncan, Westie owner and dog trainer

The day was getting on, but they had plenty of light. Little Fella looked wasted, but he was still tanking up on water. They'd survived close encounters with the coyote and the beast stalking them. And though it was slow, man and dog were strong and making progress toward the trailhead.

The kid was another story. He had dropped his bike on the path and promptly flopped down on his duffel bag. Wade looked from Jesse to the dog and back. "We can take a breather, but then we gotta keep moving."

They had come upon a long-abandoned mining and prospecting site from a century ago—now a rusty patchwork of hydraulic pipes and tunnels. Wade surveyed the remnants of crude water channels created by building low walls, the aged ditches and rotting bulkheads that once carried ore and minerals by water down the mountainside. Let's get around this mess of danger without losing the dog, he hoped.

Wade put a firm boot on his leash. He took his binoculars out of his backpack and panned beyond the site. He tried to focus on a vista of canyons and niches to the south, but the Westie tugged against the lead. This was a rare chance to scan the southern canyons from high ground. His work in the Coronado National Forest offered a limited view of passageways running north to south, gateways for wildlife moving and migrating to and from the rugged mountains in Mexico. He fought to keep a steady gaze with a terrier pulling at the line.

He turned to Jesse, still sprawled out. "Here. You think you can hold this wee monster for a minute?"

After handing over the dog's line, Wade carefully glassed farther south over many canyons, gorges, and passages leading toward Outpost, his home turf, not far from the Mexican border. He knew the Santa Ritas alone had strings of canyons, many dozens mapped and named, and many unnamed. He longed to explore new spaces in depth.

Then a sudden cry, Jesse was jumping to his feet, scrambling in circles.

"What's the problem?" Wade asked, focused on an outline of hills in Mexico.

"Little Fella got away!" the kid whined. "He pulled the line right out of my hand!"

Wade dropped the binoculars on his pack and started hunting around the immediate area. The dog had disappeared in an instant. Exasperated and angry at both Jesse and Little Fella, the ranger cursed under his breath. How could the terrier perform a vanishing act, just like that? Wade heard huffs and puffs close by and realized the dog was on another wild scent. Wade tracked the grunts and spotted the dog's lead near a bush. He grabbed for it, but the line slithered away as quick as a snake. He should never have handed the lead to Jesse.

"That loony terrier's gone to ground," Wade seethed when the noises stopped.

"Is he hunting something?" Jesse shuffled over to join him near a large manzanita bush.

"Rabbit or rodent, whatever moves! They'll tweak his predator button every time."

The ranger parted the branches and peered beyond for the leash. He spotted an opening on the ground that proved an entrance to an old, crumbling culvert-like tunnel.

Via a slight echo, the terrier could be heard heaving and panting through an old aqueduct that used to be used for mining ore. Wade retrieved his headlight, plus a small flashlight from the pack. He stooped down and searched for the dog on the runaway cord, but he couldn't see him. "Cripes, Westie, I know you're down there! Chasing packrats, rabbits, whatever catches your eye—you gotta go for it!"

"Why would he go down there, Mr. Wade?"

"He's a damn terrier! Gone to dirt and ground—a pain in the back side!" Wade yelled into the tunnel, "Blasted terrier!"

"Here, Mr. Wade, let me see if I can root him out." Jesse got down on his hands and knees to push his way into the entrance. "Could you shine that light into the tunnel again? I'll get him out."

"Don't go crawling in there, kid. It's too old, too risky." Wade beamed the flashlight along the dark tunnel, trying to assess its structure.

"No problem. You wouldn't believe the places I've crawled on my missions. Hey, Little Fella," he called in a high voice. "Come boy, come back out! Here, sir, let me use the headlight." Wade passed it reluctantly, and Jesse attached it around his bandaged head.

On all fours, Jesse peered deep into the tight, dark culvert for a closer view.

"He's in there, but he looks stuck. Ya know, maybe the line got twisted." Wade tried to train the flashlight on the line, but in the tight drain he couldn't see much ahead of Jesse. "Must be caught on something. It's not close enough to grab."

While the kid's muffled voice droned on, Wade found the other end of the drain, about thirty paces away. He got on his knees and spotted the flashlight through the passage, highlighting rusted pipe and rotted wood struts, with Jesse and the headlight moving toward him. The kid actually might be right for once: the dog could be stalled.

"Come on, doggy, come on out, boy," Jesse called cheerfully.

"You are one loopy dog!" Wade huffed from the opposite end. "How we gonna pull you free?" He vented and cussed and shook his head. "Well, what a hell of a great walk in the park this has been!" The Westie whined in reply.

Wade could tell the tunnel hadn't seen much water for a long stretch. His ranger mode kicked in to assess the safest and best rescue.

"Hold on, Westie, I'm coming for you," Jesse coaxed. Wade saw the tunnel narrowed.

"Hey, listen, kid, back off. Don't crawl any farther." It was a horribly tight fit, even for a thin frame like Jesse's.

"It's OK, sir. I'm goin' real slow, oh-so careful. I can just about grab the line."

The ranger followed the light, the kid edging along on his elbows, crawling and straining, with the shadowy Westie making little whines and groans, stuck between them.

"His line is so close, sir. If I could only push up this beam, just a little."

"Hold up!" Wade ordered. "You can't be pushing or bumping any rotten old beams!"

"I got the line! But it's hooked on somethin' ... maybe I can shake it loose—"

Little Fella gave a sudden yelp and scampered forward, bursting from the tunnel with dirt on his muzzle and cobwebs covering his body. After a couple of expert canine shakes and a quick brush by Wade, the dog bounded into the ranger's arms. At the same time, Wade heard creaking from the culvert.

"Oh-oh, sorry, Mr. Wade. I lost my grip on the line—"

"You freed him, kid. He's back out here with me."

The tunnel made another groan. "What's going on, Jesse? Back out of there, pronto!"

"Well, sir, it might not be possible," came an anxious voice.

"Why?"

"I think I'm stuck now. I'm trying to wiggle back out, but ... I can't."

"Are you hurt?"

"No, sir," came the tremulous response.

"Well, just relax and crawl forward then."

Jesse strained and grunted while Little Fella sniffed and danced around the entrance.

"Can't. One of them struts is blocking my way. I can't get by it."

"OK, steady now. Don't move anymore forward. You could cause a cave in."

"Yes, sir." Jesse squeaked out in agony.

"Take a look at that strut with the headlight. If we loosened and moved it a bit, would you have room to crawl through?"

"Uh, yes, siree, I think I could."

"Rope, Jesse. You got a string of rope in that big duffel bag?"

"Yes, yes, I do."

"Miracle of miracles," the ranger whispered to himself. "Stay put while I get it," he yelled.

"I won't be going anywhere."

While Wade and the Westie rummaged through the kid's bag, he swore he heard Shóódé off in the distance. Had the tunnel uproar drawn her attention? Little Fella would get antsy with her around.

Sure enough, the dog had a canine conniption fit. He was bored with the tunnel game, oblivious to a kid who'd just saved his furry little rump and a park ranger trying to save that kid. Given the chance, his potent terrier nose would lead him to the next reckless adventure, wandering off to who knows where, with his line dragging behind, tracking wild calls beyond—and to what? His rapid end. Doomed in no time.

Damn.

"Hush up, Bucko!" He gave the lead a hard jerk and the line broke at the collar.

Wade made a grab, but the terrier dodged him, barking and keeping his distance—just another game to him. "Hey, Bucko, that's enough!" Wade stopped and stared him down. The curt command or tone, or something in Wade's expression seemed to stop the bark-fest. Little Fella halted in his tracks, waiting and watching.

"Bucko?" Wade repeated. The Westie tilted his head and studied the ranger, decoding a new language. "Buck?" "Buck" got an even bigger reaction. The dog trotted forward, full of attention as if expecting a treat, and Wade grabbed hold of him.

He gave him a few calm, confident strokes. He tried calling him Buck again, sensing the dog responding to the sound, the name. He repeated it and each time, the Westie focused on a name that seemed to prompt a conditioned response, and he waited for the next command. Could *Buck* be his rightful name?

Well, that's it, Wade decided, you seem to be taking to Buck, so Buck it is. And what a namesake. For the ranger it was a most honorable name—like Buck from *The Call of the Wild*—a hero dog who finds the lure of wild country in his heart. The ranger quickly retied the lead to Buck's collar.

Frantic, muffled cries came from Jesse, "Hey! Mr. Wade, sir. Please get me outta here! I don't wanna die!"

"I know! I'm coming, kid!"

Wade quickly hunted through Jesse's bag. He got to thinking, going underground is a frolic for the average terrier. The last thing we need now is the dog crawling back into the culvert and creating a total clusterfuck. Except Jesse is stuck. We aren't done with that damn drain after all.

Wade had a plan brewing, one as loopy as their day was going—a plan that might even work.

After tying the dog's lead to his belt, he emptied Jesse's duffel bag. As suspected, it was mostly stuff of little use for a hike—except for that rope. There, at the bottom of the bag he found useful, sturdy quarter inch nylon cord, brand new, 25-30 feet long.

Then came that familiar whup—out somewhere beyond. And Buck, alias Little Fella, was back at it, ready to terrier-ize the habitat. In a high-pitched whine of excitement, he darted back and forth, and strained at the lead that pulled at the ranger's belt. Shóódé or her brethren always seemed to trigger this hyper state.

They rushed back to the mouth of the tunnel. The dog simmered down, nosing around and watching Wade's every move. The ranger's unlikely plan called for using the rescued dog to turn around and rescue the kid. Jesse's long rope in hand, Wade untied the dog's lead line from his belt, and, in its place, secured the long rope to the dog's collar.

"Okay, Buck, you still got work to do!" He peered into the tunnel. "Jesse, how are you doing?"

"OK ... I guess."

"How's the air in there?"

"OK, but it helps if I don't move—or breathe much."

"Well, here's what we'll do. I've got one end of your rope tied to the dog's collar."

"Then what, Mr. Wade? How can he pull me out?"

"No, no, just listen up. I want you to call him back in there while I keep hold of the other end of the rope. When he gets to you—"

"How can I get him to come?"

"Hell, they bred these dogs for crawling in tunnels. Just shout out for him. Call him Buck. He seems to answer to that. Try Buck."

"Oh—OK. Buck."

"Now, when he gets to you, untie the rope from his collar and hang onto that rope. Then I'll call him back out to me. You don't let go of that rope."

Buck stood at the opening taking it all in, while the ranger made sure the long rescue rope was secure on his collar.

"OK, Jesse, he's ready. Call him!"

"Here, dog, here, dog," Jesse whimpered.

Wade looked at Buck. The dog waited, looking eagerly for the ranger's next move.

Wade sighed. "Come on, kid, belt it out! Call him BUCK!"

"HERE, BUCK … HERE BOY! COME, BUCK!" came Jesse's call.

The dog stirred, his ears moving, as he danced and whined. He looked to the ranger for reassurance. Wade pointed him in the right direction and Buck darted back in. For a few seconds he could hear the dog's huh-huh-huhs through the tunnel.

"He made it, Mr. Wade. He's right here in my face!"

"Can you untie the rope?"

"I'll try."

Wade listened to their grunts and groans until Jesse shouted that he had the rope untied. "OK, now, hang onto that rope while I call him back out."

Wade called to the dog. "Come Buck, come boy, come Buck." Again, it took only a few seconds and more huh-huh-huhs before his gritty white face popped out of the opening.

"Well done, Buck," Wade praised. He hastily knotted Buck's lead back on his loose collar, tying the other end to his belt.

"Now, Jesse, can you loop the rope under your arms and around your back? Then you'll need to tie it in a half-hitch at your chest."

"I don't know. You mean like a knot?

"Yeah, tie a tight knot."

"I can try."

"Good. You tie a real tight knot after the rope's around you and against your chest, OK?"

"OK."

Wade listened to more grunting and struggling for a minute or more.

"I think I did it. I got myself tied."

"Good. Now, I'm going to pull you out, carefully, right past that strut. While we go nice and slow and easy, I want you to adjust, shift, and squirm your body as needed. Be patient and careful and squeeze by that strut. That's all you need to do while I keep the pressure even and move you forward."

"OK, Mr. Wade, I'll try."

Wade would have to talk him through the process. A scrawny kid like him could squeeze by the strut, he hoped, with just the right care and rope tension. The rest would be an easy pull free. "You can do it, Jesse, I know you can." Wade made some trial tugs to make sure the knot wouldn't slip loose from Jesse's chest. Then he secured a purchase with his feet against the entrance. "Now, you tell me right away if I'm pulling too hard or if you need me to stop."

"OK," came the tremulous voice.

"Here we go."

Wade pulled the rope toward him easily for at least a foot before the line got rigid.

"WAIT!" Jesse cried.

Wade heard heavy breathing, more grunts and groans, the kid's obvious attempts to squirm and maneuver his way forward. As he kept the rope tense, the struggling faded.

"How's it going, Jesse?"

"WHAT IF THE STRUT BREAKS AND EVERYTHING CRASHES DOWN ON ME?"

"WHAT IF YOU SPEND THE NEXT TWELVE HOURS IN THERE WHILE I GO FETCH THE RESCUE SQUAD TO DIG YOU OUT?"

The kid whimpered. Wade regretted at once blaring and scaring the poor lad.

"I see what you mean, sir," he squeaked back.

"Look, Jesse, just breathe easy. Forget the twelve hours. We'll have you out in another minute. Give me your status. How far along are you?"

"Not too far."

"Are your shoulders and chest past the strut yet?"

"I—I'm sorta even with it, I guess."

"Very good, Jesse. Now, I need you to rock gently from side to side—see if that helps slide you past. I'll keep the tension on the rope. If I feel you coming forward, I'll apply a little more. And keep breathing easy, right?"

"Right."

For another minute Wade kept the rope taut and steadily gained more line, amid Jesse's grunts, groans, and cries. At last, Jesse squeezed beyond the strut and the kid birthed to freedom from the tunnel. The ranger guided a dirtier, dustier Jesse to a rock to sit in the sunshine.

"Take deep, easy breaths." While he gave him water, Wade felt at his belt for the line attached to Buck. He felt it loose and pulled it in. He couldn't see the dog anywhere. He couldn't hear him. And he couldn't feel his right hand, which was numb and cramped from the struggle to free Jesse.

"You saved my life, Mr. Wade." Jesse took long drinks between nervous breaths. "Are you OK?"

"Yeah, sure, kid. Except that dog vanished again." Wade rubbed his hand, working to get the feeling back.

"BUCK?" he called, looking all around the site for him. "WHERE ARE YOU?"

"He's got to be right around here." Jesse got to his feet and turned a few aimless circles.

"Hand me the light." Distracted and tense, the ranger knelt down and flashed the headlight into the tunnel. "Buck! Are you back in there? Come, Buck!"

"Hey, Bucky, where are you? Buck!" Jesse shouted, wandering about the site.

Wade rushed to the other end of the culvert. "BUCK!" he demanded. He called over and over, his voice more uneasy with each call.

Another whup-whup came floating in from the brush. Wade felt a dark dread invading his whole body. Shóódé, still hangin' round, he was sure of it, and his worst fear: the nose-sensitive terrier running amok and chasing after her.

He shouted and whistled, darting around the old drainage grids. Jesse, serious and shamefaced, moved out in the opposite direction, calling for Buck.

Wade felt himself tumbling back into a fearful, angry panic—a zone he'd been stuck in for weeks. And over a dog that wasn't even Abby.

Between calls, he listened for more coyote whups. He sent out a silent oath through the surrounding wilderness.

Forget it, Shóódé, Buck's not for you.

11

"Many people are attracted to the Westie because of his cute, stuffed-toy appearance in pictures or at dog shows. This appearance is not the way he looks in everyday life and belies the Westie's strong and independent nature." —Anne Sanders, Westie owner

Buck was drawn to urgent whups, familiar calls from a fellow traveler. In no time, he picked up Shóódé's scent, snooping his way down the hill to another discarded mining claim. For a terrier with a powerful nose, the scene was a wonderland of rich, potent trails to explore. A decayed mix of aromas led him to another network of old drains and culverts where he stopped at a tunnel twice as large as the one he got stuck in.

A strong scent lured Buck on. He rushed in, but slowed to a stop in the darkness. His eyes adjusted to the dim light, and he peered along the musty passage. His far sight was shadowy, though a blend of odors pulled him forward. Nose to the ground, he padded slowly, tracking, until a menacing sound brought him up short. A long, breathy huff-huff echoed through the drain.

Light ahead caught his attention. Just inside the opening at the other end, he made out a shadowy profile. A big animal on its haunches, the shape of its large head triggering Buck's instincts. *Danger.*

Two shining eyes watching him. Fiery eyes. Deadly eyes. *Run.* He turned around and scurried the other way.

Buck scrambled through the tunnel, the huh-huh breaths upon him. He bounded out of darkness and into bright light. He sprinted straight ahead, putting distance between him and the big cat, running toward a tree, to find a safe place, to find any place to hide.

She followed, taking deliberate steps. Out of the tunnel, she stopped to adjust to the light and look around. The dog had disappeared. But a gray-buff blur flew at her from above the culvert. It crashed hard on her back and pinched her flanks, then it hit the ground and zigzagged away.

Shóódé.

The cat, stunned and confused, emitted an angry growl, with no prey in sight. Taking unsure steps, she paced back and forth, searching for the scent of her attacker. She swiveled her head at a slight movement and spotted a long white tail fluttering behind a small tree. She sprang toward it and the gray-buff blur shot from the brush to her left and darted back into the bushes.

Shóódé.

The cat came to a halt, as if unsure how many animals were near and whether predator or prey. A bush ahead shook and a white streak sped away. She sprang in pursuit, but the coyote reappeared. They ran parallel some twenty yards apart and eyed each other as they ran. The big cat veered off to give chase, but Shóódé kicked into a higher speed, gaining distance.

The cat, best only at short sprints, pulled up, breathy, and dropped to her belly. She looked around and stayed that way until the coyote emerged on high ground some fifty yards ahead. Shóódé dropped to her belly as well. Both remained still, cat watching coyote and Shóódé playfully aping the cat.

Buck, panting heavily and moving on shaky legs, climbed back up the slope. He followed a familiar trace, a friendly scent. Soon he heard the whistles atop the hill. He stopped to rest among oak and juniper, keeping cover and stifling the urge to bark and call the cat's attention. When whistles got closer and then the calls, he let out a little whine.

After another whistle, Wade heard a whine and then a short, muted bark from the bank below. "BUCK!" He eased down the bank and found the little escape artist. Low to the ground, in scrub and gnarly juniper, there was Buck's small white body, his button eyes peering up.

"Buck!" Wade rushed to the dog and dropped to his knees. He reached out, but the dazed dog remained as still as a fawn waiting for its mother. Overcome, the ranger found the collar intact and ran his hands over Buck's soft coat. Wade checked his legs and paws, and the dog showed no signs of harm or injuries. Wade patted, caressed, and cuddled him, but Buck had no time for it, alert and still panting, his head tilted left and right, caught by a sound out of human range.

What is it, Buck?

Then Wade heard it. Little need to ponder, for the ranger knew the roar moving downslope came from an angry cat.

Jesse, petrified, stumbled down the slope, breathing hard and hovering close. He fidgeted and turned, fearing danger from every direction.

Wade scooped Buck up in his arms, scanning the mountain slope, alert, expecting worse to come. He hugged the dog. "Buck, that darn nose of yours is gonna get you killed." Wade stayed vigilant, on high alert until the roar from the wild went silent. The dog squirmed to be free.

What now?

Wade set him down, but held him secure by the collar. He inspected the spot where the line broke and found a fraying collar. He opened his pack and offered water. Buck wouldn't drink.

"Keep a steady eye out there, Jesse," Wade cautioned.

Jesse wiggled into a barefoot dancer on hot coals, while Wade worked on rigging a sturdy tie for the dog's lead. He needed to MacGyver something, as Katy called it, for more control over the wild Westie.

Wade rousted through his pack for cord and salvaged more to cobble together a sturdier harness around Buck's belly and shoulders. He sliced out several short strips of Velcro from the pack pockets to secure the harness. While Buck's panting faded, he watched the ranger cut, loop, and tie the cord to the Velcro. An extra shoelace he always carried came in handy to tie the harness together. Buck strapped in; Wade gave the new harness a test lift. Confident the dog was secure, he tied him again to the lead line.

Buck gave a shake from nose to tail, trying to rid himself of the harness. Yet the rugged dog still seemed distracted by something deeper in the canyon. Wade knew it must be the cat.

"Let's get back on the trail," Wade commanded.

Jesse tried to simmer down, though his face betrayed him. His insides were as wary and upset as ever. Yet, the trail was still capable of exerting its magic on Jesse, distracting him from a predator they couldn't seem to shake. Like a kid on a road trip—Are we there yet? Are we there yet? —Jesse called out every so often, "How much longer to the campsite, Mr. Wade?" The ranger's not-so-patient responses were either "Not quite yet" or "Anytime now." In the end, Wade had to explain a geographic fact of hiking a mountain. "You're either goin' up or goin' down, with very few level spots in-between. You keep a lookout for a large flat spot for decent sleeping, a ways off the path."

At last, Jesse pointed to a small plot about a hundred yards off the trail. They moved in for a closer inspection and found a flat spot with partial cover, but near enough to the main path to discourage wildlife from nosing around their camp. Wade spotted a distant vista that was breathtaking and a nearby main road led south toward the small border towns.

The ranger indicated where to lay out their sleeping gear and pointed farther off in brush for the latrine.

"You know how to dig a *cathole* to bury waste out here, don't ya?"

"Sure," Jesse shuttered. "But can we call it another name?"

Buck was already conducting a site inspection with his nose. "Got that too, Buck?"

They barely had their spot staked out when Jesse began collecting loose brush, twigs, and small limbs, stacking them in the center of the campsite.

Wade eyed him, incredulous. "What are you doing?"

"For the fire, sir," came the innocent reply. "What, to send smoke signals to your friends?" Jesse chuckled.

"Signs, Jesse! You didn't see any of those signs posted at the trailheads and along the trail—No

Fires—Highest Danger, No Campfires Allowed in the Dry Season. Not here, no way!" He gave Jesse his best scowl. "Are you aware of the dense vegetation on the slopes of this mountain? We've got thick oak woodlands. A blaze," he paused, kicking at the pile of brush and wood, "your blaze, could race right up this hillside and ignite the whole forest of conifers covering the crest."

"Gosh, I'm sorry, sir, I—"

"All it takes is a small patch of grassland and your fire ladders up the slope, burning bigger and bigger trees as it goes. And the wind, in effect, acts like a giant bellow." Wade flapped his arms like a condor. "Like some mean Vulcan god bent on destroying all vegetation and every living creature!"

"Wow, I didn't realize—"

"You didn't REALIZE? We lose thousands of healthy trees and wildlife in every fire, some caused by lightning, most man-made by idiots like you! People misjudge where and when to start campfires and then they don't completely extinguish the damn things before they pack up and move on!"

He halted his harangue when a smile flickered across Jesse's face.

"WHAT?" the ranger demanded.

"Smokey the Bear," the kid blurted out. "I'm sorry, Mr. Wade, you sound like an angry Smokey. Those 'Smokey the Bear' posters, you know 'Only YOU can prevent forest fires'."

Wade's jaw dropped, and he fixed him with an icy glare. "Wait a minute. That fire back down on the trail—tell me it wasn't yours."

Jesse froze, all traces of humor gone.

"That firepit yesterday, right off the path, the one still smoldering because no one smothered it out. Was that yours?!"

Jesse got jittery. "If you're a ranger, uh, you must carry a badge."

"BADGE!" Wade hollered, purple with rage. "YOU WANT ME TO PROVE TO YOU I'M A RANGER WITH A BADGE?"

From his hard-earned break, a snarly Buck sprang alive and started barking at Wade, then turned his wrath on Jesse. As soon as he heard the dog bark, Wade snapped out of his rage with Jesse and turned to calm the dog—and himself.

"Sorry, Mr. Wade. I was only funnin'. I didn't mean disrespect."

The ranger, bent over and stroking Buck, fumed in silence.

"Alright, it was my fire. I admit it. My socks got all sweaty, and I hate wearing dirty, wet socks. I needed to wash and dry some things. And I was low on water and didn't want to risk ... giard, girard—"

"Giardhea, intestinal infection," Wade said, ice in his voice.

"That's it, sir. But it took forever for the water to boil, plus drying my socks, so I guess the fire got pretty hot."

"Kid, you win a gold medal for the most ill prepared and incompetent hiker on this mountain." He took a deep breath, shaking his head.

Trees gave some cover to their campsite, twilight dying fast. Wade kicked at the twigs and brush, dispersing the pile. "Here's an idea. While we still have some light, we oughta eat and then get some sleep."

Wade regretted his outburst—he should have explained the dangers instead—and then he recalled an argument with Katy, during which Abby erupted in a barking fit at both of them. Katy calmed the dog and assured her that she was right to exercise an "Intervention" before the quarrel escalated.

Like Abby, Buck knew things.

12

"Populations of mammals, birds, fish, reptiles, and amphibians have, on average, declined in size by 60 percent in just over 40 years. The biggest drivers of current biodiversity loss are overexploitation and agriculture, both linked to continually increasing human consumption." —
World Wildlife Fund

Jesse took a nervous turn around the camp, peeking through the foliage surrounding the camp. He gave a little shudder and went back to unloading his bag of meager gear. Along with a few soy snack bars left, his food was raw carrots and assorted vegetables in a Ziploc bag. He took out a couple of well-worn paperbacks— *Animal Liberation* and *Desert Solitaire*— plus some things the ranger didn't recognize, of little use in the wild.

"Thing is, I usually let a fire die overnight, but gosh, last night was truly strange and scary." He dug into his duffel bag as he pleaded his case. "And the racket went on all night, so I wanted out. I admit, I ran ... I didn't put it out right."

"What racket?"

"Well, same as we've been hearing, except right outside my camp. It was—real creepy."

"Predator creepy?"

"Yeah, you got it, Mr. Wade."

"What are those, if you don't mind my asking?" He spotted two Ziplocs that looked to be bathroom supplies.

"Oh, these—uh ... make-up supplies," came a hesitant reply.

Wade frowned.

Jesse quickly added, "They're for creative protests." Wade's expression turned to a blank look. Jesse had his tiny camera in hand, fiddling with it again.

"The camera still working?"

"Yup. It's a GoPro." Jesse proudly strapped it over the bandage around his head. "From my bartered labor. It might come in handy when I start my next protest. I can record the whole experience."

"OK, tell me about your creative protest stuff." He poured water for Buck and pulled out their dinner snacks.

"I'm vegan, remember? I try to teach people about why we shouldn't kill animals for our food." He sat on his pack and munched on a carrot. "Say I'm in this big shopping mall in Denver. I find me a spot along the main pathway where there's plenty of foot traffic, people strolling by the shops or sitting around. Then I find a good place to stand, like a step or a bench. And I start talking to people, see, and some stop and listen. Some stare or just keep walking by with their big shopping bags."

"So, you start jibber-jabbering like the village idiot?"

"I just start talking real natural. And I'm quiet, you see, and I try to draw them into talking about their dogs and cats, maybe. Then I get on to talking about other animals. I usually get a small crowd for starters. If I do it right, I get a bigger crowd, but I'm happy if anyone stops. That's when I start taking off my clothes, real slow and casual-like, you know, maybe the mall's too hot, so it's an everyday thing. I talk about how we kill animals for food when we really don't have to. That we can get along just fine without all that animal protein. Pretty soon I'm down to my skivvies—"

"That's when security shows up and hauls you away."

"If it goes well, they don't show up right away. And, I've got a swimsuit on. Not like I'm doing something real cheesy. Anyway, that's when people can see my body's all marked up with tattoos. I've got these tats all over different parts of my body, marking the places that show where various cuts of meat are located—like I'm an animal to be slaughtered. Butchers used to have posters for customers that showed where they carve up the body parts of cattle and other livestock. Anyway, I keep talking and change positions so people see these different cuts of meat illustrated on my body. If it works out, I start a conversation—"

"Over the shouts and jeers?"

"Well, sometimes people wanna argue—but I try to stay focused, you know, about the ills of a carnivore diet, how it shortens your life and being bad for the planet itself, what with all the livestock grazing and methane gases, and all the trees cut down for more grazing. And I try to throw in medical words, you know, how dysfunctional the human body becomes by consuming so much animal protein and fat. Oh, and most importantly, how it's morally wrong—all the ethical stuff."

"Let me get this straight. You've branded yourself with permanent tattoos, all over your body, showing cuts of beef?"

"Oh, no, Mr. Wade, the tats aren't for real. That's why I carry the make-up supplies for disguises, with fake tats and other stuff—illusory stuff. I have theater friends—actors know all about make-up and disguises—and they give me what I need. I wouldn't go branding myself permanent or anything, because you never know what you'll need to do for your next protest. You have to start with a clean body for every creative protest."

"So to speak," Wade murmured, unable to decide who was dirtier, the dog or the kid. "I suppose in the end you're arrested, or at least booted from the malls."

"Sometimes. With mall police it's always the same—demonstrating on private property."

He's lucky they don't send his sorry, scrawny frame somewhere to fatten him up, Wade figured.

"And you expect to get a few converts with these protests?"

"Well, I hope I get enough time to make a point about how selfish and shameful the idea of species superiority is. That eating other living things isn't necessary and it's very unethical. Since most of my audiences are young like me, I figure some will go away and think about what they saw and heard. Who knows? They might even consider changing their diets. Malls aren't my thing so I don't hang out in them, except when I protest or if I need to use the lavs to clean up."

In the dying light, they could hear another wild call faraway from camp.

"Coyote?"

"Coyote," Wade said, nodding. Buck, packing it in for the day, sprawling on his side, eyes shut. He'd been watered and had snacked on bits of turkey jerky the ranger stirred with trail mix.

"Mr. Wade, have you heard about the wildlife detention camps?"

"What do you mean?"

"I was with this protest group for a while in Colorado. They said a bunch of coyotes were being held in detention pens and they planned to free them. Their scheme was to sneak in at night and release every last coyote. Let 'em go back to being free and wild again."

"Probably one of those Wildlife Services' predator camps, a so-called research facility."

"It isn't the only one?"

"There may be others—they try to keep it hushed up."

"The public doesn't hear about 'em?"

"Until recently they've managed to stay under the radar, even from elected reps who supposedly have a right to know what's going on, since they fund those agencies."

"I can't see how they get away with it."

"Powerful allies—beef ranchers, lamb and pig farmers—all the usual suspects that lobby your politicians to keep things the way they are."

"Not fair to the wild animals."

"Yup, kid, life can be real unfair, especially for coyotes, as you know by now. So, did you free the pack of coyotes?"

"Oh, no, Mr. Wade, I left that group. I wouldn't take any chances on going to prison for enviro terrorism stuff. At least, I haven't yet."

"Wise decision, Jesse."

Wade recalled one terrible flap against Wildlife Services over the use of collars to locate and kill wild predators. He suggested in a National Forest e-mail that all its 'guns-for-hire', maybe even park visitors in general, be the ones radio-collared to closely monitor their FUBARs, routine foul-ups and colossal stupidities. The wildlife would be far better off. He was forced to interact with all kinds of toadies and dummies—whether at Wildlife Services, the National Parks, or US Fish and Wildlife, all separate but all under the U.S.

Department of Interior—but he didn't always cooperate with any of them.

"Do you know what a euphemism is, Jesse?"

"Uh, sure. That's when you use a word that's, say, not so offensive to cover over something awful?"

"Exactly, as in Wildlife Services," Wade said grimly. "It's a hit-man agency for killing wild animals, even though they use a name that has nothing to do with the welfare or service to wildlife. While its purpose has never changed, at least the names it used to be called fit its true tasks: Animal Damage Control or the Division of Predatory Animal and Rodent Control."

"I guess most people wouldn't want to learn how these poor animals die."

"I reckon they'd rather ignore it."

"It's terrible stuff, Mr. Wade. They even shoot coyotes and wolves from planes and choppers. And they use those horrible traps that take days for the animals to die. They feel the same pain we do! They even gas them to death—whole families in their coyote dens."

Jesse, his head bowed, covered his face with his hands. "I can't believe they let those things happen!"

"Agriculture and its 'co-operators,' sad to say."

"Co-operators?"

"The bloodsuckers who contract with Big Ag. The same farmers and ranchers who whine about the government interfering in their lives—until they call in Wildlife Services."

"Welfare parasites. That's what Edward Abbey calls them." Jesse raised his copy of *Desert Solitaire.*

Wade shook his head. He had always pondered how humanity ended up so unkind against wild canines. How could men kill and slaughter a coyote that looks and even behaves in so many ways like a regular house pet, whose only "flaw" is to choose to live free in the wild, find its own food and mate, and start a family unburdened?

Jesse, along with most people, had a fuzzy understanding about the connection between the U.S. Department of Agriculture and its killing arm, Wildlife Services. But the kid knew cruelty and senseless killing, and injustice, when he saw it. If Wade himself had any mission in life, it was butting heads with coyote trappers and resisting those who showed an easy willingness to commit cruelty and killing of animals, domestic or wild.

Yet after a time, you grow weary of the whole damn, ugly fight. Still, how often do you have a chance, right at your own campsite, to prime the pump for the next generation of protestors— already a so-called creative protestor at that?

"I agree, Jesse. While abused and slaughtered for two-hundred years, coyotes are among the most intelligent and resilient mammals on earth."

"Is that because they eat just about anything?"

"Ultimate omnivores. You couldn't find a better mammal for controlling pests or a more resourceful predator. I'd say the coyote is the ideal survivor of the fittest, a perfect animal to support a healthy genetic pool and environment."

As if right on cue, another string of vocals erupted in the dark. They listened intently until the coyote chorus faded.

"True, they can be odd and surprising creatures, but kid, if you wanted a fresh cause, you could do a lot worse than organizing a creative protest for the coyote. We need sleep now, and you still need that head gash sewed up ASAP."

As the campsite grew dark, Wade turned his headlamp on. Jesse and Buck were curled up and falling asleep, the kid on his yoga mat and the dog on Wade's bedding. After the ranger turned the headlamp off, Jesse opened his eyes.

"You are a park ranger, aren't ya', Mr. Wade?"

"I am. Though I speak as a private individual. Besides, I'm taking a little break from rangering."

"Is that how you got those scars, rangering?"

"What do you mean?"

"I noticed the scars on your fingers, sir, the right hand."

"Oh. I tussled once with a badger—he got the best of it, kid."

"Mr. Wade, sir, could you stop calling me 'kid'?"

"Sure, if you stop calling me 'sir' and 'Mr. Wade'."

For a while there was quiet, but not for long. Soon, a strange creature chorus rang out, not the cicadas from earlier in the day. This was a different noise, a clucking-cooing song surrounded the camp, like the sounds quail make, only amplified about twenty times. But they weren't quail keeping them awake. If they were, Wade imagine them the size of baby dinosaurs. He lost track of how long the weird sounds lasted. Even Buck, in a deep dog coma earlier, began to stir.

Hours later, after sliding into a stupor of half sleep, Wade opened his eyes. The hyper-sounds of quail were gone, but the distant call of a feline—not so much a cat shriek, but more a growl—took its place. He swore there were moments when the resonant growl sounded as deep as the rumble of mufflers on an old, idling race car. When a glow appeared in the darkness, it jerked him wide awake. He heard Jesse stirring. He could see the kid futzing with his GoPro again. In camera light, the boy looked disturbed by something on the screen.

Night dragged on into dawn and all was quiet. He could see dim outlines of Jesse and the camp. It was a hard night for the kid; he sat propped against his duffel, as jumpy and fidgety as a drinker coming off a hard-liquor bender. Buck, stretched out next to the boy, couldn't have offered much solace through the night of noises.

Wade went about the early routine of breakfast and breaking camp. "You okay, kid?"

"I can't take it anymore, Mr. Wade," Jesse whimpered nearby. "I gotta move on."

He studied the boy as he nervously collected his gear, tossing it mindlessly in his duffel. In dim light, he still had the crumpled bandana wrapped around his forehead, his straggly, dirty-blond hair, the smudgy face, and beard—the kid needed a serious makeover. But the lined face and exposure to wind and sunburn seemed almost irreversible. Wade was looking at a late teen, twenty at most, but with the hardened, weathered face of a man maybe twice his age.

With hands unsteady, Jesse started to stow his camera away but then hesitated. He turned it back on and after the screen glowed, he clicked on a picture and unsteadily handed the camera to the ranger. A huge head covered the frame. A wild cat, fiery amber eyes, wide-open mouth that exposed large canines. In the foreground of the frame, he could see part of the duffel bag attached to the back of Jesse's bike.

"Kiss my grits," Wade uttered after staring at it for a time.

"Mr. Wade, I got what they call hidden demons ..." Jesse's voice trailed off. "They're wantin' to chase me right out of these mountains."

13

"Emotions are the gifts of our ancestors. We have them and so do other animals. We must never forget this." —Biologist Marc Bekoff in The Emotional Life of Animals

Jesse had to keep moving, keep his boney frame in motion, away from the campsite and the eerie presence that hung on through the night.

Even Buck knew, the way dogs do, of the fear and panic that gripped him. He didn't know why, but he had made a connection with the Westie. Buck had cuddled up to him through the awful, never- ending hours, together against the cat shrieks from the surround of deadly black.

Back on the trail, he was sure he heard Shóódé hanging around, yip-yipping every now and again. But when he stopped pushing his bike to listen, he couldn't hear her. He already missed her calls. She was a strange comfort against the terrible night predator—her yip-yips curled up beside him, along with Buck, through the long, miserable, dark hours.

What a low point on his journey when he made his quick getaway. The ranger must have thought him a real weenie of a kid. He wished he hadn't said goodbye in a panic—though there was no anger in the parting, like during the campfire incident. Jesse never could talk much about his true story, and anyway, who would believe a big, wild cat leapt right up behind you on your bike? But seeing is believing. All Jesse could think to do was show Wade the scary picture of being chased in a race for his life. And he had to get away from the cat that had stayed with him through yet another night.

But after leaving camp, he heard no more horrific, guttural noises. Maybe daylight had scared the cat off for good. And mercifully, there were no more sensations of being tailed. A hopeful feeling built in his bones that the predator no longer cared about him. At last, he could travel the trail without those jumpy, over-the-shoulder glances.

Mr. Wade's stories about Shóódé and her kind, forever hunted and butchered, stirred in him a real union with the Shóódés of the wild—maybe something even bigger, a canine bond born in the same moment with dog and coyote, one tame and the other wild. And then there was the ongoing conflict over restoring a few packs of Mexican wolves in Arizona.

"The Department of Justice only prosecutes those who kill wolves if they think they can prove the person intentionally killed an endangered species," Mr. Wade had said. "The law makes it easy to kill wolves because hunters and ranchers can claim they thought the gray wolf was a coyote. So not only do they take endangered gray wolves, as always, the lowly coyote is the scapegoat, always left with no status at all, no protection anywhere, anytime." Jesse had it all written down—for the record, a record he would never forget.

He heard another yip. He pictured Shóódé and wondered if she would ever have pups—and if they would be exterminated in their dens by Wildlife Services' hired killers, never having a chance at life. In some ways, he counted himself like those pups, feeling unsafe around the very people who were supposed to love and care for him. Maybe that's why he needed to be a Shóódé, roaming and running wild, always moving on when things turned troubling or dangerous.

Jesse's father came into his mind and Jesse slid into a trauma from his childhood that happened during a family outing at the zoo. His dad, who had a habit of doing dumb, weird things, went all crazy that day. He grabbed Jesse, holding him by his wrists, dangling him over the safety bars of the cat enclosure. How a family of big cats, a whole pride of them, circled around below, looking up curiously as he hung helplessly in the air. How the cats sprang at him, trying to grab hold of his feet. There he was, caught between the terrifying cats below and a monster of a dad above who smiled and giggled like a maniac. How he cried and how his mom screamed at his dad to pull him back up to safety.

That day was the first time he planned his getaway. He had never told anyone this story and now he wished he'd had the guts to stay at Mr. Wade's campsite and share the truth about the heart of his dread.

When he came out of it, he was wet with sweat and he shivered. Jesse looked back at the trail, sighed deeply, wiped the sweat from his face, and wondered how far back on the path Mr. Wade and Buck were. He continued to plod his way toward the trailhead.

14

"Lapdogs … not! Sitting still does not compute for Westies. Their mental and physical energies require them to always be doing something. Westies have a high please mode and will try to accommodate your wishes by giving you their version of a lapdog. If you're lucky, to lie patiently in your lap for maybe five minutes."—Writer and Dog Trainer Deb Duncan

Wade remembered the oval-shaped lake, a picture-perfect stop along the route. But the water level was severely reduced by drought, and it looked as if the surrounding piñon pines, oaks, junipers, cottonwoods, and sycamores had sucked the lake dry. At water's edge, he heard the hum of insects, led by a glut of grasshoppers. His panting partner, instead of dropping to his belly to take a breather, sniffed his way over to the lakeside, and nosed and lapped at the clear, tepid water.

The ranger felt better than he ought to, having been awake most of the night with the strange drone of the big cat lurking near their camp. The bizarre murmurs and cries had pushed Jesse into a jittery, anxious state the whole night. Wade agreed the nerve-wracking bouts of sleep were enough to make a normal person come down with a bad case of cat phobia.

How the kid had acquired such a fierce case of feline fear was not at all clear. One of his creative protests gone wrong? One he might not have been ready for? The ranger could only guess—not that he had time to piece it together with a large predator at the edge of camp. Yet, while Jesse confessed to a cat phobia, he seemed captivated when face-to-face with the coyote. Obviously, the ranger realized some people were naturally drawn to wild animals—wolves, coyotes, big cats—but for Jesse, wild canines might attract him, while felines repel him.

In hindsight, Wade better understood (without condoning) the kid's need for an illegal campfire; at least it made more sense after undergoing a night of groans and bellows from a predator unwilling to move on. In the end, the kid was so antsy to get back on the trail and make a run for the trailhead that he even refused the offer of cold tea and cereal. How the boy survived on such scant protein was a dietary mystery to Wade.

Wade had tried to put the best face on it and assured him that he'd make better time on his own. "We all gotta hike at our own pace." As he'd waved Jesse on, the ranger reminded him to get that forehead mended.

While concerned about Jesse's condition, Wade was relieved to be back on his own with Buck.

They had made steady progress for a good two hours. They kept a brisk pace with eyes and ears alert, as the dog, nose rituals aside, more or less adapted to keeping up. For the open stretches when he felt it was safe, the ranger let him drag his lead and trail behind, seemingly unaware of being unrestrained and showing no signs of tuckering out. They quick-marched through flat and easy-rolling grasslands and clusters of bush and mesquite, and Buck, in spite of his short legs, kept valiant pace.

The little lake location and surrounding trees and lush meadows seemed ideal to break for lunch. Wade drank from his flask while the dog dipped paws in cool water and splashed around. As soon as dried fruit and turkey jerky were pulled from the backpack, Buck made a beeline for his share. When he gave the dog a closer inspection, he noticed flecks of rabbit blood still streaked the white hair around the muzzle from his predator chase and kill.

"How about a snack, ya little carnivore?" He tore off a strip of jerky and ordered the dog to sit, which he promptly obeyed. "You picked up some manners back home, didn't you?" Having acquired a taste for jerky, Buck chewed and bobbed his head with obvious delight. This was repeated several more times and the ranger took some for himself.

As the dog licked around his spotted chops, Wade wondered, not for the first time, if Buck had the grit to keep up during the tests to come. Could he make the many more miles to the trailhead under his own power? There would be obstacles and risks. And what about the trailhead itself? Would there be any hikers there? Would they be reliable and able to cart the dog to the nearest vet?

And what if this big cat or some other predator made a bold move?

Damn, there could be a heap of trouble.

After a few encounters with lions, Wade knew he'd put himself in more danger than he should have. Prime predators most likely would keep clear of him alone but, with Buck tagging along, a big one could turn aggressive and attack. Top predators routinely pick up animal scents, tracking, and stalking over great distances. Alpha predators were dangerous and intelligent. And after the glimpse at Jesse's GoPro, Wade had a vivid picture of the predator undoubtedly stalking them.

There was another side of the prey equation to consider, too. Buck's basic terrier instincts, his sudden shift to predator upon spotting rabbits, could put them both at risk. Wade, who liked reading about animals, recalled an on-the-road memoir by John Steinbeck; how he'd been warned against his Standard Poodle interacting with bears when entering Yellowstone National Park. Steinbeck had assured the park ranger that Charley was a peaceful, tranquil dog; a coward at heart. Yet the author was shocked when Charley became a maniacal bundle of rage and aggression as soon as they spotted a bear less than a mile from the park entrance.

There was little doubt how Buck would react—if, as Steinbeck observed, "Bears simply brought out the Hyde in my Jekyll-headed dog"—Wade figured he'd be burdened with a terrier full of pure, raging Hyde at the sight of anything on four legs that didn't resemble another canine. For both their sakes, he hoped rescuing the little runt didn't prove the biggest blunder of his life.

You don't have a choice, mister. Katy's voice rang in his head, a reminder of what they both believed. Caring for a dog was of the highest calling.

He gave Buck the once-over as they finished lunch. He seemed in good health apart from his gritty, dirty brown appearance and rabbit-stained chops—a matted mess of trail mud, dust, and desert debris from his days wandering and hiding. Wade found a small tube of organic travel soap in his pack, quickly took his boots and socks off and rolled up his pant-legs. He swept the dog up in his arms and carried him into the shallow lake for a dip in the water and a vigorous lather. Not a bit of struggle from Buck. He was a dog used to a bath, though he kept shaking a ton of water from his double coat.

Wade finished rinsing him off and saw the dripping animal beneath all the dust and dirt—a beaming snow-white Westie.

Dancing out of the lake onto rocks, shaking himself one last time, Buck stretched his head to the rocks, butt upward, and ran his paws over his face and pointy white ears, trying to wring himself dry. Wade wiped his feet dry with a flannel shirt he'd worn earlier that morning, put his socks and boots back on, then grabbed the dog by the tail and pulled him close to dry his face. Working his way along the strip of beige down Buck's back, he noticed something strange he'd missed when he lathered him up.

At the nape of his neck he found slight puncture marks just under his hair. Could they be widely spaced, large canine fangs? The lesions appeared fresh, though there was no sign of blood. An odd wound it was—though Buck didn't seem at all bothered by it.

In any case, Buck looked the regular, pampered house pet, renewed, restored, and revived by a little snack, soap, and water. What a piss-ant live wire, Wade mused, one scrappy little terrier, a fearless force in a tough, undersized body. He tracked after the dog taking in new odors and prancing about the lakeside. Wade, aware of his mood lifting, caught himself even breaking out with a hint of a smile.

What a different animal from his serene and obedient Abby.

When he had come home with her as a puppy, she was a golden-brown ball of soft hair with a cute, broad face. She reminded him of a story he'd read as a teen, the tale about an old miser whose gold coins were stolen from his cottage in an English village. One day the miser came out of a stupor at his fireside hearth where, in place of his heap of hoarded hard coins, he found a child asleep. A little girl, a fair one with gold ringlets like the miser's very own childhood sister who had died when they were poor children. A precious child that would become a more treasured gift than gold coins for the miser, same as Abby had been for Wade.

Abby, his big beautiful treasure of a Golden Retriever was gone. A runaway, maybe taken by coyotes? Lo and behold, in her place was a squeaky-clean, shimmering white marvel of a Westie—a pain in the backside to boot. As he followed this glittering white creature—his tail trailing in the breeze like a white plume on a soldier's helmet—he recalled Abby's long, flowing, gold tail. And he was startled by a frightful realization: how much Buck, with his shiny white coat, would stand out in a wild environment where it's best to blend in to survive.

What have I done? Buck might as well have a big target painted on his little white rump, like a white-tailed rabbit.

A few hundred yards across the lake, movement caught Wade's eye—more mule deer near the shore. Binoculars in hand for a closer look, he glassed to the right of the deer where a smaller form moved steadily along the lake. He focused to catch sight of a canine— coyote by its size and bushy tail—loping along the shore and meandering over to lap at water.

"Might be our new friend, Buck." But the coyote was too far away to catch Buck's attention. The ranger tracked the creature as it ambled along the lake's edge, limping slightly between otherwise graceful strides.

Well, Shóódé, my friend, we meet again. Why are you on the prowl at midday? Like other predators, coyotes typically hunt early morning and from sunset through the cover of night. Still, he knew coyotes were becoming more active at all hours, day or night these days. And Shóódé could be on a bigger move, he guessed, migrating north with many other wild creatures. Still, something seemed amiss. Were other predators competing with her? Was she changing her hunting schedule?

He pulled out his water filter and pumped lake water to refill his bottles. As he finished, he secured his backpack and tethered Buck. They moved northeast along the lake, coyote and deer herd disappearing to cover on the other side.

Then, among the trees, another figure caught his eye. Wade glassed in for a close-up. A woman with a small backpack emerged from the brush, her head down, walking in a slow, searching posture. She took careful cat steps, stopped every so often, stooped to collect stuff off the ground, and dropped the contents in a small bag. He watched her move on, repeating the procedure, head down in concentration, unaware of the deer or coyote, much less a ranger with a dog across the lake. Finally, she looked up, turned toward the lake, and listened for something. With a confident, determined expression, she returned to her careful search along the ground.

At a clearing farther on, Wade and Buck heard Shóódé's yip-yip, sounding closer. They stopped to listen. Was she actually tracking and leapfrogging ahead of them? The dog, still but alert, cocked his head from side to side. In a whoosh of noise, the coyote darted out of the bushes, bee-lined across their path, and disappeared as quickly into a thicket at the other side.

Such coyote behavior stymied the ranger. Living at the edge of the mountains and familiar with scores of coyotes, Wade found their ways, and manner of hunting and play, endlessly fascinating. Still, this showed another level of unusual behavior.

Wade stayed motionless while the dog growled quietly, his pointy ears alert, tail curling up and forward. "Stay on your guard, Buck. Shóódé may be messin' with us."

Wade glassed again for the woman near the lake, but she was gone.

15

"Protect the park from the people, the people from the park, and the people from the people."—Jerry Smith, Snohomish County Park Ranger, Quoting the US NPS Park Ranger motto

Footprints … cat paws … tracks the size of a softball or larger. Rachel Green carefully circled the prints, checking the predator's lobe marks, etched in a patch of sand near the lake. She noted the slight arc of the toes, the toe three leading. For days along the trail, she had been finding the same heel pads. As a cat biologist, Rachel knew the tracks were feline and not mountain lion. Just that morning, she had actually heard a muffled roar. But was this cat the real thing … was she onto the most elusive mega predator in the Americas? Mirage, the most cunning of cats?

Rachel found more cat tracks when she got to her next camera trap and opened it to check the memory card. The recent tracks were of great interest, but she'd seen them before and Mirage had yet to be captured on any camera. These days Rachel and her colleagues made routine checks weekly to monitor the kinds of animals passing along the trails.

Rachel clicked through photos from the last few days—night shots of a coyote and raccoons passing, and even a coati. But when the camera showed rare daylight shots, she knew she'd hit the jackpot—she had a jaguar! She almost clicked past the first image because the furry face was right up close to the camera, sniffing at the foreign object. Apparently satisfied the metal box was a thing not alive and not worth crushing in its strong jaws, the cat backed away and moved on. A jaguar spotting in daylight and captured on their camera!

Rachel had to catch her breath, coming hard and fast. She stopped the camera on a perfect side shot of the cat. She knew the coat pattern of this creature was not one of the recent male jaguars that cameras had caught in the Santa Rita Mountains. This was her Mirage, the first recorded female jaguar in these mountains in well over fifty years, and she had undoubtedly traveled north from the source population some hundred miles south in Mexico.

Rachel finished clicking through the rest of the photos, put the precious memory card in her vest pocket, and reloaded the camera with a new card. She felt a surge of satisfaction. How extraordinary—a female jaguar at last reclaiming a former habitat north of the Mexican border!

Not far along the trail, she spotted more tracks, took more shots, and moved on, easing her way through thick scrub. She couldn't help imagining how Mirage would take soft cat steps on those hefty paws, crisscrossing the paths, and stopping to lay in wait for a good meal, a javelina, a coati, perhaps a cottontail for starters. The Santa Ritas and other lush habitat in the border region offered Mirage a variety of wildlife prey close to her home range in Mexico.

With pending news of a female jaguar on the prowl in the Santa Ritas, colossal changes would be coming. After cross-verification back in the photo lab confirmed her Mirage sighting, Rachel knew it would be a game changer, not only for her field of study, but for her own career as well. Only recently, lab tests of cat scat from those mountains had proved positive for jaguar. But did that mean jaguars had moved in and established habitat? Jaguars are notoriously elusive cats. True, males had been recorded, but males roam much farther than females. But sure enough, the last scat samples she submitted came back positive. Not just jaguar, but a female—her Mirage—hugely significant for Arizona. And now she had her on camera. Unbelievable ... fantastic.

Rachel wondered why a smart, stealthy cat like Mirage—jaguars famous as night predators—was taking more chances and coming out in daylight. Of course, this gave Rachel a better chance of a live spotting of this exotic creature. Maybe just a fleeting one, but she felt it was their time to meet for real, somewhere, sometime soon.

A coyote had called out as she was trailing the cat tracks to the familiar wildlife respite at Circle Lake. Rachel knew her mission was urgent. She needed to move quickly to protect Mirage and her habitat. She and her colleagues must tread a fine line. Let it be known that a rare, wonderful, federally protected endangered predator roamed the region, while only a few trusted biologists and naturalists must know anything about Mirage's specific location, chosen paths, and habitat.

She was the last of her species and they wanted to kill her ... a line from an Isaac Asimov story echoed through her head.

16

"We need wilderness—whether or not we ever set foot in it. We need a refuge—even though we may never need to go there …. We need the possibility of escape as surely as we need hope; without it the life of the cities would drive all men into crime or drugs or psychoanalysis." —Writer and Naturalist Edward Abbey

R anger and dog hiked along a wash for a good mile, Buck still moving on his own four pads. Wade saw a big rock ahead, a huge boulder perched at the edge of the wash. As they approached, he saw water in the wash, small pools at least. No evidence of larva or tadpoles in the shallow stream, but Buck jerked his head about, following gnats and a dragonfly darting from one tiny puddle to another. Wade gave him slack and he tentatively waded in a large pool. At once, he started to paw, slap, and thrash at insects in the water. Just as soon he gave up, confused to find the pool vacated of all bugs. He settled for tanking up on cool water.

The ranger felt they were between a rock and a pleasant place this time and had found a good location for a campsite. He scaled the big boulder and surveyed a vast, painter-perfect desert to the east, a land spotted with piñon and pine trees dotting the foothills and lining the higher ranges.

From his rock perch, he could glass a whole cluster of mighty Sky Islands to the southeast, distant swells stretching toward borders east and south. He was high enough that he could sneak a hazy view of the massive Chiricahua's farther east to the New Mexico border.

Buck, tethered to Wade's backpack below, sprawled near the water pools, his short legs splayed, playing the part of road kill. Wet and tired from hiking and chasing anything that moved, he lay quiet, tongue hanging loose, the soul of patience, the urge to explore on hold.

Wade eased off the boulder and set up sleeping gear nearby. A quiet site, except for the periodic ping of insects upon water pools. He found a deeper pool to filter water, passing a bowl of water to the dog, his tired button eyes watching the ranger's every move. Food next, Wade pulled cold snacks from his pack. The usual—jerky and a little trail mix with water.

Buck stirred and came over to sniff at the backpack but snubbed the usual grub. Gingerly, Wade opened the bag of smelly dead rabbit and tossed it on a rock well beyond them. He put the snack mix under the dog's nose. Buck ignored him and nosed up to the foul-smelling bag.

"Oh, of course," Wade sighed. "Not too tired for stinkin' raw rabbit, eh?"

Two things dawned on him: Buck craved real protein, but how could he risk feeding Buck raw day-old rabbit. Wild faunae can carry infectious parasites like trichina worms from undercooked meat. And this was a raw, stinky dead rabbit. Wade broke down and decided to start a tiny fire, to roast the damn rabbit as fast as possible for the little canine carnivore.

At times the ranger packed a mini-camp stove, and fuel canister, along with an all-purpose frying pan. He'd left them behind, over Katy's objections. "I know how you like to eat, at least 'til a month ago." Then she'd added, "How will you ever live it down when a rescue crew recovers a starving park ranger—for want of a few survival items, like a food stash along the way ... and a frying pan in your pack?"

Wade bitched to himself as he gathered some sticks and dry brush for a fire next to the creek, thanking the camp gods for an absent Jesse. With the dog still tethered, he pulled out his all-purpose knife and sat at a pool of water with rank rabbit on a flat rock. He hadn't gutted and skinned one in ages but once the procedure is performed, it's much easier the next time.

The job finished, the game rinsed in a pool of water, he was back at the fire with the rabbit skewered on a sharp branch, supported by a Y of limbs on each side of the fire. Plenty of well-cooked rabbit with leftovers to seal and dole out later to the hungry little beast. After all, he figured Buck would need all the energy he could muster for the final leg to the trailhead in the morning.

Buck nosed up close to the skewer to witness each turn of the spit, until the ranger removed the still sizzling meat and dabbed it with a bit of cold water to cool it.

"Have at it, little predator." He set chunks of rabbit in a bowl in front of Buck. Watching him devour it as the camp darkened, he swore he'd never seen an animal enjoy a meal more—and no house pet was more deserving. Wade even sampled a bit, but couldn't get much past the pungent odor.

Cleanup was easy and quick. Making sure to carefully dispose of rabbit skin and innards, he double wrapped the leftovers, the entrails separately. As the western light faded beyond the mountain, he hung the sealed eatables from a Palo Verde tree well away from camp, per camp-food protocol. With any luck, the ranger and dog would survive the nose of nightly predators roaming the slopes.

Lying on his sleeping bag, Wade gazed at a sky of diamonds, the ragamuffin tucked under the bivy against him, fast asleep except for quiet groans and the odd yelp.

The ranger's thoughts turned to dogs and their human companions. Would the Westie's family give up all hope of finding their Buck? You never give up on them; never easily, not ever, really ... words as familiar to Wade as a mantra. Since Abby disappeared, he'd pondered the misfortune from every angle, right into the ground. That she might have run away, that dog behavior could be like human behavior, like that of homeless souls, even street kids like Jesse. Does something snap and they just need to run off on their own, however miserable or frightened they are? Perhaps they can't find their way out of the maze of their minds, let alone find a way back home.

He must have dozed off in the quiet and darkness. The calm came alive with familiar, comforting coyote calls. He recalled Ed Abbey describing coyote's "weird, unearthly song, like the legendary wail of banshees." As he listened, he wondered if Shóódé was near, maybe among them, her solitary voice floating through the clear night air. Or was she on her own and on the move farther north? Wild calls were having no effect on Buck, flat-out oblivious to the night sounds after the day's forced march, nosing and hiking the trail.

Forget the call of the wild, if this wee dog's goin' native, it ain't happenin' tonight.

That old nature poet had it right, the English chap who grumbled that "the world is too much with us." What a joy to put some time and distance between us and the human race.

Out there in the pitch black, among the cactus, ocotillo, prickly pear, greasewood bush, with a woodpecker or a cactus wren offering background music, he felt free of sloppy, braying humanity. Oh, humans are OK, at least some—well, a few anyway—but apart from Abby, his real love and compassion always tipped toward wildlife and nature. "Biophilia." An odd word that popped into his head as he closed his eyes on the sparkling constellations. Biophilia: having an innate love for the natural world. Calling yourself a naturalist, though, seemed a mite better than claiming to be biophilic, which sounds more like a crime or a disease. Even so, he'd live with it either way.

He seldom let on much to his fellow humans about his natural-world affinity. He knew how weird and unfeeling it would sound to a species as self-centered and destructive as humans. "Are you some interspecies weirdo?" somebody might ask. Better to let things be (except for those serial killers who work for organizations that hide under mislabels like "Wildlife Services"), and he mostly didn't share his sense of how much healthier, how much saner, living among animals could be.

When the issue popped up, his counselor asking about his cynophilist tendencies, she seemed surprised that he'd even heard of the word. As for any special communication with animals, any uncanny knack for communing with wildlife, he could scarcely claim any talents. Cripes, he was pretty sure that a *wildlife whisperer* was strange and well-nigh impossible, that talking to animals was just another wacko claim he would never want pinned on him.

He tried to doze off again but Abby kept coming into his mind. When he brought her home from the animal shelter, just a puppy, he never for a moment considered her a rescue. He was the blessed one, the rescued one—from the very beginning. And he knew they would be the perfect pair after their run-in with the badger.

It was a quiet morning in early spring, Abby not a year old, a curious, sprawling puppy, weaving her clumsy way along a foothill trail not far from the ranch house. She was on a long line ahead, snooping around a tight corner when he heard a sudden yelp, then a string of agonized cries. When he rounded the bend, the creature had hold of Abby's face—in its jaws! Wade pulled back on her lead, but the beast held on firmly. A badger with a vicious grip on her nose and would not let go. He rushed in, grabbing at the badger to pull it away, but the darn thing had loose skin, hard to take firm hold of. He managed to work his way up to its jaws, got a purchase, and yanked its mouth open enough to free poor Abby. But then the badger clamped down on his right hand and he was in a struggle with a varmint that might never let go.

With blood running out of the badger's mouth— ranger blood—he had to find another way to get free. That was when he went all calm and left off struggling. OK, OK, you win, was all he could remember thinking, and darn if the badger didn't let up on its vise-like hold, and the furry thing dashed away without taking his right hand with it. For Wade, another incident in a series that got him wondering if he might at least have an unusual way of relating to wild ones. Maybe passive resistance was the way to go. But try telling that to a hunter being chased by a grizzly.

Fortunately, they were close to his pickup at the trailhead. He got to Doc Ruth's vet clinic, pronto. Abby needed nose stitches but it turned out he got the worst of it with lacerated fingers and a hand with nerve damage which taught him the hard lesson to never use a retractable leash for walking a dog. After hearing his story, a native friend advised that if he ever tangled with a wild animal again, he should sing to it. Go figure.

Yet, if ever two beings fused over a shocking mishap, it was he and Abby who became perfect companions. Henceforth, he never doubted he was capable of deep devotion to another being, if not a human, then an animal for sure. Even now, he felt the choke of emotion as he recalled all their minor hassles with neighbors and their adventures against the world, especially among his brief liaisons. Lady friends who had to audition for Abby to see if they fit in, to qualify for hanging around the place.

There was the spick-and-span lady who always washed her hands after petting Abby; another he pegged a discipline freak as she considered a dog unacceptable up on any furniture, and God forbid, never on the bed. There was even one who wished Abby to be strictly an outdoor pet. And when he found out that the shopper lady tied Abby up like a horse at the hitching post outside the outfitters store, he practically had a conniption fit. She didn't last long at all.

Then "vet gal" entered the picture. That was what he took to calling Katy when he learned she was studying for a second career in animal care— "like a nurse practitioner," she said, "but for pets." He knew at once she was a serious contender for Abby's affections—and his. After dating for a while and having their first serious argument, Katy stopped seeing him. Shortly after that, Wade realized Abby was gone, as well.

He couldn't find her. Whatever special animal empathy he possessed, vanished.

At his wit's end, he broke down and called Katy to tell her Abby was missing—could she come and help look for her?

"Did you check underneath the house?"

"Why would she be under the house?" That would be odd, but when he went under to check, there she was. And when he called her to come out, she wouldn't move. Even treats wouldn't lure her out.

Wade called Katy again. "She won't come out."

When Katy arrived and got down under the house, she talked real quiet with her. Abby came out right away.

"What was that all about?" he asked.

"Oh, it's a girl thing," she replied, matter-of-factly. "But she's OK now—we're both OK."

Must be a girl thing. From then on, he knew Katy was the right one—if she would have him back.

At last, he was drifting off when another wail rang out. He sensed something peculiar going on with this wild coyote creature. He'd read those early trappers and settlers figured coyotes the most intelligent animals in the world. Of course, they used a highly scientific phrase, *smart sonsofbitches*. Was it possible Shóódé had actually been tracking them for the last two days? Plum odd ....

Buck rolled over. The ranger felt his short legs poking him in the ribs as the dog stretched out. Must be dreaming, imagining those short legs of his got suddenly long like a coyote's, so he can run and keep up with the big ones. Wade smiled. Now it was a soft muzzle up against him. Abby did that when she wanted a treat. Back home, there were even moments when he was sure she was still there. He could feel her pushing her muzzle against him—her touch like the ache of an amputee's phantom limb—but when he looked down then, it was only Buck, too tired now for a treat.

What a mess, out on a big mountain with a small white dog. And hardly anything decent to feed the beggar.

"Guess I get sort of emotional about my dog, most dogs," he found himself confessing to the anger management counselor. "That would include coyotes."

17

"Explore, Learn, and Protect!" —Junior Park Ranger motto

Jesse stood on a wide pathway in early morning light. *Where am I gonna stash my gear?*

Late the day before, he'd wandered to a more familiar pathway, like one of those utility trails—maybe for off-road vehicles—because he couldn't imagine it being used for anything else in such a deserted place. It seemed as good as anywhere to camp the night, with no predator lurking, no sight or sound of anybody or anything.

Yesterday had been exhausting, nothing but hike-a-bike, no chance to hop on and ride. Rest breaks became as long as his walks, the weight of his duffel bag heavier by the minute. Having slept so little for the last two nights, a short nap turned into two hours. He woke in a panic and, jumpy and nervous, he skittered on, ending up at that very spot for an early camp, hoping to thumb a ride on a passing ATV in the morning.

There he was, still waiting the next day to put his thumb out for someone, whether on foot or with wheels. Still, he'd caught up on sleep without spooky noises during the night. Until he got snapped awake, startled by a distant whistle, an unexpected alarm jangling his nerves. But at least it wasn't the beastie cat that wouldn't let go of his life.

For breakfast he ate his last soy bar and the rest of the dried-up raw vegetables, his stomach as empty as he'd ever felt. He nosed around the campsite for a time and found a juniper tree with its small purplish berries. He knew as a kid that you could eat the plentiful berries, that they were sorta' more a nut than a berry. His stomach growling back at him, he picked a few and tried them. They tasted kind of oily and bitter and had a pit. He picked a bunch to take along, and if it got really bad, like he felt he was starving, he could always pick more to eat along the way. If his stomach could take the dang things.

Drowsy and weak, he couldn't figure how he could go on with all his gear. He had sat alone and cogitated for a long while, like his mother advised. He spun a wheel on his bike, passing time, hoping someone would show up, maybe even Mr. Wade and the dog. Maybe they weren't that far behind. What to do? He must stay to join up with them again, but a quiet voice inside reminded him that a dangerous cat still roamed, "claiming the slope" or whatever. And the voice urged him to get off that mountain, pronto.

OK, here's what: *I gotta have a plan. First step, find someplace to hide my duffel with my gear. Then I'll go for the trailhead and hang around.* He would be safe and he could check that Mr. Wade and Buck made it out. But there was the bike—he would have to face more hike-a-biking if he took it with him. As light as it was, it felt heavy now, so he would have to leave it behind too. He would take only the most basic survival stuff, like the tiny flashlight and the last of his water. *Oh, and my GoPro for sure.*

He headed out feeling weaker than the day before, weaker than he'd ever felt. And he was sure those juniper nuts didn't agree with his stomach. Yikes!

18

"And not only did Buck learn by experience, but instincts long dead became alive again. The domesticated generations fell from him. In vague ways he remembered back to the youth of the breed, to the time the wild dogs ranged in packs through the primeval forest and killed their meat as they ran it down." —Jack London's The Call of the Wild

In a cool, easy dawn, instead of the black nose of Buck in his face, Wade had half-expected the yellow eyes of Shóódé. Serenaded all night, he wondered if the strange coyote ever slept.

Though drawn to wild desert creatures, Wade followed a set of natural commandments for interacting with them—for starters, *better not to interact at all.* Which, considering his fascination with wildlife, was the toughest rule to follow. Minimal interaction was essential, especially around predators; otherwise, the consequences could be unfortunate and even tragic for both human and animal. Doubly on his guard with the dog in tow, he was careful to avoid a wrong move or poor decision. Shóódé, for one, would show little interest in a full-grown park ranger, but a nosy little terrier was another matter. Best to sidestep this daring, opportunistic coyote and the slightest chance of easy pickings.

But above all, Wade's top commandment: *Do no harm.*

Together, he and Buck would make the best of it and limit the risks. This was their second morning alone and Buck already knew the routine. He promptly took to the first order of business—hurry-ups and collecting waste. Then a swift Spartan breakfast, improved with a few bits of rabbit for Buck, and they were ready to break camp.

Buck was a quick learner. *We're off for a quick walk—oh, I get it, we're off for another hike.*

Daybreak and a gleaming wide valley to the east served up an epic panorama. They kept a decent pace for a good hour, Wade satisfied with moving steadily but not breakneck. Dragging his line and skipping many morning nose rituals, a staunch Buck held his own, close on the ranger's heels.

The trail changed and ran through a thicket of ash and pine. Wade felt a sudden grip of anxiety when he heard familiar but disturbing sounds— snorts and grunts not far away. *Javelina.* He turned and lunged for Buck's lead and reeled him in. He knew these wild, pig-like animals were aggressive around any sort of canine. And there wasn't a chance the herd would keep grazing on their prickly pear cactus while a man and a dog were around. Similar to feral hogs, yet not related, Wade could only hope their poor vision would save them both from those sharp long fangs.

Wade kept a tight lead on Buck and glanced about for an escape route, even the near impossible with the one good hand—swinging from a tree, monkey-like, clutching a dog. Louder grunts came from the brush some twenty yards ahead, and a beefy alpha emerged from the undergrowth. He had a grizzled-grayish coat and a white band of hair at the shoulders. Others appeared, following the leader, a whole snorting herd with their keen sense of smell. His head down, the alpha had the ranger and Buck in his sights. Capable of charging up to twenty-five miles an hour, could Wade reach the bear spray in a side pocket of his pack in time?

A slow, deep growl erupted into aggressive barking—Buck, ferocious defender. Looming large and mean, the alpha let out a horrendous squeal and mounted a high-speed charge. The whole screeching herd followed, with awful howls and menacing snorts in rapid, croaking intervals.

And there was Buck, pulling at his lead, right out front to meet them!

Wade lunged for the dog and swooped him up in his arms, the herd closing. Buck squirmed and barked his little lungs to bursting. The ranger stepped to his left as the angry male brushed past him and turned to re-charge. Wade grabbed a hefty tree limb, the dog clutched in his left arm. Standing his ground, poised like a gladiator, the ranger gripped the limb in his lame right hand. Bull-like, the alpha huffed and puffed, stomping hard hooves, while the others behind moved about excitedly. On blind instinct, Wade mimicked the creature and scraped at the ground, huffing and puffing, to stare him down.

A standoff at hand—until a loud whistle rang out somewhere up the path. The alpha abruptly retreated with the herd into thick brush of juniper and pinion trees.

Wade stood dumbfounded, drowning in a rush of adrenaline. He dropped the limb as Buck wriggled out of his arm and leapt to the ground. The ranger grabbed at the lead but his right hand cramped and he lost the line. A plumed tail was off and running, a white blur of snarling dog in pursuit toward the brush.

Wade suddenly bellowed, "NO, BUCK ... YOU STOP ... RIGHT NOW!" The severest and angriest of commands, a tone he'd never used with Abby— or any animal in his life.

Incredibly, it brought Buck up short. Somehow, against instinct, he snapped right out of predator mode at the sound of such a strident, passionate roar. He slowed to a trot and circled back, avoiding eye contact with the ranger but stopping in his tracks. One more turn toward the javelina, then a direct look back at the ranger, locking eyes. The ranger, tense and shaking, bounded toward him, moving between the dog and the javelina. Buck plopped down, panting heavily, lying flat on his belly, in a submissive posture.

Wade reached down and lifted him into his arms, their bodies trembling against one another. They stayed that way until another whistle snapped them to attention. With the javelina gone and the dog in his arms, the ranger worked at uncramping his right hand.

Drained from the close encounter, they returned to retrieve his backpack. They sat down on the path and swilled water while the ranger held firmly to the dog's line. "Having a wonderful, obedient, eager-to-please retriever like Abby," Katy once told him, "could make you a teeny bit smug and comfortable." She said he needed a tougher, willful pet to deal with—but a terrier?

They didn't hear more whistles, but he sensed someone approaching along the path. He raised his head, and a woman stood on the trail. She was the backpacker he'd spotted across the lake.

"What's with all the racket?" she asked. Buck advanced and pulled at his line, growling.

"We had a tangle with a herd of javelina." Wade gave the lead a sharp tug, as he nodded toward the undergrowth.

"One hell of an uproar." She twirled a whistle on a string, letting it drop to dangle from the side of her backpack.

Wade sized her up: tall, mid-to-late twenties, dark hair beneath a broad-brimmed hat. She wore outback clothes, the usual, a tan vest with many pockets and hiker boots. Fit and confident as if she belonged on that mountain, *her* mountain, by the tone of her voice—and she was not too pleased to run into a man with a dog.

"Thought I might have to go for the pepper spray," he volunteered.

"No wonder. Dogs are a big threat to javelina," she replied in a lecturing tone. "Your dog'll scare the wildlife away from the entire habitat—from here to the next passage."

"Well, this fella here is not my dog, and he sure didn't scare off that pack of javelina," Wade countered testily. "Your whistle scared 'em off." He shrugged off his backpack and unzipped a pocket, pulling out a whistle. "Guess I better tie mine somewhere handier." He quickly attached the whistle to his pack.

"You're not a newbie out here, are you?" she asked.

He looked down at Buck. "I'm an off-duty park ranger, and this fella—who seems to answer to the name Buck—lost his dang pack leader."

He eyed her and got a skeptical-irritated look in return. During the silence, Buck nosed his way over to her, put his front paws on her pant leg, and zeroed in for a good whiff at the bottom of her backpack. Next, he sniffed at her ankles, lifted a leg, and peed on her boots.

"Buck, stop it!" Wade jerked at the line, took a deep breath, and emitted a long, noisy sigh.

"Not a problem," she said calmly. "He's marking me because he smells wild feline. I'll take it as a compliment, Buck. Where'd you find him?"

"South a ways, just off the trail. Couple nights ago."

"Probably belongs to day hikers. Can't believe the crazy stuff they get up to."

"For sure on that point."

"So, you're a park ranger, eh?"

Wade reached in his pocket to pull out his park badge, then remembered he'd surrendered it. "I'd show my badge, but it's not on me this trip."

"Badges. Who needs badges?" She grinned.

"Couldn't agree more." He nodded, extending a hand. "Wade Conrad."

"Rachel," she said, shaking his hand. "Rachel Green. So, Mr. Park Ranger, no Smokey-Bear lemon squeezer hat when off duty?"

"Long, painful story, Rachel." He turned away.

"I hear you, we all have those. Painful stories, I mean." She studied him for a moment. "You know, if you replaced the cap with an old fedora, you could pass for Indiana Jones."

He turned back to her and she broke into a big smile. There was something different and rather striking about her that he couldn't put a finger on, perhaps those dark-brown eyes. Then he realized they weren't just dark but totally black, made even more striking by a fair complexion—contrasting features that he seldom saw. From the get-go, he sensed an openness and independence, a woman with an easy fit in a wild and natural environment.

"We saw you earlier across the lake. What're you doing, rock collecting?"

"Rock collecting?" Rachel echoed with a chortle. "No, I'm into scatology, you might say."

"Oh, you're looking for critter crap."

"You got it, collecting mountain scat—I'm a wildlife biologist."

"Well, Rachel, you may collect it, but I reckon you don't take any."

"You got that right, Mr. Park Ranger."

While they chatted, Buck wandered over to the edge of the brush and resumed sniffing near the javelina retreat. He tugged on the line, and Wade pulled back in resistance.

"He's a bit of a drag, isn't he, for hiking the trail?" She watched the dog.

"I'm hoping to run into someone back at the trailhead, a person I can count on to take him into town." He paused, but she wasn't offering. "Someone to find his owner?"

Something extra special caught Buck's powerful nose. He stopped and leaned forward to the end of his tether, rigid and intense, pointing at a spot he could scent in the bushes and trees.

Horrific squeals and grunts erupted deep in the tangled undergrowth, a fearsome uproar coming from the herd of javelina. Buck whined and paced back and forth, trying to break free and charge into the danger zone.

They moved forward cautiously, the ranger holding back on Buck's line. Another sound brought a halt to their forward movement—a different undertone, a deep bellow amid frightful squeals. Somewhere in the thicket, not more than fifty yards away, a violent struggle exploded. Without a word, Wade and Rachel backed away with Buck, and rapidly retreated down the pathway—tripping, slipping, and sliding along quick turns and switchbacks as they went.

19

"Experienced hunters and trappers can read a landscape for a sign, such as tracks, scat, and clues on the ground, and vegetation the animal had disturbed or eaten. The landscape is like a giant crime scene. Evidence is everywhere." —Writer Rich Landers

Quiet returned to the mountain's east slope, but not calm. Not even a bird chirped. Biologist, ranger, and dog sheltered in a small niche off the trail for fifteen minutes. Wade knelt on one knee, edgy and alert, clutching Buck, ready to quell the slightest bark or growl. But the dog stayed quiet and remained curiously passive, wrapped in the ranger's firm embrace.

Wade kept a keen eye, mostly toward the steep bank of mesquite and scrub brush above their path, a natural position for a wild predator to launch an aerial assault on careless prey. *Prey.* Wade had an eerie feeling they were fast becoming prey, same as desert animals. Rachel seemed composed and confident, though she spoke little and only in whispers. She sipped from her water bottle when not checking her cell phone, which was out of service.

"It's time to move," she whispered. "We can't hide here forever."

"Might be safer to hunker down for a while," Wade replied. He was damn sure he heard a far-off coyote ... Shóódé? He hoped she was a good omen for a clear path.

At last, they agreed to move out and cautiously make their way back up the trail, stopping every five or ten yards to listen and check their flanks. The ranger kept eyeing that high bank. A mountain lion could spring on prey from twenty to thirty feet. Naturally, Buck had his nose to ground.

Rachel boldly ventured off the path and quietly eased through a thicket to the site of the encounter. Wade gingerly followed, figuring he had little choice. A rancid, fleshy odor permeated the air around a small, open patch in the center of the clearing. Buck tugged eagerly on, taking in the heavy stench of carnage. Wherever the air reeked of dead kill, Buck was on it. Wade countered, pulling him back, as Rachel spotted a bloody heap of mammal and went to inspect. She ignored the stench, the metallic odor of blood and the swarming flies, no doubt conditioned to inspecting such scenes. Eyes to the ground, she methodically circled outward, noting any tracks and predation signs left behind. In surgical gloves, she worked her way closer to inspect the carcass.

The herd had long fled but for one dead javelina, a bloody mess, riddled with bites and gashes over the upper torso. As she examined the head wounds, she gasped in surprise, and made a quick draw for her cell phone to take pictures of the kill.

"Lacerations quick and severe, but this head wound's incredible," she said, as she clicked away.

Wade kept his distance, maintaining 360-degree surveillance of the clearing, while holding Buck away from the carcass.

"Pretty weird," she mused. "If this was a big boy, he didn't even cover up his kill for a snack later."

Wade knew it was standard practice for mountain lions to cover a kill and return later. "We could have scared him off," he said, still watchful.

She moved on to inspect the attack site from a different angle. Something caught her interest, and she pulled out a Ziploc and deposited hair, blood, and tissue samples in the bag. Satisfied, she kept moving, caught up in the process of inspecting and noting a predator kill scene—a change from the routine of scat collecting, checking cameras, searching for prints. She seemed especially keen on the last of these.

The ranger gave the gray, bloodstained carcass a wide berth, holding Buck well clear to prevent him from nosing in for a messy inspection of the mangled, bloody creature. As they followed Rachel, Buck strained at his lead to pull out front of her.

From the clearing, they came to a dry riverbed. Known by multiple names in the Southwest—sand bed, dry creek, dry wash, arroyo, or just plain wash—dry rivers and streambeds were a way of life and travel over a wide expanse of desert and mountainous terrain in the west, for wildlife, humans, and water. Water being essential in the post-monsoon season for survival. Buck hopped into the wash and carefully nosed the sand, quickly reeling out his lead and circling one spot. Wade assumed he was about to take a poop, but he was zeroed in on something in the wash.

Rachel knelt to examine some tracks and scrapes.

"See the drag marks." She ran her fingers along furrows in the sand.

Wade took a closer look and spotted dark stain marks on the rocks nearby, still damp. "Blood," he muttered, and got up quickly for another wary 360 degree look around.

Rachel studied the troughs in the sand. "This is looking like a double-kill—very unusual. Our greedy predator dragged one away from the kill site, a young javelina most likely."

"A takeout order," Wade said wryly.

"Might have been dragging twenty to thirty pounds or more, even with a young jav."

Wade did the math. If the young javelina had some bulk, then the cat had to be one big, hefty tom. Other candidates were few—bear, wolf, perhaps coyote, but that would be a stretch. Coyotes tend to hunt alone and are unlikely to attack a herd.

Rachel was up and heading to the brush on the other side of the wash. Then another quick jerk on the line and he realized Buck was already out ahead, nose in the lead.

Wade had no idea of Rachel's intentions, but without even checking his GPS, he knew the simplest, quickest way out was back to the path and on to Bedrock trailhead to off-load Buck to day hikers willing to take an adorable West Highland White Terrier out of the wild and deliver him to his owner. He hadn't the slightest interest in holding to their present course farther off trail. This mountain was not his domain, but he had a good idea they faced nothing but rugged slopes, along with some tough bushwhacking. They could easily end up far afield if they were unwise enough to keep tracking a predator and its kill.

And for what reason? They had rushed forward after finding and inspecting the prey. For Rachel, a curious wildlife biologist, duty required that she stop to investigate, take notes and photos, record facts and details of a predation encounter. For a park ranger on LOA, such encounters were just part of the ongoing story. Darwinian survival of the fit and hungry in the wild. Being a diligent and responsible ranger, he could go along and stick his nose into one of nature's predatory struggles to some extent. But in this case, it was much riskier with his sidekick Buck. Having a potent nose out there in the wild, Buck could end up both instigator and victim, which made the ranger even more regret the bath at the lake.

As he followed Buck, he made a quick check of their GPS compass position, and he could see they were veering left in an arc. Though far away from his own rangering patch, he was confident of guiding them back to the trail. He calculated they could soon reconnect with the main path, as early as mid-afternoon, for the best chance of handing Buck off to an animal-loving backpacker departing the trailhead.

Wade took a stumble on their quick-forward march, caught himself, pocketed his GPS, and went back to keeping one eye out for predators and the other eye on Buck and Rachel. They broke out of the shady cover of the brush to warmth and brilliant sun. They entered a divide, trudging over gently rolling foothills with the looming Santa Rita's above. While there were no further signs of prey blood as they left the wash, Buck's powerful nose pulled them steadily along the flatter, grassy terrain, passing oak and mesquite and agaves. Rachel kept right on the dog's tail, but from the ranger's perspective, she wasn't paying much heed to the spots he was nosing in on.

Crossing those shallow fields, Wade figured their chances slim of picking up more evidence of predator and dead-prey tracks. At least until Buck brushed around a shindagger and moved to an agave plant with spears jutting upward a foot or more from ground. Parts of the plant's prickly spears were freshly crushed, so Rachel stopped to examine them. Buck, head down, crowded in next to her to sniff at the spears, nostrils flaring, his nose running a bit of fluid.

"He seems onto *something*," she allowed, watching him. "He's zoned in on this agave. The javelina might have been dragged right over this plant." Buck gave the plant a good final sniff before moving on to others. "It's hard to tell what he's scenting; he might be on a cold trail—it can be a guessing game."

In her typical analytical way, Rachel mulled over the olfactory capabilities of canines, specifically male dogs with longer noses.

"A terrier like Buck might have some 150 million scent receptor cells compared to, say, a German shepherd with a whopping 225 million."

"Size is important? The bigger the nose the more smell receptors?"

"Size isn't always the deciding factor. A thirty-pound Beagle might carry as many scent receptors as a German shepherd twice the size."

"So, Buck's receptor count could actually be much higher."

"Maybe. Would you be surprised to know that male dogs scent better than females?"

"Of course, because a male dog's nose is more sensitive."

"Well, not exactly. The theory is males are just more interested and focused on smells."

"Considering male and female relationships, that's something perfume producers have traded on for centuries."

"Can't disagree with that," she said.

"How many of these scent cells do humans possess?"

"Oh, we lost our capacity for powerful scent receptors, if we ever had them. The human nose contains a measly five million smell-analyzing cells."

Wade knew that even the best-trained tracking dogs often end up cold trailing—following an old, unrelated scent left by an animal some hours or even days before. He gave Buck some slack as he tugged forward, his short little legs churning through low, tufted grass often as high as his head, in possible pursuit of whatever scent he picked up earlier. He was doing his best, a gutsy little Westie following a scent trail that could stretch out over miles through the wilderness.

Since the javelina attack, Rachel played the skeptic to Buck's tracking talents. Even as she followed him, she implied that such skill required lots of specialized training, insisting that truly effective tracking was best handled by the finest European-bred German Shepherds and Belgian Malinois trackers. Yet Wade knew about Conservation Canines, a Pacific Northwest group devoted to finding and training shelter dogs that exhibit a strong drive to hunt—but not to kill. They rapidly train dogs to find scat from coyotes, wolves, bears, big cats, and certain ungulates. Like many educated professionals, he figured Rachel was doubtful that a common house pet or shelter dog could have a special knack for scent tracking equal to those highly trained, pricey European scent dogs.

But something was leading Buck away from the foothills. He was moving back to higher elevations. Their path had meandered back and forth between brush, bushes and trees, and back into another dry wash. Meanwhile, Buck's nose was drawing them ever farther away from the trail and nearest trailhead.

Nearby there was a loud, startling animal howl, a sound rising to a shriek, except this time Buck seemed to take no notice. Wade took notice, figuring it for a warning. Maybe a cry of both fear and caution from Shóódé?

20

"Cruel wildlife-killing contests are proliferating in Arizona. Over the past two years at least 40 of these contests have been held in the state—mostly on our public lands. Cash and prizes are given to those who kill the most, largest, or smallest animals. Sometimes, at the end of these barbaric events, hundreds of carcasses are left in piles. As if that weren't tragic enough, the dumped animals' bodies expose scavengers like bald eagles and condors to deadly lead poisoning from the bullets that were used to slaughter them." —The Center for Biological Diversity

Jesse tried to stamp his memory so he wouldn't forget the exact spot where he ditched his gear. He hid the duffel and bike near the path and followed the only way ahead. His terrible behavior ate at him. Especially the last scary night and not showing more gumption and staying with the ranger and the dog. He just couldn't tell Mr. Wade the real story. Even now, a picture of the big cats leaping at his toes crowded his mind. So long ago and he still felt the panic.

He had hiked for about an hour when he got a sinking sensation he was no longer on the main path. *Any* pathway. How could he have missed the trail signs? He knew that parks—all parks—had pretty poor trail signs, but he also knew the Arizona Trail moved to the South.

The trailhead had to be nearby. He carried an old, unused compass in his duffel, but it never crossed his mind to include it in his small travel bag. He searched the sky for the position of the sun. With so much forest canopy, he couldn't get much of a fix on it either. Oh well, it's still morning and the sun isn't that far south yet.

Jesse couldn't keep from looking back over his shoulder, which he did a lot when in the wild. But instead of fear of a big cat pouncing on him, he worried how Mr. Wade and Buck were doing. On he went, though, anxious to reach the trailhead, wherever it was.

He found himself deep in thought. He ran through a picture of events from the last day and night, and all the stuff he'd done wrong, especially building the fire. He searched his soul over why he always ran away from people, even Mr. Wade. He mulled over the things in his life he wasn't proud of—lame stuff, dumb stuff. Around and around in circles he went, his mind always coming back to the ranger and Buck, and a simple fact. He shouldn't have up and left them like that. He should have had more self-control. It wasn't right, no matter how afraid he was.

Jesse was good at finding escape routes, but where they led him was another problem. Where would he go this time? Before joining the Arizona enviro-volunteers, he hung out with some young street people in Tucson, which he learned was kind of a gathering place—like a sanctuary site—

for thousands of homeless youths. One kid said he got kicked out of his home for doing some really crazy things. But most of them said they'd plain run away just like him—one girl to escape a creepy stepfather who wanted to touch her; another because he was a middle child in a pack of brothers and sisters, and he didn't want to be a burden on his mom who was single.

At last, Jesse reached a trail with a small signpost— an old wooden one. *Footbridge*. Nothing more carved on it, a simple notice between two paths.

The sign wasn't quite lined up either left or right, so how to choose which way? He decided to fudge the sign a little more to the left, mostly because that path looked more worn. Besides, something piqued his curiosity, so he went that way.

Got to be the right way, he hoped, the one to safety.

21

"Half of tracking is knowing where to look; the other half is looking." — Pro tracker Susan Morse

Wade listened for more calls from Shóódé, but the curious coyote had gone silent—or moved on. Was her call a signal, a sign of alarm?

Tracking through the sandy wash was proving tougher for Buck. He was sniffing less and lagging behind Rachel. Wade figured the little terrier had lost the scent, or he was too darn spent to bother. Little Buck wouldn't have the stamina of a big tracking dog— that much, Rachel would be right about.

Wade was fairly certain Rachel hadn't identified a single track since circling back into the sand. Yet, she claimed the wash the best locale for finding evidence of wildlife, because predators prefer hunting the borders between one habitat and another, like riverbeds adjoining thick vegetation. Of course, a wet wash was better because of fresh tracks.

Since they'd joined up with this "scat specialist," Wade and Buck had learned a whole lot about the world's three dozen or more different species of wild cats.

"All cats have scent glands," Rachel lectured. "They leave their scents randomly, or not so randomly, often in spots covering a large territory or habitat."

"They *want* you to know they're around," Wade said.

"Oh, yes. For cats, scenting promotes their presence and often their status and availability. Or they want to warn off other cats and rivals."

"Back off and keep away from my territory."

"Exactly."

Rachel would stop at each prominent tree to check for signs of cat tracks and markers. Larger mesquites acted like lighthouses. She kept a lookout for them because they harbored scent aromas for attracting bobcats and lions. They were ideal for depositing their own scent markers, and for detecting other cats passing through. "In effect," she observed, "they're like a feline social network—Facebook for wild cats."

Facebook for cats. Wade rolled his eyes, but he mostly listened. Much of what Rachel had to say was solid stuff, though it hardly took years of graduate study in "felids" animal biology to know what all pet owners already know. Dogs and cats mark their paths to communicate with other animals. Wilderness hikers can detect traffic corridors that animals use, or recognize places where they find water, food, and shelter. Wade never considered himself a Sherlock Holmes of the wild, but simple observation showed the day-by-day behavior and activity of wild animals.

People don't always agree on things, he knew. Better to combine forces for safety— and he considered himself the responsible one. With Rachel, it was harder to say. Not that she struck him as irresponsible, but her interests and work could be risky and dangerous. Professional, curious, and relentless as a bloodhound, she craved more trail knowledge about "apex predators" like bears, wild cats, and wolves.

Apex predators. In rangering, if Wade used phrases like apex and alpha mammals at the top of the wildlife food chain, he often got a negative reaction or nonresponse from ordinary park visitors, whose vocabulary was simpler and more direct. Yet, Rachel was also direct and candid. "I majored in scat detection," she quipped. In her study of animal scat, she was happy roaming the mountains and gathering samples to detect what biologists call "species-specific scat."

Buck approached another mesquite, so full and healthy its limbs hung over the wash. Wade called a halt. The terrier deserved a break, as he was the only one likely to find any more cat crap. Still, Buck showed an interest in the tree, tugging hard toward it, the ranger pulling back. It was not easy restraining about twenty pounds of determined terrier.

"Yeah, Buck, it's just like the one yesterday," Wade murmured impatiently. He couldn't get over how this flyweight canine was able to generate so much explosive forward thrust when he wanted to. He'd also acquired an annoying whine when he didn't get his own way. "Buck, enough," he scolded. "Time for some lunch." Wade sat with his back up against a shallow bank. Buck grudgingly gave up on the mesquite and found a shady space, plopping down on his belly and panting to cool off. Rachel slipped off her backpack and dropped it near Buck.

"This one fits the profile." She stood in the wash looking at the tree. Wade told her about Buck sniffing out the cat marks on a mesquite the day before, and she showed interest, having a good idea which one he referred to.

As soon as the ranger opened his backpack, Buck was on it, his nose deep inside the pack. Nosing the water bottle and the rabbit in the ranger's grip, the dog opted for a hunk of rabbit first and then the water.

"Well, we've come too far for the cat to be dragging a jav," Rachel said. "Anyway, we're not picking up any more drag marks. Probably settled down under cover to feed."

She sat nearby, pulled out her cell phone, water, and a snack. Wade eyed her futzing with her cell again. When next he glanced, Buck was stretched out on his side in the soft warm sand, fast asleep. While Rachel fiddled with her cell, Wade pulled out his GPS, frowning as he checked their position.

"How much water have you got left?"

"Why?" She looked up from her phone. "Are you running low with Buck?"

"Got plenty for both of us. I always carry more than enough so—"

"So that you never run out," she replied, to finish an old trail tip. She rummaged inside her backpack, little more than a day pack, filled with a lot of cat scat, for sure.

"I was asking if *you* had enough," he added.

"Yeah. Well, I've got a couple bottles. I should be fine." She pulled one from her pack, a small liter. They both knew the chances of finding water in the wash were dicey; that's why they called them "dry washes" outside the monsoon season.

"It hasn't taken long to stray way off the trail." He glanced at his GPS and shook his head. "Do you pack a headlight?"

"It's been a while since I had to use it. The batteries might be weak." Rachel searched a couple of side pockets.

Wade got quiet, turning to check on Buck, still asleep. The last thing he wanted to face was a lot more hiking, or maybe bushwhacking, the rest of the day into darkness with only one small headlight to guide them. And most likely with a trail-tuckered Buck slung across his shoulders.

"What's the problem, Mister Park Ranger?" Rachel stared at him.

"Buck's, well, dog-tired, and we're off-course by a mile or more. We're getting toward mid-afternoon. I think we're pushing the scale toward higher risk."

"There's always risk-reward."

"Well, I see some risk. What's the reward?"

Rachel studied her phone, ignoring his question, and then dropped it back in her pack. "Damn, I'm not getting a single bar. I know there's coverage out here!"

Rachel's outburst startled Buck. He jumped up wide-eyed emitting disgruntled harrumphing noises, ready to go into a barking fit. Wade caught him before it started, stroking and calming him. He offered him a snack and water. Buck took the snack but ignored the water. His attention turned to the mesquite again. From the wash, he hopped up on the bank and pointed his nose toward the tree, Wade and Rachel watching.

He circled the tree, then doubled back and stopped, nudging this way and that among the limbs until he reached the base of the tree. They watched his snout carefully follow an unseen path up the trunk, nosing his way higher between the limbs. Then he stretched as high as possible, front paws against the trunk as if searching for something out of reach. They quickly climbed up the bank and gathered near the tree.

"What is it, Buck?" Wade asked.

Back on the ground, Buck resumed tracing an invisible scent around the base. Rachel peered through the branches as she circled the tree.

"Aha!" At nearly eye level, Rachel gazed at the trunk.

Wade leaned in to see what excited her. There were long scores in the trunk just like the mesquite the day before. "Good work, Buck!"

"Yeah, Buck, nice work," she echoed. "Of course, it's one thing to find them. The trick is deciphering what he's found."

Wade reckoned this "professional" had an answer for everything, or a new problem for each discovery. Exactly how many tricks was Buck expected to perform?

"I think these are fresh scores." She reached in and ran her fingers along the troughs.

"How fresh is fresh?"

She shrugged, "Perhaps twelve to twenty-four hours. There's a wild cat definitely staking its claim and announcing a local presence. 'I'm here, everybody, so you better respect my space.'"

Buck moved a few yards away from the tree where he stopped and put his nose to the ground. They monitored him methodically digging paws at the dirt, leaves, and brush. When they went over to check, they found him uncovering scat recently buried.

"This is very fresh," Rachel declared excitedly. She pulled out a Ziploc to collect a generous sample. "Fresh is best, for what the lab can detect about the animal. A bit strange, though."

"Why?" The ranger noticed Buck taking a studied interest in the scat.

"There's something different about it." Rachel whipped out her cell and took a couple of pictures of the scat.

Abruptly, Buck became agitated, circled the scat, sniffing and whining. Then he seemed to follow another hidden trail away from the scat, moving atop the bank along the wash. He stopped and homed in on something. Wade saw a round object on the ground and he stepped forward for a closer look. Buck pawed it and the ranger picked it up.

"Buck's found a tracking collar." He held up a sizable collar as Rachel rushed over.

Hell, Wade realized, *Buck's back on a scent, and it could be that big cat on the prowl.*

22

"After we radio-collared the big male jaguar, we left him to let the drugs wear off. Back the next morning, I heard his radio collar but it didn't signal him on the move. His collar emitted a mortality signal—an animal not moving. I heard the beep, beep, beep, and I froze. This cannot be. Something's wrong with the collar." —Biologist Sergio Avila-Villegas

Rachel examined the collar carefully, holding it in her hands like a relic from King Tut's Tomb. It had an oblong hard-plastic box attached to a sturdy and broad leather strap. "It's a GPS-tracking collar for a large mammal," she allowed, guardedly.

Collars like that with GPS receivers enabled wildlife biologists like Rachel to monitor the movements of "megafauna" or "keystone" species from the convenience of a computer. Wade knew the older—and less expensive—radio transmitters required tracking the animal on foot, by vehicle, or by aircraft. Whether tracking via receiver or transmitter, Wade believed that, in the grand scheme of animals, such research was ultimately counterproductive. Researchers ran the risk of endangering themselves and the animals during the process of sedating and collaring them. In spite of the standard biologist argument—a few will inevitably be sacrificed for the greater good of the entire species—the ranger wasn't convinced. For many species, only a few still survived.

So much for the grand scheme.

Rachel was sure the collar came off a predator from a Mexican wildlife reserve south of the border. However, she wasn't prepared to share this with Wade, and she needed to contact her colleague back at the lab. She wanted to confirm who placed the collar and the animal to which it had been attached. She turned it around, inspecting the box. "These are securely attached, but they're designed to fall off in a couple of years," she mused aloud.

A couple of years, Wade griped to himself, while some poor animal's roamin' about with a stiff, bulky, two-pound collar strapped to its neck.

"Hey Buck, how'd you like that thick belt choking you at the neck?" He shook his head. "While the so-called higher species monitors your every dang move."

"Well, Buck's wearing one, isn't he? Just not radioed."

"How about a heavy-weighted slave collar to really piss you off, eh, Buck?" Wade felt himself tempted to fall into a tirade in defense of mammals held captive or collared.

Rachel ignored the snide comments. Anyway, she had cam traps and scat collecting—other methods of tracking—since it was impractical to fit more than a few jaguars with GPS or radio collars, a project costing thousands of dollars.

Besides, to dart, tranquilize, and collar big cats had proven risky, with so many unintended consequences. Rachel believed it only sensible in the rarest of circumstances. As an undergrad, she got furious whenever a biologist had an accident while collaring a wild cat. Cats died, cats ultimately euthanized, sometimes induced by the stress of capture as much as from the cat's age and condition. Well-meaning animal biologists, some she even knew, made plain dumb decisions. Along with the risks, for Rachel, it was arrogant science and deeply immoral.

She peered at Buck, lounging in the sand, his eyes drooping shut and then opening when he heard his name.

"Buck's the hero of the day," she purred, reaching over and stroking him warmly.

Having sniffed out fresh scat and finding the collar, Wade noticed her change her tune. Who knows? She could become a true believer that a small, untrained dog had a sensitivity for picking up wild predator scents.

As she fawned over Buck, Wade came over and sat on his other side. "What do you make of these?" He drew back some short hair at the nape of Buck's neck to show the punctures he'd found with the bath at the lake.

"My first night on the trail, I pulled him out from under an oak. Hunkered down there, he was in a hole for a fox or small animal."

She examined the punctures while Buck enjoyed the attention, his eyes closed now. "They're very strange." Rachel used her thumb to gauge the size and spread of the marks, took a quick picture, and jotted down some quick notes in her field notebook.

For Wade the break was a relief to focus on something besides straying farther from the trail. It was becoming clear, if yet unsaid, how differently they responded to risk. Rachel seemed ready to follow tracks wherever they led, or wherever Buck's nose led them. But the dog was running on low and the ranger more concerned about compromising their safety. He suspected finding fresh scat and a collar had changed their situation, and that their risk was higher than ever.

"So, the nice park ranger found you in a den?" Rachel cooed to Buck, smoothing his nape.

"It wasn't much more than a small burrow, hollowed out, tucked in among the tree roots."

"But there were other sounds in the dark—besides the coyote ..."

Wade took a long look up and down the wash. "Yeah, there was something else up there in the blackness. And a sound, more like a roar, like nothing I've ever heard in these mountains."

"Like what we heard in the javelina attack?" Rachel probed for more as she tried to clarify the difference in cat roars. "Definitely more roar than cat squeals?"

Wade nodded. "I sensed a different creature lurking above my camp. One on the prowl, a mammal with a pair of penetrating yellow eyes."

"Not the yellow of a coyote?"

"Yellow—but probably not coyote. Yellow and fiery."

Rachel had a stranglehold on her cell phone, the screen showing no coverage—a no-service screen in a remote area on the eastern slope of the mountain. She tossed the phone back in her pack.

"Supposin' you get through. What are you expecting to find out?"

"It's what I *have* found. A very special kind of animal wore this." She raised the collar. "One big cat that prefers traveling the wash, clever enough even to rid itself of a collar, maybe hours ago." She stashed the collar away and packed up, anxious to move out.

"Well, for the record, I've had a sense something's been stalking us for the last two days." Wade pulled out his GPS and got a blank screen as well. "Hard to find any satellite coverage in these narrow trenches. Even on higher ground out here, coverage will be iffy."

"We'd better get on the move." She stood and waited for them.

Wade looked at Buck, sprawled out in the sand, trying to keep his eyes open. "Buck's got an On-Off switch. He's in the Off position for now."

"I've got to go on before the trail goes stone cold."

"He's worn-out, as you can see. If you mean to use him, you'll have to put your tracking on hold for a while."

Wade could tell finding that collar was a big deal for Rachel. She was determined to reach higher elevations, where she claimed she could access cell coverage along her regular path of scat collection and camera monitoring. For Wade, though, going to higher ground would add more distance and time to reach Bedrock Springs trailhead.

Decision time. Go their separate ways or stay together? As a ranger, he always encouraged hikers to stick together for safety, but circumstances varied. Rachel would make better time on her own, being more familiar with the slopes and unburdened by the dog. He and Buck, on the other hand, would head back to the trail, with the ranger prepared to carry Buck on his shoulders if necessary.

They came up with a loose game plan. The threesome would go on until Rachel found a good path to head off and arrange a meetup with her colleagues. The ranger would keep to a shorter route and try and join up with them later at the trailhead, still miles away.

Under cover of afternoon shade on the south slope, Wade loaded Buck in his arms. The willful, rugged dog would not have it. He set Buck down and easily coaxed him into a slower pace. Rachel soon halted where she recognized a game path carved into the hillside.

"This is as good a place as any for me." She looked down the bushy path.

"Try to limit your scrambling," Wade cautioned. "If you start bushwhacking, you'll run out of water in no time, so try staying on animal paths."

"Wise advice, Mr. Park Ranger—for a tourist on a day hike," she said, with a smile.

He handed her a canister.

"Bear spray?" She gave it a skeptical look.

"We don't know what's out here."

She started to hand it back but changed her mind and tucked it into her pack. Before taking the path, she reached to the side of her pack and unclipped a medallion.

"For safe travels." She tossed it to him. Puzzled, Wade gave it a cursory glance. "It's a pendant from Central America," she added, "made by a fine artist and crafted from a carved conch shell. A Maya elder in Belize gave it to me for luck and safe travel, especially through jungles and wilderness with predators lurking and tracking you. If nothing else, you can admire how it radiates and glimmers when the sun hits it at the right angle."

"You sure you ought to part with this ... now?"

"Pepper spray or a simple pendant." She used her hands to signal weighing the choices. "I'm a biologist; I'll take the spray." They both smiled.

Wade looked at the engraved pendant, depicting a fierce-looking jaguar within a circle, the great predator curled in an action pose with a blood-red tongue. The mighty cat appeared to be devouring a desert creature, the imprint made more startling because the prey itself showed a cluster of fangs. A doubtful ranger reached down and clipped it to Buck's harness.

"Excellent idea!" Rachel gave him a thumb in the air as she headed up the path.

As soon as Buck quit vacuuming for scents along the ground, the ranger stretched into a naturally long, steady stride. Wade knew he was taking another chance by letting the dog's lead drag behind, but it did the trick, and Buck put all his effort into keeping up. Abruptly, Buck came up limping, coming to a quick stop, holding his paw off the ground.

Wade bent down and lifted the dog's front pad to inspect. The pad, fine, tough, and black, showed no evidence of cuts or blood. He got in closer and picked around with his finger, and found a vicious desert sticker. After he tweezered it out, Buck gave the paw a few healing licks and resumed walking just fine.

"We gotta keep movin', Buck. How much ya got left in the tank?" He sensed the dog's alert, intense focus, turning his head to one side and the other, seeking the meaning of Wade's words.

They sure as heck pay us close attention, Wade mused, returning eye contact.

"They try to interpret our every sign and move," Katy would say. "By sheer instinct, they lock onto your eyes, then do a beeline to your heart and soul." It always touched him deeply when he recalled what she said.

"Let's get movin', Buck."

But Buck lagged behind. Wade recalled a story about an African bush tribe, and how they carried their hunting dogs, Basenjis, loaded across their shoulders. He knew he would make far better time if he straddled the dog across his shoulders, atop his pack, giving him a longer break, maybe a light snooze as they trudged on. A Basenji doesn't have an actual bark like normal dogs, which reminded him of how quiet Buck had been—for a change. Their last encounter with Shóódé—a few growls, yes, but no barks. Of course he had created a canine tsunami of barking during the javelina attack and was probably exhausted. Considering the dangers out in the wild, a no-bark dog had its advantages.

"Now listen up, you. We got miles to travel and, no, you won't cover all of 'em atop my pack, but we gotta move before it gets dark." Buck eyed him warily, making more head tilts and antenna-like ear adjustments. Wade lifted him on his shoulders and Buck instantly squirmed and resisted the high perch. When he wouldn't settle down, Wade pulled him off and set him on the ground, sitting down in front of him, right up close in his face.

For some time, Wade stared straight at him without saying a word. "Now listen, Bucky Boy," he began again. "I know this is hard to understand, but I'm trying to save you so we can get your little hiney back to all the comforts of home. Understand? HOME." Wade gave his best penetrating stare, with both of them still and trading mute glares. "So, you've gotta stop fidgeting and fighting and trust me on this, see?"

"OK?" He lifted and placed Buck back up on top of his pack. He slowly settled down, the ranger containing him with a steady, sometimes firm hand on each side as they went.

How strange to be conversing with anybody these days, he thought, let alone a stray dog. He couldn't recall any magical chats with Abby. Perhaps he should have tried working more on animal communication with her. Then again, it could be only a guy thing—man talk with Buck.

23

"I saw the jaguar laying under a tree, not moving. He was dead. I found a lifeless jaguar—a muscular 110-pound body with huge claws and a beautiful coat of fur soft to the touch. They are very clean animals, but you see the scars of life. He was a dead jaguar that had roamed for over 10 years, and there was that collar around his neck, and I questioned my own career and the goals of such a study." —Biologist Sergio Avila-Villegas

Mirage tracks led toward the border, moving through her own cat corridor.

Jaguar Canyon—Rachel's private name for a rugged passage she and her colleagues planned to reconnoiter. Soon they would have camera traps set there, although Rachel was leery of making such an intrusion. Hunters and unlawful border crossers from Mexico tracked through the canyon and often damaged the cameras. Nevertheless, she and other biologists were convinced that wildlife found their way through Jaguar Canyon, a major artery to and from the border. And trail cameras could capture rare shots of them. But for now, Rachel needed to keep Jaguar Canyon under wraps, for fear of hunters and other human traffic endangering wildlife movement, including a jaguar like Mirage.

Rachel had never encountered a wild jaguar outside a zoo, but she had come very close to one as a youngster. Her passion for big cats came about in a strange way, though at the time she never felt it strange. On a school outing to an animal reserve, the group made the rounds, petting farm animals and enjoying up-close looks at less than exotic creatures like a wolf, a coyote, and a llama.

Then the keeper guided them into a more private enclosure. There, Rachel came face-to-face, eye-to-eye, almost nose-to-nose with a cat more fascinating than any picture book or nature film ever revealed.

Less than a foot away, her little body faced a furry, feral being more than twice her size. Startled by its presence, she realized their only separation was a clear Plexiglas barrier. She could only imagine its feline odor, as it heaved breaths from its bulky head, and nosed and fogged the barrier a couple of inches between them.

How could she ever forget its penetrating stare with those luminous, fiery eyes? Would she ever see another wild animal with such a rich coat of browns and reds and pale yellows, sprinkled with dark butterflies, circular black markings in rosettes enclosing smaller spots? All combined in one hypnotic creature.

She still felt the same arousal and rapid heartbeats; even now, imprinted on her soul, she recalled her restless fidgets, while those radiant topaz eyes remained fixed on her every nervous, little-girl tic. Years later, she was still unsure what her younger self faced in that momentous encounter—a devil or an angel, a wild angel, if so. And much later, she also realized this so-called animal exhibit had harbored exotic pets, which in many places today would count as illegal animal trafficking.

Sadly, she knew some biologists spent whole lives without a true encounter with the exotic animals they study, never in their natural, wild habitat. Would a close brush, while Mirage stalked and killed javelina, be her only chance? The attack on the herd got Rachel thinking about Buck. How could an untrained house pet be a credible tracker? Of course, family dogs could be scent trained, but such cases rarely amounted to more than amateur, impractical trail tracking.

She considered the dangers Buck faced on the mountain, which brought her back to Wade. In spite of so little time with him, she suspected his soul mate was the natural world, if he had a special mate at all. Deep in her heart she related to him, a man in tune with the wild—people and society be damned. She imagined herself a few years ago, meeting and maybe falling in love with such a spirit, instead of becoming tangled up with a mentor. She hated the consequences, to study and work under an older, "wiser" colleague, ending up in a student-professor romance. The whole episode an ugly cliché that still made her sick—sick of men, of people, and for a time, sick with self-loathing—caught up in nothing more than a tawdry campus affair. And so many charges of sexual harassment still end up ruining careers for young women only starting out.

She regretted accepting the bear spray. She knew the ranger and dog were in greater danger, Buck being a magnet for many different predators, with Mirage the overwhelming threat.

Rachel came out of her restless musings and realized she was already on a path near Jaguar Canyon. In just twenty minutes she'd scrambled and bushwhacked to a ridge that would lead down into the canyon. There at Horseshoe Ridge, an aptly-named horseshoe-shaped rim, she found herself so breathless she had to stop.

As she took water, she felt a slight tingle against her right thigh—her muted cell phone alive with a text message.

24

"And all this time the dog is only a short twenty feet behind the coyote, and to save the soul of him he cannot understand why it is that he cannot get perceptibly closer; and he begins to get aggravated, and it makes him madder and madder to see how gently the coyote glides along and never pants or sweats or ceases to smile;" —Mark Twain

Under a shady paloverde on the slope, they grazed on trail mix. Unburdened of backpack and twenty pounds of twitchy terrier, Wade felt light enough to glide onward to the trailhead.

Side by side, they sat before a canyon, with layers of hills and mountain ranges spreading to the east. It was time for another "silent dialogue" with Buck. He turned to him, eye to eye, and reflected on Buck's owner, imagining different scenarios of how they lost their dog. Perhaps an elderly couple day hiking the trail for the first time, or a vacationing family on a quick hike with their feisty little Westie. Where had they lost him, and where had they searched for him, and for how long? Whoever and wherever Buck's owners, were they as sick and grieving over their loss as he was over Abby?

I should have pulled out at once. Should have found a better way to get Buck to town right away.

I could have located his owner. At least found a vet to check for the owner's I.D. chip.

He recalled the days and nights that stretched into weeks, searching for Abby, with regular checks in, around, and under the house. He imagined her bolting off on her own for some odd, unknown reason. Over and over, he tried to root out why she disappeared. He never let her loose to risk running across roads or highways. Always, he left her inside when he was away, or when he was home, enclosed safely in the backyard, and never out at night unattended. He tried to picture her safe somewhere with a dog-loving family.

A soft, wet nose pushed up against him, looking for more to eat. Abby, nuzzling up next to him? Another muzzle nudged him now. Buck, begging for a treat—a little fella with a big appetite and a long way from home. Wade pulled out the jerky.

Wade thought of man's best buddy and the ways they sacrifice their freedom to please humans—which to dogs are never sacrifices. After more treats, Buck settled back down, and groaned and moaned like an old dog. The ranger was already used to his distinct smell, different from Abby's, but a canine scent as familiar and pleasing, especially after his bath at the lake.

Buck got back on his feet, tensing with a rumbling low growl. The ranger reacted. The dog pointed directly up the hill; his tail raised stiffly above his butt. Wade made a careful 180-degree scan of the slope. No signs of movement, not a sound in the air. Still, something troubled Buck as he made his comical, gruff complaints. A few yards ahead, a rock squirrel stood in place, sniffing the breeze. Buck spotted it and was off and running—brought up short by the end of the line.

Wade smiled at Buck's surprise. "You got a nose for brains, Buck."

Wade pulled him back and Buck tilted his fuzzy, white head left then right, trying to decipher the ranger's meaning. Wade reached in his pocket for the last half bit of biscuit left. Not just a treat, but a precious morsel of hope he was saving for the day he'd find Abby. Buck waited, but an empty hand came from the pocket.

"Gotta settle for trail mix, Buck." He pulled out some and tossed a raison in the air, watching the dog snatch it before it hit the ground. After catching a few more, Buck curled up at ease next to him. Wade ruffled his soft hair and looked again at the mysterious puncture marks.

Quiet and calm, like Abby for once, Buck barely raised his head at the sound of a distant yip. Most likely the here-and-there Shóódé. The ranger tried to keep alert, while Buck lay quiet and drowsy. Abby ambled through Wade's mind, now as a puppy, claiming her spot at bedtime, pushed up against his feet at the corner. Many a sleepless night, exhausted after hours of searching for her through the desert and foothills, Wade listened in a kind of sad agony to the howling, hooting chorus of coyotes. Troubling images seldom left him.

Wade flinched at the sound of more whups. Buck sprang up and dashed off, a startled ranger no longer holding the line in a right hand gone numb. Dang! Gotta be that crazy Shóódé. Fed up with chasing the terrier and more fed up with taking a pain med that had a numbing effect on the entire hand and arm, he resolved to live with a right hand in mild pain.

Wearily, he slung the backpack on his right shoulder and chased after Buck.

Shóódé, sure enough, perched on a slope about two-hundred yards ahead of a barking Buck heading straight for her. Not to be rushed, the coyote casually stretched herself and gracefully carved out a diagonal path on the slope. In elegant strides gaining distance, she soon stopped to look back, and there was Buck, his short piston-like legs churning away in mindless pursuit, and Wade at the back taking long strides. He gave up shouting at the dog, in predator or play mode Wade wasn't sure, and settled on keeping pace with the dog's trailing line.

The chase went on for several hundred yards, Shóódé galloping with little effort. Seen and unseen, Wade believed she somehow wished to make herself a constant presence. On she led them, keeping mostly in sight, bobbing and weaving, popping up at the next bend, peeking out from brush or bushes, always well out of Buck's reach. He can't be aiming to take down a coyote. Nah, he only wants to play tag or something. Bringing up the rear, a lumbering ranger with a backpack was confident Buck wouldn't win any races. It was enough to jog like Shóódé, though he felt a volcanic irritation building. Chasing Westies and coyotes was never in the plan for his escape along a wilderness path.

Buck chased her toward partial cover of brush and trees higher on the slope. Wade, breathing hard and well behind, kept a close eye on Shóódé in a small gap among trees. Some twenty yards in front of Buck, she decided to take a quick ninety-degree turn to the right and disappeared, leaving him in his tracks.

"Buck! Stop, Buck!" the ranger shouted.

Buck approached the gap, closer to the cover and the coyote, with Wade now weary and worried. The dog slowed to a bouncy little strut and stopped at the gap, panting heavily, then listened and sniffed the air. As he turned back, the ranger closed the distance on him.

"Stay," Wade softly instructed, reaching out, and picking up the lead. Buck still panted and dropped to his belly, a trace of a puppy smile, one that seemed to say, 'Sometimes I just gotta do stuff.'

Utterly soundless, Shóódé reappeared. Buck lunged forward, foolish to pick up the chase as bushed as he was. Wade held him in close. Shóódé, something furry dangling from her mouth, moved in playful little circles, keeping an eye on Buck. The ranger stood agape at her weird behavior—once, twice, the circles expanding, like some zoned-out whirling canine. In ever-widening turns she rotated, revolving around them like a satellite. Buck strained at the line while he watched; the ranger wary, but captivated by this complex creature and her crazy-eight circle game.

She's just plain strange, he had to admit. When she came in closer, he studied her delicate face and nose, her inquiring expression, her shiny coat a mix of black, gray, and rust. The only distinctive feature, aside from the oddest behavior, was the slight limp so noticeable when she kicked into a higher speed. A bit on the gaunt side, maybe she weighed ten pounds more than Buck. Yet he figured her for a young female with a fair chance of a hard, free life of nine or ten years.

For this go-around, Wade kept a firm left-handed hold on Buck, antsy, whiny, and eager to join her circle game. She played with whatever she held in her mouth, a feather maybe, tossing it about on the ground. Like dogs and coyotes do, she had to be gaming them, taunting Buck with her prize, since her attention had to be for Buck. Legend has it they have a rich sense of humor, however bizarre or crazy by human standards. For anyone who has a dog, a coyote with a comic streak is no stretch. And what playful, alert creatures they are!

Wade had witnessed such antics and acrobatics with coyotes around the ranch house. From his back porch, he once watched a young coyote jump his seven-foot fence as if hopping over a dead log. Abby had levitated from the porch and chased the interloper from her yard as the yearling bounded the fence just as easily a second time.

Wade observed Shóódé swirl the feathery object in the air and pretend to munch at it, all the time making dervish circles at a safe distance, out of Buck's reach, the same way dogs do with toys and playmates. Wade rejected the Wile E. Coyote cartoon stuff, yet considered them shrewd and resourceful, as bright and obviously fun-loving as any family pet. Shóódé made one last revolution, peeled away with a sudden burst of speed, and vanished back into brush and trees.

Wade shook his head and took a few deep breaths. They waited, giving her a good interval, but she never reappeared for an encore. Coyotes were such tricksters, letting predator or prey chase after, playing every manner of crafty games—spinning around in circles, running and wearing down less resourceful animals—until the chaser goes ragged and exhausted, then sometimes moving in for an easy meal.

Wildlife, neither friend nor foe, like the mountains, sturdy and constant, only looking to survive in this devil of a climate. Everything having its place, the natural order of things, to be left unharmed and treated with respect. Even if they take a pet dog.

25

"The Sky Islands are the only place in the world where mountain lions, jaguars, ocelots, and bobcats all exist in the same environment. It's kind of a nexus of a lot of different regions coming together." —Shipherd Reed, Flandrau Science Center

Rachel stood on the ridge looking for an optimal entry point into Jaguar Canyon. Along the southwestern slope below she spotted baked grasslands, a vast complex of canyons holding smaller passageways with scores of dry riverbeds and tiny slot-ways leading down the mountain. She knew no better view of wildlife passages toward the border than that very spot.

She also knew where the high ridge offered rare cell phone coverage. She'd received a message, a report regarding the lab tests she'd been waiting for—news she longed to hear, news hugely significant for her and likely for wildlife across the entire mountain habitat. Mirage, no longer a dream or imagination, was Rachel's chance of a lifetime. She dashed off a text message to her colleagues to park at Bedrock Springs trailhead and to hike to meet her at Jaguar Canyon. Rachel had a plan, that day before nightfall, an attempt to further reconnoiter Jaguar Canyon.

With a bit of luck, Mirage would thrive in a brave new world, a place from which jaguars had been driven out many decades earlier, retreating to habitat in Mexico for a better chance to survive. But there was the issue of a border wall, a juggernaut, hair-brained scheme that would never prevent humans from illegally crossing the border. A thirty-foot steel barrier that would surely kill wildlife movement and migration.

In spite of the existing crossing challenges, Mirage had found a way to roam from Mexico into southwest Arizona. From her source population located in the rich, resilient ranges of Mexico's Sierra Madre Occidental region, she had managed to cross north some hundred miles or more from where she likely was born. Now the human forces of greed, fear, poverty, and politics could put a permanent block on the rights of keystone predators like Mirage and other wild animals. They would no longer be able to roam freely and survive as a healthy species in a place where they thrived long before the first humans appeared.

Rachel tightened her pack straps and hiked along the rim, keeping a fast pace where possible. She gained quick access into the canyon but encountered bear grass, and slow going over sharp-speared agaves, traversing switchbacks on game paths to shorten her way.

Soon out of breath, she lost track of real time. Her throat was so dry she could hardly swallow. She slowed to a walk, bent over, and heaved for air like a marathoner at the finish line. Catching her breath, she consumed most of her water and took up a slower pace. Jaguar Canyon proved an ideal animal corridor with plenty of water, and sure enough, soon she found water in a creek bed. She stopped to inspect imprints in damp sand, evidence of cat tracks, positively, the same as those they had found for weeks in and around Jaguar Canyon. Tracks left by Mirage.

A euphoric Rachel imagined how Mirage sashayed her way through the washes, her supple, rather delicate stride contrasting her muscular, solid body. Filled with joy at the sightings, she continued along the wash as if floating through air. She felt overcome by a silly mood and actually caught herself blissfully walking a cat gait. She tracked Mirage through the wash for some time, tracing more sets of prints, until she came to more cool, shallow pools of water. She pulled out her water filter and refilled her bottles, while she soaked her bare feet and splashed water over herself.

On she went, tracking fresh unbroken prints, noting obvious points where the cat splashed through puddles and streams. She took a few quick photos, her six-inch ruler laid next to tracks for scale, showing sand prints so clear even an untrained eye couldn't miss them. These prints circled back and Rachel found herself following the prints up the other side of the wash and back the way she came.

Then the tracks disappeared. They plainly indicated Mirage must have jumped out of the wash. Rachel got a weird feeling that the tracks were making her confused. It got even eerier. Was *she* being stalked? Mirage in a turn-about to pursue *her*?

Rachel moved cautiously above the wash. She spotted a juniper tree nearby, one among the many types Mirage would mark. And a familiar scent in the air, an odor she recognized from her work in the university's feline lab. A sound as well, carried by a gentle breeze—a low, quiet, breathiness, like the wild cats she knew rehabbing in cages.

She got closer to the tree and the cat odor grew more intense. The juniper, as gnarly and thick as any she'd ever seen, had abundant protruding branches that held her back. A sudden faraway thunderclap startled her. She sensed rain and turned to see a darkening sky to the southeast.

How wonderful. A thunderstorm in May.

When another thunderclap resounded, followed by a heavy breeze wafting up the southeast slope, she abruptly retreated. But the breeze brought another sharp odor ... of wild feline mammal ... a pungent scent rarely sensed in the wild. She followed it around the juniper's lush tangle of branches.

As she angled higher for a better look, she heard a different, distant sound, like a whistle in the wind. Or a bird farther up the winding wash. She jumped back in the wash and pressed on briskly with much ground to cover to catch up with her colleagues in the canyon.

On the other side of the wash, high in another juniper, an immobile form loomed above the biologist. There the creature quietly rested, motionless on a thick limb. Dozing through the thunderclaps, she opened her huge jaws to yawn and observed Rachel's departure with large, fiery eyes. As light rain fell, she raised her massive head and, like a child in a storm, she tried to catch a few raindrops dripping through the branches. Then she sniffed at something in the breeze—perhaps the intruder's trailing scent. She leapt from the tree and swiftly followed her nose. Sprinkles of rain having passed, the creature crept through a soft creek bed along the wash.

26

"At some point we must draw a line across the ground of our home and our being, drive a spear into the land and say to the bulldozers, earthmovers, government, and corporations, 'thus far and no further.' If we do not, we shall later feel, instead of pride, the regret of Thoreau, that good but overly-bookish man, who wrote, near the end of his life, 'If I repent of anything, it is likely to be my good behavior.'" —Writer Edward Abbey

Jesse suffered from regret and frustration for making so many wrong choices. The more he went forward, the more the urge to go back. He needed to find the ranger, to let him know how sorry he was about the fire and for walking away from them.

He tried to follow the sun to keep track of his direction. He felt the temperature changing. There were gray clouds swirling and racing over the mountain. The weather was about all he could be sure of, as he zombie-walked along the path. Was he even on the right path south? Maybe if he found an easier way to higher ground, he'd have a better view. There was a long, high ridge ahead that he might gain to mark his way, but it looked awfully steep to climb. He had no idea how much farther to that footbridge, let alone how far to the trailhead.

He wasn't sure he could think straight any longer—with so little to eat for days and nothing left but juniper berries. He tried popping a few more in his dry mouth, but he couldn't decide which was worse— his empty stomach or the oily, sour nuts. His hunger was almost enough to make him turn carnivore again. He recalled the meat-eating volunteers. You are one protein-starved dude, they chided, their mouths dripping of greasy hamburgers. But they did not sway or deter him.

The next moment he was overcome with the sensation of blood rushing to his feet. The footpath teetered at the very edge of a rim overlooking another deep canyon. Overcome with dizziness, he stepped back from the precipice, knelt on the ground, and lowered his head to regain balance. Somehow, he had reached the long high ridge, and he peered out at the vast chasm, trying to restore his equilibrium.

He struggled to his feet and edged along the canyon rim, careful to stay well back from the brink. The path to his right was a high solid bank covered with dense brush and trees, and to his left, the steep canyon running south. After looking into its void, he knew the trail beneath his feet and straight ahead was the only option. It was a well-worn path that animals must have plodded for ages, forever, keeping away from the dangers on each side.

He soon came upon a section of the rim that must have fallen away, eroded over a long period.

And sure enough, in its place loomed the footbridge across the gap. He quickened his pace. But when he got close to the brink and the bridge, it looked really old, made of dried-out desert wood, rotting and falling away, with flimsy foot-planks and decayed ropes for handrails. He guessed the span at about thirty feet, with only room enough to walk across single-file—or crawl if you were a small animal. Miners in the mountains might have used it long ago, though he figured a "paw bridge" would be a better name now. He imagined four-legged critters crossing—coyote, fox, some bigger predators, maybe a small bear.

Jesse edged in closer to this bridge from another age, a different world. A crossing he never saw except in nature pictures about Africa and faraway lands. He glanced at the other side and beyond to the south. If he ever hoped to make it to the trailhead, he hadn't the strength to double back. He needed to go ahead and cross that footbridge. He inched forward and reached for a handrail. As he shook it, the wobbly bridge started to sway and shudder.

How would it ever hold him? Again, he looked for another escape route. To the left, the steep drop into the canyon, to the right, the brush and trees covering steep high rock-face. *No turning back ... no other escape*—words he dreaded.

He eased a right foot onto the planks. He put the left foot down and crept ahead, stepping softly, testing his weight on old timbers. Gripping the rope rails where they still hung, he moved a few feet ahead. He came to a section missing the rope rail. He grabbed rope on the other side with both hands and went ahead cautiously. He was halfway across when he stepped off a large chunk of planking and it fell away. He watched it drop below on a steep bank and plunge into the deep canyon. Like falling into a black hole, he felt shivers above a canyon ready to swallow him up.

He craned his neck around and faced a four-foot gap with nothing but air from where the plank fell. With Jesse shaking and the bridge shaking, he moved forward until a noise froze him in place—a low rumbling, an awful echo that plunged him back to a horrible place within himself. He was caught up in a terrible groaning and growling from the past, and the same muffled roars from camp the nights before. Then a long, agonizing howl of human pain—before he realized it came from his own throat. And if he wanted to live, he couldn't cover his ears and curl up against his knees. He had to hang onto the rope on a rotten bridge over a deep canyon.

But the noise wouldn't stop from the deep abyss, the creature aroused from its hiding place. The past returned like an evil, phantom tracker. Jesse no longer stood on a collapsing footbridge. He hung in the cage over cats with their sharp canines and powerful jaws below. His crazed father held the rope he clung to, Jesse pleading to be pulled away from the wild predators staring up at him.

27

"Jaguars can't use Google Maps to find tiny gaps in hundreds of miles of impermeable walls. Without reintroduction in the Southwest and cross-border connectivity, isolation, and genetic problems may doom jaguars in northern Mexico." —Michael Robinson, Center for Biological Diversity

Wade and Buck were well along to the trailhead with no distant whistles from Rachel. And no sign of Jesse, who should have reached the trailhead by midday, providing he had a bit of luck and kept that bike clear of cactus and ditches. The kid would have a fair chance of finding a ride out, but he and Buck might arrive too late to hitch a ride, even with the longer days. Better to stick close to the trail as darkness set in, rather than camp at an empty parking lot, or worse, tramp along a narrow, pitch-black, country road with tired, distracted drivers.

Best to push on, he judged, keep to the path and maybe meet up with Rachel.

Wade knew he shouldn't feed Buck much more of the salty jerky, which was unhealthy for dogs. He also knew he should have considered Katy's offer of a resupply stashed at a trailhead up the line. Having rejected her idea, he felt an imaginary rap on his knuckles and heard her voice. Why don't you carry your cell phone? You could call, and I could pick you up at the trailhead. At least take the dog off your hands.

As a ranger, Wade was compelled to carry a cell. He'd be damned if he would let the miserable device cling to him on his own time, especially on a mountain where cell coverage was mostly non-existent. Besides, it was time to stop ruminating on stuff he couldn't control. Time to put his grievances behind. He and Buck would trudge on. Enough said.

They hiked for another twenty minutes. "Let's take a breather, Buck." He checked his GPS but it wouldn't position a thing, and he shook his head. At a Y along the rough path, he and Buck pulled up when he noticed a small sign between two paths. It pointed a tad to the southeast and read *Footbridge*—no way was it an official park sign.

They were in a stretch of unfamiliar terrain and Wade was troubled, with his GPS still drawing a blank. Time to get this dog back home—to wherever. Lolling at his feet, Buck panted and gazed in the same direction—a path through which they could expect more scrambling over steep terrain, with obstacles to avoid on a hot afternoon, and a Westie on your shoulders. For Wade, having no cell coverage was one thing, but hiking off trail without GPS reception was quite another.

"We don't need this, Buck."

As he reached for water, he got hit with the odor of left-over rabbit. In glaring afternoon light, he saw outlines of a horseshoe-shaped ridge above a large canyon he vaguely recalled skirting by years ago. He pulled out the rabbit for Buck to finish, and while they rested, he considered their options. He was fairly certain the ridge had a game path to traverse south toward the trailhead.

Wade gave the dog a skeptical look. "Buck, you are an unfit animal for this grade of hiking."

Along about now, Buck was like any other house pet, ready for his afternoon nap. Yet, there was nothing left but to load the dog onto his pack again. He had a hunch the ridge ran roughly parallel to the trail, and with a bit of luck, the route would have advantages. The trick was getting up to it without expending too much energy.

They took the nearer route, but he soon found it hard going with the dog draped across his pack and shoulders. It was a slog up a grade and around boulders, with some rugged, steep, scrambling to boot. Seasoned climbers might easily class it as an "A" hike, when they expect to struggle through, around, and up over rough vertical terrain. Wade had to keep readjusting his backpack, sweating and puffing for his balance, and not just because of the added dog-weight.

Minutes later, the top of the ridge still a goal, Wade set Buck down to go some on his own. The ranger ended up on all-fours like Buck as they traversed their way up the steep grade. He was startled to see that the quicker he went, the quicker Buck went, even scrambling when they had to scramble as if to mimic the ranger's every move. He couldn't believe Buck, still moving under his own power, a real champ on a sheer "A" climb.

Then Buck slowed down, hesitated, and stopped dead in his tracks. *His tank's gone dry*, Wade saw. He needs another breather—but not hanging from a steep slope. Strangely, Buck grew more hyper, sniffing and darting about on the sharp embankment.

"Buck, come on, we gotta get on with it." The ranger grunted and pulled at the line impatiently.

Buck paid no heed, anxious and antsy. Wade called out repeatedly, tugging at the leash. Buck resisted, making fitful moves, agitated and whiny. What to do? How could he ever keep hold of him, let alone carry him up and over this steep face?

"What is it, Buck?" The ranger slid over to him, but Buck shied away, darting and slipping, turning panicky. When he tried pulling him closer, Buck jerked away and skated farther down the hill, twice rolling over. They tugged at the line in different directions.

Something's dead wrong, Wade realized, leaning backward to keep his balance on the incline. Buck resisted, digging in with all fours, the ranger dragging him up, shaken by the strength of the small terrier at the end of the line.

What's going on?

Somehow, he had to carry him, but it was too much of a balancing act on the high shoulders sling. That was when he heard a hissing sound in the rocks—the rocks he was backing into. They both heard the rattle. Buck made a complete backflip that took him into a long downhill slide. The ranger spotted the diamondback and nearly lost his balance, too. The rattler gave another clear warning before slithering away, avoiding a confrontation. The white-and-black banding at the tip of the tail disappeared below the rocks. The ranger took a quick, deep breath and slid down after Buck. He gathered him up with a few calming words, ready to resume the challenge and this time carry him like a sack of groceries for the scramble to the top.

As they broke over the rim, Wade was convinced Buck must have had rattlesnake aversion training. Buck might have saved them both with his early warning anxiety. But he regretted not picking up on the signs quicker, not to mention taking on the sheer slope in the first place.

Atop the crest, they found access to the vast horseshoe-shaped canyon running south. Not expecting any more trail signage, though, Wade was surprised to pass a crude wooden marker, *Horseshoe Ridge*, painted in scraggly, faded block letters, likely something going back to the old mining days.

Horseshoe Ridge, rightly named. They stood on an imposing rim, high above a deep canyon. Wade stepped forward to survey the vast expanse and his foot gave way on the jagged, narrow rim path. "Son of a bitch!"

His expletive echoed into the canyon. Buck tilted his head and listened to it trail off, turning to the ranger for their next move. Wade regained his footing and plopped down on the path, towing Buck in for water. Wade pulled out the binoculars for a closer look across the vast canyon. Horseshoe Ridge cut along a vertical line as if its rock and ground had been sliced into the shape of a humungous loaf of bread, the sheer canyon wall on each side running horizontally for miles to the south. He imagined it a colossal loaf that could only have been cut by the gods.

With Buck back on his shoulders, they moved gingerly along the west ridge, the gap below expanding and deepening, with rocks gradually replaced by large boulders. For sure, the trek was a well-worn game path, a deep drop-off from the rim on their left, and on their right, mounds of granite under cover of trees and overgrowth.

They came across something stranger, weird enough to start Buck squirming from his perch atop the pack. They heard a low, muffled croaking noise from a crevice far below.

"I don't blame you, buddy. Sounds like some eerie, never-seen thing," he said to Buck, "like dinosaur frogs, ugly and malformed, a subspecies evolved and lodged in an old, poisoned mining claim." Whatever they were, they had Buck's full attention with every fidget, twist, whine, and whimper, Buck doing his best to wiggle off the ranger's pack. Wade kept a firm hand on his canine cargo. "You're staying put, Buck." The ranger wanted no part of any side trips below to investigate.

He held steady and swift along the rim path, but Buck wouldn't let up. The more the ranger restrained him, the more the dog squirmed and resisted. *What is triggering you now, Buck? Whatever he's hearing, scenting, feeling—only he knows. What wild creature is down there, Buck? Was the dog witness to a mystery while the ranger worked at a human level of awareness?* Whatever lurked below, Buck grasped it. For Wade, it was an unknown, a presence to avoid. They were not venturing down there.

Buck assumed some composure, tilting his head, listening, and reacting to the presence—one too deep, too high, too distant for the human ear. A current of cool breeze swept past them along the bank. Another yip followed from beyond the rim. *Now that I recognize ... Shóódé.* Buck paid no heed, as if he couldn't hear her, fixed on another presence and sound beyond Wade's hearing.

Wade kept an eye over the bank below and on unknown overgrowth to the right, while he held to firm footing along a section of tricky, rugged path. The strange sounds from the canyon faded, but Buck would not relax. He stirred, sensing another presence that needed telling. He kicked his legs in four different directions. Wade stopped abruptly, reached up, took hold of the harness, and lifted him like a bread basket off his sore shoulders. Buck hit the ground and charged ahead along the ridge, Wade following, turning his stiff neck from side to side, keeping tight hold on this small sled dog.

Buck ran nose to the ground, on a scent, tracking something, picking up speed. Wade steadied his backpack as he trailed behind, Buck's lead held tight in his left hand. Crazy bushwhacks up a slick slope had turned into a frantic Westie running amok in the wild, and not a sign of one soul all morning.

Damn dog! Now what?

An ancient, well-worn game route turned rugged, but the dog rushed on. Wade tried to rein him in so he could glass ahead for a footbridge. But the dog would not slow. Farther on, Wade spotted a gap across a missing section of the rim.

"Enough, Buck, stop it!" He pulled Buck up short and hard. He glassed in on a wide breach but no footbridge.

Moving closer, he saw that a bridge still spanned the gap, a footbridge collapsing—*in real time*. Dust still billowed under the gap. Moans from below, and a roped bridge sagging badly in the middle. On the far side of the gap, a familiar figure teetered on the span, now hanging more vertically than horizontally. At sight of the ranger, Jesse cried out and started waving one hand frantically, the other hand clinging to a rope railing for dear life.

Ah, Jesse, of course. Good job, Buck.

Wade spotted an old footbridge sign, staked in the ground off to the side where the span used to be fully attached to the pathway. It said *Danger. Bridge Fit for Critters Only.*

28

"The federal Endangered Species Act defines 'take' as 'to harass, harm, pursue, hunt, shoot, wound, kill, trap, capture or collect, or to attempt to engage in such conduct.'"—The Endangered Species Act

From the edge of the canyon, Wade and Buck beheld a wide-eyed and petrified Jesse, marooned on a collapsing bridge, clinging to a hunk of bad rope.

The aged structure sagged so deeply that Jesse was on the verge of dangling in the air. He was so excited to see them that Wade feared he would lose his grip and slide from the planks into the canyon. But this was no time to get all twisted inside-out over the kid's crash-prone disasters.

Wade kept Buck on the tightest rein as he surveyed the scene, the damage, and the danger. For sure, the gap was too steep and risky to rappel from on either side, and no rope at hand for rappelling, anyway, since Jesse's rope probably was in his pack at the bottom of the canyon. Wade assessed the void below and cursed to himself. He glanced at Jesse and cursed again. The kid could only cry out as he made incomprehensible shouts and appeals. Allowed free reign, Jesse's panic and fright could be fatal.

"Jesse, shut up and listen!" Wade yelled. "Keep focused on that rope."

"Yes, sir," came a whimper.

"You must climb up to the ridge!"

Jesse looked up toward the edge and cried, "OK, sir."

"Wrap your legs around that rope for better grip!" Jesse struggled to wrap his skinny legs around the line. "Good. Now try taking the rope, a little at a time, and move your legs and feet as you go. Then get a re-grip." He managed to climb a foot or so but quickly came sliding back almost to where he started. "You gotta use your legs and feet to press and hold you against the rope as you go."

Wade looked around again, frantic. He was helpless to do anything but offer advice. "Now, try again. Work with your hands. Grab up a bit and pull up, little by little. Legs and feet follow, and use those feet to help hold and re-grip the rope." Jesse swayed and struggled, trying to summon strength in a weakened body, straining to power up with lean to little muscle mass. But this time he made progress. Wade watched Jesse struggle to climb toward the ridge. "Good! You can do it, Jesse!"

Wade peered out over the precipice, figuring it could be a free drop of sixty feet, landing on a steep, hard bank of rugged bushes and rocks, then the risk of a second fall into a deeper canyon. And there was Buck's crusty growl, Jesse's whimpers and help-me faces, and more deep groans from below, drifting up to surround them.

Nasty stuff below—but no Shóódé.

The noises faded and Wade focused on Jesse, ever vertical. He pulled the dog back farther from the edge and he tried to figure what else he could do for the boy.

First priority, keep Jesse cool and clinging to the fraying lifeline. He was wrapped around the rope, but hardly safe on the opposite cliff. And as Wade coaxed him into climbing higher, would the rotten line hold, or snap?

Then came the loudest cat roar Wade had ever heard, reverberating through the canyon. Jesse let out a strange wolf-like howl and slid a foot lower, losing any progress he'd made. A startled Buck barked into the gap, then barked at the ranger for good measure. Confused and aggressive, Buck pulled forward near the edge of a slippery and sandy, rock-hard incline.

Nothing but a total FUBAR ... Wade struggled for calm in chaos, holding the dog steady on a tight lead.

In the midst of surreal sounds, one after another, Jesse and Buck vied for loudest and most agitated. Until Buck lost his footing and all four paws slid down the steep bank. He went over the edge, landing on a bit of collapsed bridge. Wade held tight to a taut line; Buck perched on a tilting piece of plank some six feet away—stranded.

Wade tried for secure footing on the bank's edge and pulled harder on Buck's lead. It wouldn't budge, the line hung up on a bridge plank. He gave it some slack, wiggled it, and tried pulling again, but the lead held fast, tangled in the plank. There it was: A shaky bridge about to collapse with too much gap to reach across, untangle the line and grab the dog. If he tried jerking line and dog through the air by the lead and harness, would the mended harness fall apart with so much tension?

Wade was used to jams with more than his share of deadly dangers. Hell, how could you live with yourself otherwise? You gotta take the risk when it's an animal that needs help.

"Keep using your feet as a grip, Jesse, and stay wrapped around that rope," he ordered.

Wade took a deep breath and inched closer to the bridge. He leaned forward at the edge of the bank, reached out and shook the dog's leash line caught under a plank.

"Buck!" he called across the gauntlet. He held out a hand in appeal, hoping Buck's movements, any movement, would free the line. Buck took a step toward him, as if to Westie-will his way across. Wade took a tentative step from the bank onto the bridge. It started to wobble as he gave the lead another hard tug and the rope untangled.

The line free, Wade held an arm out. "Jump! Jump, Buck!"

Buck, hesitant and whiny, reared back and sprang through the air like a flying Wallenda, and landed in the ranger's arms. Another chunk of plank fell away from where the dog jumped, the bridge creaking and swaying. Wade tried to stay still in place, balancing one foot on the bank, the other on a bridge folding into a V-shape. He held the dog close, struggling to stay upright on the rickety structure.

Overcome, Wade sensed Buck's heavy heartbeat and his own gasps for breath. He tried to breathe slower and deeper, catching another glimpse at Jesse, struggling to climb the rope. In the next moment, the bridge gave way completely from the middle—the kid was now on his own. *And so-the-hell are we.*

Buck went still in Wade's arms, as if sensing his sole job was to keep motionless. Wade felt the bridge folding and strange, deep groans from the canyon below.

In slow motion, Jesse moaned and cried a reply. Then the splitting of planks, and Wade's footing gave way. Jesse screamed.

The bridge cracked and groaned and finally broke cleanly in half.

Wade grabbed at rotten rope from the rail, clutching it in his left hand, the other holding Buck close to his chest. They swayed and crashed against the vertical face. There they hung, dangling from a piece of fraying rope, swinging, and bumping against the rock wall.

"Jesse! You there?" He shouted overhead but it was barely a shout. He got no response.

He tried to listen for the kid, but he couldn't hear or see him. He gripped the rope tightly and peered down at the rocks, boulders, and gnarly bushes, a steep drop some fifty feet below.

He steadied himself for a fall, but the rope held, though he knew his grip would soon slip away. They would take a hard fall to the slope no matter what.

He felt for the dog's lead still looped around his right wrist. He slowly let Buck slide down his leg and dangle by harness and lead in the air below him.

The harness is holding!

But his fist was cramping so badly that the lead would be the first to go.

Wade's breath came hard as he strained to hold fast to the rope with his left hand, the right hand so numb he knew he would lose the lead any moment. The line was stretched as low as it would go. Buck must endure the fall on his own.

"Buck, be lucky, champ—my grip's gonna let you go." No longer feeling any right-hand sensation, the line slipped away. "Fly away safe, champ, fly away," came an agonized whisper. He tried to track his free fall to the bank below.

He wished for a soft landing on a strong juniper bush. But he could only imagine Buck landing and rolling down the steep bank, his small white body swallowed up in the shadowy canyon. He strained to keep hold of the rope with both hands, his right now useless. He listened for Buck.

No yelps ... no whimpers. He strained to glance above for Jesse, but the rope kept turning away and slipping from his grip.

No calls, no sounds. Nothing but dead silence from the rim above and the deep canyon below.

He felt a sharp spasm of anguish at not hearing a bark, a whimper, a call from the boy. Cramps and piercing pain ran through his burning left hand, running up to his shoulder. He tried to gain a grip on the rope in his right hand, but the hand was as good as gone. Then his left hand cramped and slipped off the rope, and he took the drop toward Buck. A timeless fall as he pictured Buck falling and rolling before him.

Then he felt whooshing, whipping, and scraping against his body. He was engulfed by stiff, thick bushes and branches that whipped and cut at him, slowing him down, and cushioning him from a hard fall. Reality returned in the next instant when he met solid ground, and he glanced off rocks and boulders. He tumbled farther down the steep, rugged grade, maybe a replay of Buck's tumble. He rolled over and over, pushing off a boulder here, a tree or bush there, until he came to rest and waited for the pain. He lay still on his side, his shirt and pants torn, his arms and legs scratched and burning. He listened for the life of a boy and a dog around him.

29

"Do animals have souls? Of course they do. Don't be an idiot."—Author and former park ranger Nevada Barr

Wade lay quiet in a shallow dry ditch on a steep bank, a yawning canyon below. His limbs burned in holy hell; his innards ached like someone pummeled him with a battering ram. From his side he carefully rolled over on all fours. He didn't feel any broken bones. He panicked that his backpack was lost, before he felt it intact on his back. His pack must have cushioned him in the fall and rolls along the ground. Incredibly, not only could he stand, he could walk. Never had he hurt like this, but never was he so driven to move and listen for the life of a dog.

He started calling out for dog and boy, but pain from his ribs stopped him. He fumbled for his whistle from his side pack and blew a sound so weak, he wasn't sure he could hear it, let alone Buck or Jesse. He edged sideways down the bank one painful step at a time. He stepped over rugged scrub amid small pines rooted on the hillside, denser brush stretching into the canyon.

"Buck! Hey, Buck!" he called weakly.

Buck wouldn't answer—or couldn't. He turned slowly and whistled harder in every direction, but no response. Though his chest throbbed each time, he shouted anyway. "BUCK! BUCK! WHERE ARE YOU, CHAMP?" His calls rang out through an enormous chasm, an infinite echo chamber.

He looked back up toward the crash scene. "JESSE!" he called. He whistled toward the rim, but neither Jesse nor any four-legged creature answered.

He blew ever longer, blowing as hard and as long as his breath and the hurt would allow.

Staggering back up the slope, he saw where portions of the footbridge lay strewn on the slope, but no Jesse, nothing in sight. He traced the line along the fallen path. Would Buck stop higher up, a lighter body not falling as far? Or would he roll farther down the hill?

He glanced again along the ridge above and the gap where the footbridge had fallen. What the hell happened to Jesse? Did he make it up the rope to the rim, or did he take a fall too? Without so much as a yell or a peep? Was this his end? A poor kid who seemed to live a life of total disaster? To the rim above or the canyon below, he sent him a message: *Focus on what you can do now, Jesse, on what's in your own power. You're back on your own now, kiddo.*

"BUCK," he bellowed, "WHAT THE HELL HAPPENED TO YA, CHAMP?"

An image lingered and haunted him, stalled in his head. Buck hanging helplessly in his harness at the end of the leash. And a streak of *whys* haunted him too. Why didn't he hold him tighter, on a shorter line? Why risk taking a route from a bogus detour sign? Why ever stray from the trail with a small white terrier? And how much chance was there ever out on the Arizona Trail for a muddled, feckless lad so easily distracted by screwups beyond belief?

"BUCK," he appealed, "show yourself!" He waited for a bark, a groan, a whimper. Nothing. He strained to hear any sound. His dread and alarm mounting.

He forced out deeper breaths, though it hurt to breathe at all. He shouldered his pack off and took out water. He fumbled for his ibuprofen and swallowed three pills. As he washed them down with water, he realized he was dehydrated after the trauma of the fall.

Come on, he's gotta be near ... "YOU GOTTA BE HERE, BUCK."

Wade was never much concerned with man-made concepts like fate and destiny. But he did believe in luck and that's what they deserved, he and Buck, right now. Pronto.

He needed to focus on the bank directly above and below the drop zone. That dog must have rolled along the same path but just not as far. He took one last look at the wide gap above where the crumbled footbridge hung. Against the odds, Buck would survive like him.

With reference points from the drop, he searched for any signs, any white object that stood out, amid the pale brown and green, before moving down into a deep rift.

Hell, a small white dog's gotta stand out!

"BUCK!!!" Nothing.

Why wouldn't he respond to his calls or to the whistles? He tried not to think of the alternative; Buck injured, unable to bark or whine ... or worse.

"BUCK!" He cried out. "I'M GONNA FIND YOU, CHAMP."

Back down the slope, he called out, halted, listened, and trudged on at an unsteady pace.

When he stopped next and listened, a frantic voice echoed through the canyon.

"NOT ON MY WATCH ... GET A MOVE ON IT." *His* voice. *His* pain.

What an eerie place it was, stranger still as he made his way calling for Buck. He came to a swale, a deep cavernous swath of ground, where day seemed to be turning to dusk.

Whup-whup ... whup-whup.

Shóódé ... her calls brought him up short.

He listened closely and sensed her unique call, her voice, her downward inflection just before the yip went higher. For sure, he knew her tell-tale signs, a language as familiar as her limp. She had her quirks and traits and she was sounding off. Her calls were coming deeper and farther to the south. What was she trying to tell him this time? That he and Buck's deliverance was out of his hands. Were they in the paws of Shóódé--a wild, barely thirty-pound coyote that traveled the slopes with a limp?

Listen up. But for what? For menacing sounds from a deadly predator? No, keep a listen for Shóódé.

If he had any true affinity with animals, this was damn well the time to prove it.

But what the blazes is Shóódé trying to tell me?

30

"Don't let a Westie's small size and cute appearance fool you. Westies are physically stronger than their size indicates, including their jaws." —Deb Duncan, Westie owner and dog trainer

Jesse huddled at the far side of the rim, stunned, shaken, and curled in on himself. As the footbridge collapsed, a rush of adrenaline took him up and over the rim. But as soon as he made it safely onto the path, he went into a daze, a mental paralysis, the ranger's shouts from below having no effect.

When he opened his eyes, the whole disaster on the footbridge came roaring back. He sat up and started dry heaving at once. He pictured brave Mr. Wade hanging onto a piece of rope from the bridge as he tried to save Buck by lowering him real easy, so Buck wouldn't take such a deep fall. But he never saw poor Mr. Wade take the drop. He was too involved struggling to make that frantic climb up to the rim like the ranger told him to do. But he knew Mr. Wade took a bad fall like Buck. He struggled to breathe deeper and stop shaking, in agony over Mr. Wade falling into that deep canyon with the big cat down there.

He tried to calm himself by imagining positive pictures, like a counselor taught him long ago. Did

Mr. Wade ever think of brave dog owners and hero dogs? Did he have a dog of his own? Was he too busy to have a dog? He couldn't imagine Mr. Wade at home without a dog.

Jesse was startled by a whistle. He looked toward the rim and realized it could be the ranger still alive and whistling from below. That he might be hurt and needing help. How could he stay coiled up and live with the shame of not doing anything? Mr. Wade might need him to go out for help. He had to do something. He took deep breaths and battled over what to do.

Shouts. He could hear human sounds deep in the canyon to the south.

31

"I have looked for and studied jaguars in northwestern Mexico and the southwestern U.S. for 20 years. It has changed my life. Two observations are most relevant to recent sightings in Arizona: jaguars are secretive, stealthy animals that don't want to be seen; and jaguars know where the food, water, open space, and mates are, but have no concept of country, whether they're in the U.S. or Mexico."
—Biologist Sergio Avila-Villegas

Wade followed a yawning, meandering canyon to the south, leading to another wet wash. The mountain slopes were full of these isolated channels, perfect terrain for wild predators. These passages fingered out into smaller and larger pockets, like the ones he and Buck had struggled through earlier. Pine and oak woodland landscape offered the correct balance of erosion, optimal for creating ground springs with plenty of water and cover for large mammals.

He moved on steadily, listening for Shóódé or Buck. Each time Shóódé called out, he responded. If she yipped, he shouted back. He even tried yipping. He tried to keep the "talk" friendly, easygoing. He had never tried to yap with the coyotes around his ranch house. He was basically clueless as to how to get any sort of message into a yip or two but he was beyond any embarrassment. He was in the wild and he was desperate. Shóódé's calls drew him deeper into a remote south canyon.

He had a hunch about this passage, a sense that it was special and mysterious. A deep corridor, widening then narrowing, heading toward the border. He knew naturalists and biologists who swore the whole region had the best wildlife passages, a rich triangle of land within Mexico and southern Arizona and eastern New Mexico. Those who knew about these stretches, at least those with the highest integrity, kept quiet about them to hold the hunters at bay. He was sure he'd literally fallen into a special passageway, a habitat that would attract many wild animals.

He shuddered when he imagined the crazy construction of a so-called security wall across such a corridor, which would stop wild mammals dead in their tracks and threaten wildlife conservation.

"Human stupidity all over again!" He listened for Shóódé, his sound beacon. Deep down he had to believe she would lead him to Buck. There *would* be a happy ending. They *would* make it out of this mess together and stumble out of some side canyon. Even after a perilous fall, they *would* regroup as partners on the path, and reach the trailhead.

"YO, SHÓÓDÉ, WHERE ARE YOU?" His call was edgy and impatient. For good or ill, there were fewer yips, or so faint he wasn't sure he was hearing them at all.

"BUCK! GIVE ME A SIGN, CHAMP! BUCK! GIVE ME ONE BARK!" He could hear his pleas for Buck echoing back, becoming louder and angrier, carrying along the gap ahead. He pictured Buck out there somewhere—wandering, tired, thirsty, disoriented—no longer caring to sniff at anything. Maybe he found a burrow like the one where he'd rescued him, and maybe Buck just curled up to sleep ....

Sleep. Wade let out another barrage of shouts and heard a whistle in response. He yelled out hellos as he reached for his whistle. He blew a long response, when a muffled shout came back from a wash close by.

"Hey, Mr. Park Ranger!"

He trampled into an adjoining wash and found Rachel, resting on a soft mound of sand.

"I got another lab report," she said, with barely contained excitement. "A positive, confirming the scat is a jaguar's—from a female!"

"A jaguar ... and a female," he repeated, as if he was hearing the daily weather update.

"I can't believe it. I've been collecting cat scat on this mountain for nearly a year," she bubbled on. "I expected more lion scat. When you expect something, it can bias what you think you're tracking, what you think you're going to find, what you think you've actually found—though all along both the samples and tracks never quite fit lion."

Shaded by overhanging tree limbs, Wade stood still, nearly trancelike.

"Hey, what happened to you, you're cut and torn up? You look like a zombie." Rachel came up close to look him over. "Did you take a fall?"

"Yeah, I had a slight fall."

"Where's the dog?" Rachel looked around. "How'd you even end up down here?"

"Stuff happens." He was again in motion, looking up and down the wash.

"Are you okay?"

"Yeah ... Look, Buck's gone missing ... somewhere in this weird canyon."

"Oh, no." She peered about. "A coyote was yammering away a little while ago."

"Shóódé, I believe. Been trying to track her." Rachel waited to hear more. "She's my only lead. I've been tracking along here after him—I suspect the coyote's connected ..." His voice trailed off as he threw up his hands. "She's all I got."

"Well, Mr. Park Ranger, we've got this place in common. I've tracked Mirage down here and found plenty of evidence. And jaguar scat I'm sure, now that I've opened my own eyes."

Wade took several steps along the wash, focused on the path ahead.

"I mean, I know the difference now," she said, following him. "Maybe I didn't believe that a female jaguar would come this far, would make it into these canyons ... Jaguar prints, especially females', are similar to lions'. Her paw, smaller than the male's, threw me off."

Rachel realized the ranger was clearly on another planet, but she plowed on anyway. "We used to think jaguars are mostly nocturnal, but now we get diurnal sightings. Of course, at dawn and dusk—"

"Shush!" he hushed.

"What—what is it?" she whispered, ready for action.

"More *whups*—did you catch that?"

He was sure the *whup-whups* were sounding from deeper in the gap. Whups, rather than yips or barks.

Rachel shook her head, having missed the calls, in her rambling.

"The coyote." Wade tightened his backpack. "I'm following the calls."

"How do you know it's *your* coyote—there's a whole mountain of them."

"Shóódé whups and yips in an individual way, in a cadence I recognize."

"A cadence?" she asked with growing interest.

"She's got a sort of downward inflection when she starts a whup."

"Can you mimic it?"

Wade sighed and considered. "Well, more like a *wuh-whup*, so the *wuh* sound is slow, low, and drawn out, while the *whup* sound is faster and upward, you might say. *Wuh-whup*."

"*Wuh-whup*," she repeated. "For most humans, a coyote—or a jaguar—makes the same basic sound, generalized according to their whole species.”

“Well, as an animal biologist, you know there are differences among individuals, just like dog barks.”

“Of course,” she said and nodded. “According to personality.”

They were both silent, considering the matter in their own ways.

“How could Buck stray so far? On a scent? He doesn’t cover that much ground.”

“I lost sight of him!” The ranger felt the anger—with himself. “As if he vanished. Look, Shóódé’s all I got to go on—to follow her calls.”

Right on cue, another wuh-whup, and Wade froze to listen.

“I heard the change of intonation, for sure,” Rachel said, pulling her gear on.

She trailed the ranger, following the wild calls. She recalled the jaguar’s distinct calls to her own kind, or warning other cats to stay away. Mirage might possess an acoustic fingerprint of her own particular sounds. Quite likely jaguars have a list of calls unique to each of them, like Shóódé.

Rachel was convinced Mirage was moving through Jaguar Canyon, and her prints indicated she was dragging something along with her, like the young javelina from the earlier kill ... only now she suspected it might be Buck.

Shóódé’s whups led Wade into another wash. Rachel stopped when she spotted signs. “These are canine tracks." The ranger rushed over to examine them. "*Wild* canine tracks," she added. "See the short claws. Probably very recent, and purposeful. Shóódé's ... not Buck's."

"What about the other marks?" He pointed to blotted tracks beside the prints.

"Hard to tell—they're so brushed over in the sand." Her tone sounded guarded, even evasive.

He tried not to pin any hopes on a few blurry tracks. Enough that Rachel agreed Shóódé was near. He took careful steps along each side of the wash. He combed through fine-grained sand where he might find Buck's small pads, frustrated when Rachel couldn't verify any.

They moved on another few minutes until Rachel stopped abruptly. "Yes! Big cat tracks!" she exclaimed, squatting over a mosaic of distinct indentations in moist sand. "Hers! You must trust what you see; the round shape, both in the pad and toes that touch the ground."

Mirage. They stared at the size and shape of the tracks. Wade gaped at a pad almost the size of a circle made by a coffee can. Bad news for any prey in her path—and surely for a dog.

Rachel took pictures and followed them up the wash, absorbed with her find. The possibilities crowded in on her. At last, a better chance their trail camera would pick up Mirage-specific photos, adding to shots they'd captured of male jaguars. Yet she knew female jaguars had a reputation for almost playfully evading trail cameras.

While Rachel tracked the jaguar, Wade had an ear tuned for Shóódé, all the while looking for imprints of Buck's little paw pads in the sand. He would not give up, convinced there was a good chance of finding him through that coyote. He considered the last couple of days, the wild things that had happened, things that, as a park ranger, he would never have seriously considered in the past. Somehow, he believed that the three of them—park ranger, Buck, and that one of-a-kind Shóódé—were caught in a strange web. Was Shóódé a wild card, a wild friend?

Through the late afternoon, however nutty, Shóódé seemed to be leading them south along one finger wash after another, some narrow and some wide. But the tracks were so dried up or trampled over that Rachel gave up trying to decipher them. She knew Mirage was in those canyons. She would stay with the ranger because all the drama and players were there.

Wade tried to visualize Shóódé's actual presence and route as they pushed on. All he saw were paths that led deeper south. Given the same course, they might end up in a loop into ever narrower confines of the border region.

"Have you tried your GPS down here?" he asked.

"I have, but there's never reception here. Jaguar Canyon is too deep, narrow, and restricted." She pulled out her GPS but drew another blank.

He wasn't at all surprised—the canyons a natural shield to satellite reception. He would keep his trust in Shóódé as his compass and beacon.

"Hey—" came Rachel's voice, in a long, whispery call.

Wade lurched to a halt in the sand. Rachel sat on a big rock at the side of the wash.

"You OK?" he asked, backtracking.

"Let's take a breather and think this through." She took some water. Wade expelled another impatient breath, sat down, and pulled his water out.

"We've stumbled on a rare find—a confirmed jaguar in our midst," she began.

"They're not *that* unusual," he countered. "Others have been sighted, right, going back?"

"Not a *female* jaguar," she said, growing testy. "Not one *pregnant*."

For an animal biologist, Rachel had the triple crown—a positive for jag scat, a proven female, and the zinger, a positive pregnancy test from the last lab report. "Mirage almost certainly came from jaguar habitat in Mexico. She's found new habitat to raise her cubs."

She studied the ranger for a reaction. He appeared to be listening, but she wasn't sure he was listening to her. "Which means the whole region might be rendered off-limits to mining and housing developments—strip malls and golf courses and more fun parks."

"So, a pygmy owl becomes small change when we've got a pregnant jaguar."

"Well, yes! A rare endangered jaguar north of the border—a pregnant female? Around here, that's the gold standard in jaguar conservation. The impact would be monumental for local habitat and top predators."

Wade shook his head. "You really think anything's going to stop a juggernaut mine?"

"Mirage might put a halt to industrial encroachment. Jaguar Canyon and regions beyond would be expanded as critical habitat for jaguars."

"Jaguar Canyon," Wade mused. "Is that even on a map?"

"No, and it won't be, if we can prevent it. We won't expose a prime location where top predators have an ideal corridor, just so a hunter can take a rare jaguar for a private trophy room."

Wade knew she had a point. A rare predator like a jaguar or ocelot receives critical habitat protection under federal law; going ahead with a huge project like a copper mine that threatened critical habitat of endangered mammals would be illegal. And Wade was sadly aware of the hunter mentality of 'shoot and kill,' and stuff and mount your trophy.

Still, Rachel was into Big Issues. Wade's concern was small but vital to him—finding Buck. Not another lost dog. Not on his watch.

He fidgeted when he swore he heard Shóódé.

Find her, find Buck.

"If we can delay a monster mine from carving into this mountain, it'll starve for lack of capital funding. Mirage could hit the Santa Rita's like a meteorite, but with no damage."

"Well, she definitely won't leave the carbon footprint of a half-mile deep open-pit copper mine." Wade stood looking ahead into the canyon.

"No gaping mile-wide hole in the earth from Mirage."

Rachel sensed his eagerness to move out. "Wade, even though I'm more a fan of felines than canines, I'm on your side too. We fight for what's wild—all animals." She hesitated then added, "Maybe we *can* find Buck."

There was an abrupt explosion of yips. Did Shóódé have some good reason for luring them on, the ranger had to wonder.

Yes!

They both stood still in the wash, listening.

"What is it with this coyote?" Rachel wondered.

Wade listened for another call.

"Well, friend or foe, she shows the strangest behavior." Rachel said. "Maybe another lone disperser, like Mirage, out to claim new habitat."

"Canines. They're jam-packed mysterious."

"Ya think?"

He looked at Rachel. "I gotta move." He rushed off down the wash and she followed.

32

"Predators are perhaps our most accessible experience of the wild … an experience that is marked by gross alterations in attention, perception, body language, body chemistry, and emotion. Which is to say you feel yourself as part of the biological order known as the food chain, perhaps even as part of a meal." —Wildlife writer Jack Turner

Jesse willed himself to crawl carefully back to the rim. He didn't dare try getting to his feet because he was still shaking so much. He reached the edge, and eased up on his hands and knees. He forced himself to take a peek, but all he found was a gaping space where the bridge was.

Mr. Wade and Buck had fallen, for sure. Waves of shame and nausea swept over him, and he closed his eyes to stop his tears. But the worst wouldn't pass, and he opened his eyes and peered into the canyon. The shouts much earlier had long faded to the south, and no movement caught his eye. Though he was sure he heard a distant whistle farther down the gap.

Rattled and unsteady, he pulled back from the brink and managed to struggle to his feet. He put one slow foot in front of another along the rim path, building to a steady pace, listening for odd sounds floating up from below.

"Olly olly oxen free," he shouted weakly, hands cupping his mouth. In a token of false bravado, he called louder and quickened his way along the silent canyon.

Life and deathly stuff gnawed at him as he went. What happened to them ... Mr. Wade and Buck? Gotta get down there. They must need help. Must find them, no matter what ....

All the while, he dreaded that monster cat prowling and sounding off.

33

"Jaguars have the biggest brain-to-body mass of all big cats. They're extremely intelligent, which makes them independent, unpredictable, and dangerous. You'll never see a jaguar tamer in the circus. If you do, buy a ticket, because that'll be a one-time show." —Writer Richard Mahler

Wade and Rachel covered rough and rugged ground, in and out of one dry wash after another, the deeper sandy ones holding run-off water from the high slopes. They scrambled through Jaguar Canyon, pushing aside thorny brush and trudging through more washes. Wade suspected they crisscrossed a few of the same ones. His voice had gone raspy, lips buzzy and numb from whistling and calling for Buck. The dog did not answer. Apart from their own huffing and puffing, the only other sound was Shóódé's erratic, familiar wails.

Eventually Rachel got around to probing the ranger about losing Buck. He was forced to tell her about the bridge fiasco. It was hard for him to talk about Buck, so he steered the conversation to Jesse, suggesting that he was skeptical about the kid claiming to be a seasoned enviro defender and protestor.

"And I'm pretty darn certain we heard your jaguar in the canyon," he allowed, "maybe right below us, just before the footbridge gave way totally."

"Well, thanks for adding the vital bits, Mr. Park Ranger," she replied sarcastically.

"The thing is, that footbridge might have held but I think the kid went ballistic with your cat around. Buck and I ended up taking the fall."

"You think the boy's OK, then?"

"I'm not sure that boy's ever going to be OK, but I think he survived. He was close to that ridge when the bridge collapsed. I couldn't find him at the bottom. He's probably still trying to figure out how to get off this mountain."

"With any luck, he'll make it to the trailhead."

"If he's a no-show, I'll report him missing and request a search, but I don't think I could have missed him."

Rachel, though in fine physical condition, was irritated by the relentless pace. "Wade!" she called to the ranger out front. She'd all but given up tracking Mirage, even though damp washes offered a better chance for spotting the cat's recent movements. "At this pace, with her retractile claws, we might miss her prints in the sand," she pointed out.

Wade heard her, but didn't slow. He had heard more than he cared about jaguars. For sure, Rachel knew A to Z about the jaguar's physical characteristics; its round pupil, iris the color of golden to reddish yellow, its more powerful bite than other big cats— yadda yadda.

Tired, testy, and thirsty, Rachel shouted to pull up for a break on a sandy wash. They found pooled water, and reached in their packs for water bottles and filters and swilled what they had left. He noticed her latest easier-squeeze water filter, a method that required no laborious pumping.

An early monsoon hovered, ready to drench the mountain slopes. Rachel, feeling the heavier, humid air, pulled off a long-sleeved cotton shirt. A sleeve of colorful cat tattoos was revealed on her right arm. She knelt beside a deep pool, cupping water and running it over her head and face, letting the water drain down her neck and body.

With a splash of water from a pool, the ranger expected this cat biologist was good to go—her dazzling black eyes and fair complexion restored.

"She's still out here. Mirage hasn't left Jaguar Canyon," Rachel said, watching Wade's slow, laborious process of pumping and refilling his bottle.

"Well, for sure, she's covered a hell of a lot of ground."

They rested, leaning against the bank of the wash, each silent and weighing the next best move. Rachel pulled out the GPS collar and leaned back to examine the release mechanism. "She's at least three years old. A collared jaguar from a breeding population in the Sierra Madres. This collar's designed to drop off when the battery dies after about two years."

A kaleidoscope of ugly confrontations with Wildlife Services flashed through the ranger's brain. Recent and long-ago face-offs—they all revolted him, but he was never able to put them behind him. "Radio collaring wild animals serves no useful purpose," he stated flatly, wiping the sweat off his face and neck.

Rachel adopted a tolerant expression she showed in familiar arguments with students and trainees. "The thing is," she said, "we learn so much when we can GPS collar and follow these predators on the move. How can we not collar when we collect abundant knowledge to help these wonderful animals and their long-term survival? We might as well reject the scientific approach and join the climate-change deniers."

Wade knew about the wolves, even a few coyotes, collared and tracked over vast distances, showing how top carnivores roam great distances through mountains and ecosystems. As a park ranger, he tried not to get caught up in the "Wolf Wars," and those endless debates and battles over wolves and their reintroduction in the Western wilderness.

"Yeah," he said. "I'm familiar with the collared wolf stories. I understand how essential top predators like jaguars and wolves are for maintaining a healthy genetic pool, as vital as the grizzlies. But I'll never be a part of collaring them." He brooded over the many sinister ways Wildlife Services used technology to wreak havoc and death on wildlife.

He recalled a clash against Wildlife Services in Idaho. "Specialists" place a radio collar on a so-called "Judas wolf," so it will lead them to a wolf pack the ranchers want to eliminate. Judas wolves see their own species, sometimes their own family, exterminated, while the Judas is recaptured and used the next season when another rancher calls the specialists to repeat the treacherous method to locate another pack for killing.

To use a species to help kill its own, sickened Wade. Only humans drum up such evil methods and technology. But Wade had to choose his battles, so he could hang around for the long run and do good for other creatures ... like coyotes.

Something distracted him, heightened anxiety wearing at him. Something amiss out there, a feeling that Buck wasn't the only target, that they were in danger too. Something besides a change in the weather wafted through the wash, and not just the scent of greasewood after a storm. Was it another rumble or growl nearby? He tried to reorient himself by moving to the other side of the channel. It didn't help; he still felt distracted and disturbed. But it was a natural aura of something he was unable to see.

He glanced at Rachel who was still fiddling with the GPS collar. She planned to meet her colleagues who would bring a few days' tracking supplies. They would rendezvous at an agreed-upon spot in Jaguar Canyon. They might even take Buck back out—if he ever found him.

"Whatever the predator," Wade piped up, "wherever it's wandering, collared or not, it's still the same basic issue. Human expansion, suburban and exurban roads and developments, spreading everywhere over at least the last fifty years. And many wild species may not be on the official lists yet, but they're already endangered."

"We are so invasive," Rachel said. "Humans and our fast-track negative impact on the planet." She recalled wisdom from a trail-and-field-worn animal biologist, who questioned her own career and aims, and who opposed any more efforts to trap jaguars as a mission unsafe, benefits uncertain.

"Well, Mirage is pregnant, and that's such good news for the jaguar population," she added, keeping her focus. "Given a chance, she'll soon give birth to a litter of two, perhaps three or four cubs."

Wade paced about the wash, stopping to listen for Shóódé.

"Her gestation period is about a hundred days," Rachel continued. "The cubs are born blind and won't leave the den for two weeks. Imagine, while very young, they'll have blue eyes."

An edgy ranger could not shake off his apprehension. He didn't hear Rachel's words. He was certain a wildness stirred deeper in the canyon. Down there, the light won't last as long.

"Mirage won't end up in some animal snare in these mountains," Rachel declared passionately. "Not if I have anything to do with it. But this," the GPS-collar in her hand, "this will give us vital knowledge about her pathways and how to help her species survive." Wade was still in the wash, keenly listening.

"The coyote?" she asked.

Wuh-whup.

He nodded, grabbed his pack, and strode out in the lead, following the whups at a quick pace. Speculations and questions pelted his brain. He was convinced Shóódé was speaking to him. Calling out just enough to keep them on her trail. But would she lead a path to Buck?

What a series of snafus and blunders his "hike" had turned into, he reflected as he led the way. The call of the wild was an illusion, a false path for humans, including this ranger, no longer equipped for such a fierce life. How could a total life in nature be anything but a fool's quest? He pictured Katy, so sensible and grounded, which made him feel even more a jackass. Katy, back in his thoughts and feelings. He missed her.

Rachel saw the ranger retreating within himself. They were solo hikers. She lagged behind and kept a slower pace, dropping farther back and hardly searching for any stray tracks. She struggled to find any creature signs, let alone any evidence of Mirage. Searching for Buck was so distracting.

When she checked again, Wade was out of sight.

34

"We add 227,000 people to the planet every day ... And we take up a lot of space. 7 billion living human bodies weigh in at 125 million metric tons, or more than 12 times the weight of the planet's wild vertebrate land animals. But if that weren't enough, when you add in our livestock, we tip the scales at 425 million metric tons—42.5 times the collective weight of all the elephants, ocelots and polar bears, as well as every other wild land animal on Earth." —Kieran Suckling, The Center for Biological Diversity

Jesse lay on a large flat rock on the rim, facing the canyon, watching and listening for Mr. Wade. He recalled a story about dogs the ranger told him. Two strays showed up at his house—a black Lab and a brown runt of a mix—both in bad shape and hungry. He took them in, and fed and cared for them because they wouldn't leave. He had them checked over at the vet's, but neither had an I.D. chip. And the local animal welfare might euthanize them if nobody wanted to take them, and there was little chance of both being adopted by the same person. Yet he knew how bonded the two had become, so he posted a notice on the Internet. It took two months because he wouldn't let them be split up, but he finally got a couple willing to take them both and promise not to ever separate them.

Jesse wondered why Mr. Wade didn't adopt them? He realized he should have asked—but he didn't need to dwell on another thing that made him sorry about what he hadn't done. He didn't understand how he could always be sorry and shamed, yet never do anything about it? Then and there, he promised himself he would do good for animals. How and in what way, he didn't know yet, but he wanted to make a difference for their kindness and brave deeds. Dogs don't ever expect rewards, except being fed every day and getting a little kindness in return.

Whup-whup.

Shóódé?

He ran through talks with Mr. Wade and how awful coyotes are treated. He cogitated about how Mr. Wade said coyotes in the West needed saving from abuse. Maybe he was one to help, or he might help with all those brave shelter dogs. But he wouldn't want to spread himself too thin. He learned from the protest groups that you couldn't do everything for every creature. He could leave shelter animals to pet owners and settled people who foster and adopt, at least for now. As Mr. Wade said, you had to pick your fights, and take one at a time. It might be wiser to help raise the cause for coyotes, get people aware of their plight, and how they manage just fine when they are left alone.

He knew it wasn't the time, but his brain raced on, forming an idea for a creative protest to attract public attention over the wicked treatment of coyotes. He would expose the cruelty and the slaughter and the evil against coyotes all over the West. He would let people know about the Shóódés of the land. And it made sense because he wouldn't be dependent on any enviros or conservation supporters to make it happen. He would plan and stage the whole protest on his own, and be responsible for its success or failure.

Jesse scanned along the canyon. He heard nothing familiar, no more whups from *Shóódé,* no Mr. Wade, no Buck. Something, though, made him feel more confident about the path ahead.

35

"Why are jaguars coming back? What has changed? Well, jaguars never left! They are a secretive species that thrives in anonymity in remote locations."—Biologist Sergio Avila-Villegas

Naturally curious about mammals, animals, *and* human animals, Rachel wondered what made the ranger so troubled. He mentioned Abby, his poor lost Golden. And she was sure there were other past and current unresolvables. Then there was Big Ag. Anyone tangling with Wildlife Services would be tangling with Big Trouble. She imagined he needed a life, a life among the human species, greedy and self-centered as we are. She could relate.

After lingering behind the ranger, giving up on cat tracks, she mulled things over and opted for her usual method—some in-your-face straight talk.

Wade heard Rachel huffing and puffing, coming up on his heels.

"So, Wade," she asked. "Have you found the right woman in your life?"

"What?" He twisted toward her and then back to the trail ahead. "Where'd that come from?"

"Don't be coy. You must have someone in the picture—I *am* a biologist."

He snorted. "An *animal* biologist."

"We're not animals? Come on, out with it. Why is she the special one?"

He slowed to a stop. "OK, for one thing, I found a woman who doesn't nag and probe." He resumed hiking.

"Nag and probe. About what, for instance?" she probed, falling into step with him.

"Well, for one thing, she never nags me when I leave the toilet seat up."

"What's the problem with leaving it down?" He stopped again, hesitant, avoiding eye contact. He decided to tell her. "Because of Abby."

"Abby, your lost dog. Well, what's that about?"

"Before she was lost ... I left it up in case I didn't make it home."

"Yeah, so what if you didn't make it home?"

"If she ran out of water, if I didn't come back ... she'd have another spot—to find more."

"I don't figure—in the toilet? Wouldn't she have enough in her water bowl till you got home?"

"Unless I didn't make it back—for days, maybe ever—with no one except Abby in the house. Who knows how long it'd take before they got to her? You know, after I was gone?" He resumed his charge along the wash.

Wow, Rachel thought, this is a man who's lived alone far too long. Taking care of your animals, Mr. Park Ranger, is only one of a hundred reasons for having friends in your life. Human friends.

Deeper down the same wash, she got him to stop for a breather. Time to come to a decision.

"You know when we were talking, Wade, about weird animal behavior?"

"Weird like, say animal biologists?"

She felt he was anxious to move on—but this strategy wasn't working. They weren't going to find Buck or Mirage or any sign of them the way they were going at it.

"I don't want to guess on likely outcomes for Buck, but I do have something to tell you."

Wade was mute, having run many horrible scenarios through his head.

Rachel was itching to huddle with her colleagues, but she was hesitant to up and leave Wade on his own. As long as she remained, at least he might not charge ahead and scare away the wildlife, Mirage included. But she was so conflicted—support the ranger and his single-minded effort to find a dog likely already gone, or the biggest break of her life to track the only female jaguar detected in southern Arizona in the last fifty years? She wanted to help the man but ached to follow Mirage before the path got any colder. Criminy, she knew animal biologists who would happily sedate their colleagues with a dart gun to be the first in their field to score such a huge breakthrough. Would it make her a psychopath or something? Biologists have values too.

"Hey, are you ignoring me?" she blurted and poked his arm. "I think we both know Buck might already be a victim of a predator kill. On the other hand, he might be out in the bushes somewhere, under cover, hiding, like before when you found him. Still, it's only a matter of time till some predator—"

"I know all about the law of the wild." Wade glared at her.

"Well, Mirage is getting closer to giving birth." She took a deep, tired breath and pulled out a headlight. "We're losing our light. Anyway, what I'm trying to say is—Mirage might be planning a stash of food in a den somewhere ... for when her cubs are old enough in a few months to eat meat."

"Mirage?" Wade asked, restless and impatient. "What's with the name, Mirage?"

"Oh." Rachel looked apologetic. "It's the name I gave to her. I've used it for so long, I don't always remember to explain. A simple story about the first time a local rancher-hunter spotted a jaguar in the desert. How such a beautiful, powerful, wild creature surprisingly appeared in this dry, thirsty place? He imagined he saw a desert mirage. I started calling her Mirage and I always imagined one day she would wander into our mountains. Now my dream has come true. She's roaming right here in our own neighborhood. Her neighborhood, now."

"Rachel, you should head out now and meet up with your colleagues." He was waiting in the middle of the wash, desperate for the next coyote calls.

"It's all set," she said, fiddling with her headlight. "My cohorts will be up the slope in no time, with supplies to continue our search."

"Head out now," he replied. "You'll have a better chance of not missing them."

"We won't miss them."

"It's a huge canyon that goes on forever."

"I'm not worried. We'll connect. I'll tag along with you, and we'll keep searching for Buck."

"It'll get dark. Head out and find—"

"Still got light," she said, switching on her headlight. "It works."

"Go meet them, Rachel."

"What's going on here, Wade? What're you trying to prove? What's this all about?"

"You know—I'm looking for Buck." They were both silent, only a noisy Canyon Wren protesting above.

"Wade … it doesn't feel right leaving you now."

"I'm equipped and supplied to stay in these canyons for days."

Rachel studied the ranger's face, his strained, weary features. A sad, resolute expression in place of the plain hardness from before. How should she respond to an obsessive attention over finding this dog? Couldn't he see a rescue mission gone too far? Yet she understood obsession. She knew she was hardly in a position to criticize.

"OK, Mr. Park Ranger," she said, trying to sound upbeat. "I'll head out, on one condition."

"What's that?"

"Promise to hold close to the wash here, and I promise to return with help, and we'll all keep looking together."

Wade peered along the wash, squirmed a bit, and readjusted his backpack. "OK."

"Good. That's the plan then." She slung her pack over her shoulder. "When we come back, we'll mount a group search for Buck ... and stay alert for more signs of Mirage, of course."

"Sounds like a plan."

"Great. And where do you figure that crazy coyote is heading?"

"Straight ahead, bending back down to the southeast," he said, gesturing along the wash.

"Haven't heard her for a while. Keep a listen, and we'll join up soon."

"For sure."

"Oh, you still got your whistle, right?" He nodded. "And you've had plenty of practice." She smiled, but sensed him already drifting into some faraway zone. "She's the largest wild cat in the Americas, you know."

"Who's that?" he asked vacantly.

"Mirage the third largest cat in the world."

"So I've been told."

"Proportionate to its body, it has the biggest head and strongest bite of any cat on earth, capable of crushing a bowling ball, some say."

"Like a few of my ex-girlfriends."

"Shame on you." She chuckled.

"Well, thanks for sharing that bit." He turned away, shaking his head.

Rachel called after him, "Forget about her being at the top of the food chain. Just remember Mirage's condition. She'll likely keep near the washes—a thirsty cat, a soon-to-be-mom of several cubs."

Wade distanced himself from her advice—a soul waiting to be truly on his own.

"Don't forget she might be getting hungry, Wade—so stay alert!" Rachel headed out, turned back and put two fingers in the air. "Two hours max, so go easy until we meet up."

As she went, the ranger nodded and waved. The moment she was out of sight, he moved swiftly along the wash.

36

"It ain't wilderness unless there's a critter out there that can kill you and eat you." —Doug Peacock, Author, Naturalist, and wilderness warrior

A peculiar quiet enfolded Wade as soon as he halted his angry assault along the wash. Where were all the birds on a mountain famous for many dozens of species in the spring? In all his years in the Arizona wild, never had he suffered such silent menace, and standing only a few hours hike from trailheads on National Forest paths in several directions.

He listened for Shóódé while he searched for paw prints in the sand. He battled a muddle of emotions—anger, pain, and fear over awful images of Buck as prey in some horrible end. But this was a new level of apprehension. Maybe as a kid he'd felt it, but not as a man, and never as a ranger. He felt a pulsing adrenaline, a feeling of being humbled by fear and helplessness.

But mostly he was gripped with fury, a mounting rage mixed with the vague sense of being caught in a cat-and-mouse game—him the mouse to a big cat like Mirage. And a growing realization stunned him. The risk he was willing to take, as he grasped how much saving Buck meant to him—and how it all happened in a tick of time.

He recalled Abby and the days and nights rampaging in search of her, storming through foothills and along the edges of National Forest. And how miserable and exhausting those failed searches were.

Buck's loss hurt him deeply and in the next instant, he heard himself bellow into the wild, "NOT ANOTHER IN THE SAME MONTH!" He roared again. "I AM NOT LOSING ANOTHER DOG!"

As a slow, festering anger returned, he knew he could not fall into a reckless rage.

Determined to toss aside anger, fear, and despair—emotions that would only exhaust him— he slowed and tried to recover before struggling on.

He stopped abruptly when he saw a fresh pool of water.

Rachel was no longer there to read the signs, but her basic tracking wisdom echoed in his head. "Keep to the washes ... Mirage will need regular water to nurture those cubs she carries ... watch for large round tracks and those paw prints from your coyote friend."

While Mirage would use cover of brush and scrub, he knew that her need for food and water would bring her out of rugged terrain. Did that big cat have Buck? Is that why he hadn't answered? Checking for signs, he would keep to the washes and watch for her large round tracks—and coyote paw prints too.

And yet, how could he begin to imagine trailing a wild predator like a jaguar? It was a strange muddle—Buck somehow connected to Mirage and to Shóódé, the oddest coyote on that mountain. But he must stick to the arroyos in Jaguar Canyon and follow it through to the end.

Abby and Buck's loss tore at open wounds. Old wounds caused by his love of kindred creatures like coyotes. His mind drifted, seeking refuge.

He thought of the young man acting on impulse to save his little terrier, jumping in the water and fighting off a shark until it let go of his adored puppy. And a heartbreaking incident of two brothers drowned as they tried to rescue their dog fallen through ice. The dog survived. And a hiker falling to his death from a bridge trying to rescue his dog—again, the dog surviving. An incident in Seattle floated through his head. A loose, disoriented Labrador stopping traffic on the I-5 for hours ... the local news covering a heartening story about people popping from their cars to help corner an animal in distress, in spite of the danger to everyone on a perilous, clogged freeway.

Buck would turn out a great survivor like the dogs in the stories. And Abby, too! He took comfort in the great hearts that dogs and other animals possess. He would push on with a passion to let the wild be free and he would face up to what lay ahead.

But could he be at a lower point, a moment any weaker in doubt and despair? As a slow, festering anger returned, he knew he had to wrestle free of it before it led to reckless rage.

Wuh-whup. His mind did a flip-flop. He strain to figure out how far along the wash Shóódé was.

Keep steady ... stay calm. Suck it up and find a way to that poor Westie. Always Katy's wise voice, always there in support—when he would listen. But for her, he was certain he would've gone into an awful tailspin. He knew it all along but how to tell her? He knew in his heart it was time to face a plain fact. He hadn't lived a decent, full life for a long time. He had to face up to it and let a human companion into his life. Katy—the only other of his species possible. Katy—the only one.

Wade came to a stop and reached for water. He drank and squinted as a brilliant shaft of light reflected off something ahead in the wash. He shaded his eyes and moved closer. A shiny beam shimmered off an object in the sand. He halted and stood rapt, the object reflecting a radiant glow from the sunlight. He stepped toward it.

The pendant. There it lay below him, the lucky pendant he had attached to Buck's harness.

Buck ... He heaved a deep, long sigh.

37

"Wildlife Services bears the burden of proof to justify the indiscriminate killing of predators—economically, ecologically, and ethically. I'll go to my grave saying that." — Ecologist and coyote expert Bob Crabtree

Late afternoon, a strange quiet along the rim, Jesse was up and moving through rough territory. The trail was a fierce path to him. He'd been no more than prey, like a small wild animal and a part of the food chain, ever since he arrived.

Old anxious habits took over and the mounting urge to escape. Like when he got away from the girl from Phoenix and those enviro-volunteers. Fear made him scamper away rather than cuddle up—every time.

Yet something beckoned him deeper into the canyon, despite his inner voice telling him to 'go now.' Would his actions distance him or bring him closer to his terrible fears? He couldn't work it out, but he needed to look for Mr. Wade and Buck. They might be injured—or worse—but he wouldn't let himself think about that. He had heard the coyote below and if she went deeper, he would go deeper. For sure if he found her, he had to believe Mr. Wade wouldn't be far away.

He listened for the ranger's voice beneath the wind. No coyote calls, no dog barking below.

Nothing but silent currents of air. He spotted a narrow trail, like a switchback or another animal path. He took it without a thought of turning back, and it led him down, deeper and deeper. He followed twists and hairpin turns, struggling through a gauntlet of razor-edged sticker bushes until he reached what he took to be the floor of the canyon.

He was surprised to be surrounded by such a change in landscape, with pine trees and oaks and others he didn't know the name of. It was confusing because this new terrain had a calming effect, yet he still imagined more terrible predators lurking in a perfect and wild place.

Yip-yip.

There it was, her comforting call coming ahead.

Even before their first encounter with Shóódé, Jesse had a belief he never told Mr. Wade. That he might share some awesome cross-species kinship with the Shóódés of the wild. He had met a street kid and his dog in a Tucson city park once. The kid claimed his dog was half-coyote—a "coy-dog," he called it. Jesse saw coyote resemblance in the big ears, except the dog didn't have a bushy tail and its nose wasn't so pointy. Still, the coy-dog had some of the same independence, caution, and reserve of a coyote. Sorta' the same as Jesse felt about himself and people—a coy-dog fit with neither dog nor coyote. Jesse imagined Mr. Wade kidding him ... *Oh, so now you're a coy-boy.*

It made him feel warm inside, the chance of caring for coyotes. Sometimes he wished for a coydog companion or even for a Shóódé on the road. An animal still wild and free of pet people and their weird dog breeding habits. The more he thought about Shóódé, the more he sensed he and she were a lot alike. Yet he realized the coyote was meant to be free. They are wild and only take to their own kind—and then not always. They were so aloof when they wanted to be—almost always. Mr. Wade claimed they shared survivor traits with humans, except coyotes wouldn't kill their own kind like wolves do, and coyotes never killed other species just for the sick thrill like some humans do.

Oh, well. He knew if he had a Shóódé friend, it would end up running away—same as he always did.

He felt ready now. He would push on below.

38

"Today, jaguars are classified as endangered. Hunting them has been banned in Arizona since 1969 ... But the female jaguar's presence a half-century ago looms over the current debate over whether—and how—to protect habitat for jaguars in the U.S." —Tony Davis, Arizona Daily Star reporter

Wade turned the pendant over and over in his hands, trying to decode it. If the fierce-looking jaguar depicted on a locket offered anything to decipher, he wasn't getting it. He studied its imprint. A creature clutching its prey and the prey revealing a flaming cluster of fangs. What did it tell him?

Even before Rachel offered it, he was aware of the importance of the jaguar in Mexican and Central American culture and mythology. A potent figure of the so-called underworld, an icon of power, terror, and esteem, even of worship in Aztec and Maya life for thousands of years.

Could the pendant or its symbols mean something, other than an ornament he'd attached to Buck's harness and fallen off? For sure, it told him Buck had passed that very spot, someone or something catching hold of ... That was something.

How might ancient Maya customs, with the jaguar as its God of Night and Guardian of the Underworld, untangle Buck's strange disappearance on that day, on that mountain in Jaguar Canyon? What a tangle of myth, religion, and superstition. He tried to set aside jaguar lore for what it was —so much mythology. He tried to erase horrible pictures it conjured up.

He must stick to Shóódé and her wild calls. He knelt over the site where he found the pendant to check for tracks. He carefully examined the sand for paw prints from different angles, unsure of what he saw. He made a wider inspection zone, heading back down from where he'd come, checking the banks on either side for signs. He felt like a sighted person blind to what was before him. What could he see, save his own footprints?

Yet he felt renewed and hopeful with the pendant in hand. Though a rescue was against all odds, he would persevere and deliver Buck safely home in spite of the odds. A good-luck charm, Rachel told him, one on which he would keep a firm grip. He would move forward with his simple and resolute search. Shóódé somehow would hold him alert to the right path—he had to believe that. She had, after all, guided him this far.

He sprang forth along the edge of the wash, listening in the way a blind man sees.

39

"The central question: Does the fact that no female jaguars have been spotted in this country for 50 years mean they can't exist here? Or does it say that if jaguars lived here before, they could again?" —Tony Davis, *Arizona Daily Star*

For good or ill, Wade's gut told him he was on the right track. He had long suspected a unique bond with wild creatures. It was now or never, time to put his kin-connection to use. Was Shóódé after Buck as a playmate or a meal? And what about the ultimate in lethal threats, being stalked by a top cat like a jaguar? Buck was doomed without him.

"I'm not giving up, Shóódé!" Wade protested. "I'm on your tail to save him!" Keeping close to the coyote was his only hope. Yet deep in the marrow of his bones, he sensed there was more to this rough path he was on, a mystery to unravel.

Daylight would die, twilight turn to darkness, with nothing but his small headlight for tracking. Intuition hinted that he was oh-so-close to Buck and that he must stay vigilant for Shóódé's faint whups. But for one remarkable coyote, could he ever walk out of that canyon with Buck alive?

Running across the pendant was a stroke of good fortune. Rachel had said little about archeologists uncovering this prehistoric artifact and its significance. Could it be related to religious symbols and themes appearing on Mayan stone carvings? If so powerful to ancient people, why not take a leap of faith to the here and now? Could its power have drawn Buck, Mirage, and Shóódé together somehow? And he and Rachel? Was a paranormal, even dangerous force pulling him on?

With a huge dose of speculation and the widest open mind, he pondered the mystical and magical, and the fantastic without answers. He had little more than his knowledge of the wild, though tracking skills were untested in these conditions. Was it really now or never, time to put his kin-connection in action?

Farther and deeper into the canyon he went, alert to any movement, responsive to the slightest rebound of sound. Echoes from his lightest footfalls, even the breeze itself, became odd and eerie. A shocking barrage of monstrous roars erupted and swelled upward. They came once, twice, a third wave that reverberated and bellowed and swarmed around him. The creature seemed to envelope the whole canyon, resounding waves carried to the rim and back down to the abyss where a ranger stood rigid.

The roars faded to an uneasy silence.

As he waited, fear and anger returned and gnawed at him, until something more—a bold, wild urge—pushed him to protest those roars, to resist a predator that seemed to demand that he turn back.

Oddly, the earlier trail encounter with Jesse came flooding back. He recalled the young enviro's pleas and shouts, "Whatever it is, I'm on its side!" Wade pictured Jesse flailing his arms in the air and shouting, "Come on, beautiful monster! I mean no harm!" A dazed and exhausted kid shouting bold and inane appeals of self-sacrifice to an unknown power in the wild had seemed crazy and juvenile at the time.

Wade sat down and took deep breaths to calm himself. Maybe he'd pondered the situation too privately—and too quietly. On impulse—no pondering at all—he began slowly in a reasonable voice. "Hey, creature down here ... I know you must be near. Hear me out, Guard of this Underworld, when I say he is just a dog ... Buck is his name. Buck's worn out, in shock, I reckon. Let him be, Spirit of the Night or whoever you are ... He's only a dog, not even wild. Let him go."

But then an impulse caught hold, rousing something in him. He started to pant like a dog and he clambered to his feet and scrambled to a spot in the middle of the canyon.

"HERE I AM, YOU AWESOME CREATURE! HERE—I—AM!"

He heard his voice bellowing through the void, as if someone else's voice. "COME, TAKE ME," he blared, against an awful faraway echo. "BUCK'S A TINY HOUSE PET! TAKE ME, MIGHTY CREATURE—COME! TAKE ME AWAY!"

Wade stopped to catch his breath, his demand reverberating up the rim and rolling back down into the canyon. An eerie calm returned. With heavy breath, he waited for a creature response. An abrupt microburst of wind came hissing through the passage, unnerving him. Then one faint *whup* from below and a dead calm after.

Wade followed the faint whup like a lifeline. Charging on, heedless of the nearest trailheads, ignoring any exit strategies, he entered wider, deeper terrain. When he was sure the canyon couldn't go any deeper, down it went along the southeastern slope toward the border. He was drawn through a huge ravine of ponderosa, piñon, and pine; he passed varieties of needle trees he couldn't identify. And on he descended to the lower depths of leafy oak and sycamore. Strangely, it felt like home turf to Wade.

He could tell this deep, wide rift offered everything a big cat needed. Evergreens, woodlands, desert grass, and scrub grasslands, and plenty of water through a network of slow-moving creeks. As Rachel would have it, "Where there's water, there's predator and prey."

Was he about to enter a wild game of hide and seek? He pursued Shóódé and Mirage, wherever they lurked, moving in crisscross patterns along wildlife paths, washes, and rugged terrain.

Riveting, disturbing sounds forced him to pull up short. He counted the hoarse utterances, each one slightly different and coming quicker and closer together. Wild voices would fade to a whisper one moment and a wheeziness the next, and then die out.

He caught his breath and lurched on, amid a new round of grunts and cough-like *uh-uh-uhs*. Resonant rumblings surrounded him, rising in volume, maddening sounds from every direction on the canyon floor. The predator was no longer somewhere out-there but wrapping itself around him with rough calls from everywhere.

Wade held an absolute conviction: He had heard the same relentless calls the night he rescued Buck.

It was not just any wild cat ... it was a jaguar—Rachel's Mirage.

Mirage on the prowl, protecting her new habitat. From him.

40

"An organism without a sponsor is an organism without a future." —Writer Edwin Dobb

Wade blindly pushed on. He'd lost track of how many small and large passages he'd stormed through. Exhausted, with little left but grit and sheer stubbornness, he kept moving. He longed to hear nothing but coyote calls. Instead, he heard startling roars and rumbles, a ranger alone in deep earth crevices that smothered daylight.

Shóódé's whups had stopped. He paused, and there before him was a wildlife path leading into a vast field of boulders. He held steady to the path and moved over rocks and grassland, no longer fearing a predator tailing or circling for ambush. Why should he fret when he knew for sure what had actually happened? From the very beginning, he and Buck had been stalked. Mirage had Buck before, which accounted for his neck wounds. And somehow Buck had escaped and Mirage wanted him back! She wanted *her* prey back!

The burrow rescue lingered in his mind. It all started with Shóódé and her warnings behind his campsite the first night. An encounter with those fiery eyes and tracking the whines and wails to the hiding place, to Buck. Whether the jaguar had stashed the dog there, or Buck escaped and found cover on his own, Wade would never know. For sure the big cat had a hold of Buck for a time, and the dog had those nape wounds to prove it.

Incredible events started to fit together, a surreal experience from beginning to—no, not the end. Not yet, though he despaired of the outcome. His rampage through a remote canyon was only another step to what might come. What *would* be next? And what could *he* do?

Buck had to be out there somewhere and he could never give up on him. He would never accept a sad, grim end after all they'd gone through in two very long days and nights. Buck gone missing after the fall from the bridge was not the end because the ranger would darn well find the right ending. He would find Buck and carry him out of Jaguar Canyon and off that wild mountain.

Wade could never be sure of Shóódé's intentions, but he had puzzled out a few of her ways. Whenever Mirage prowled about, the coyote kept her safe distance, probably always downwind of the cat. As the ranger got better at locating the cat's wild calls, he managed to calculate about where the coyote would show up. He reckoned the three of them—Mirage, Shóódé, and ranger (along with Buck until he went missing)—had tracked each other in triangular movements over many miles. Shóódé would have stayed well clear, never risking the jaguar picking up her scent.

Instinctively, she would never risk becoming prey to a surprise attack from a new and deadly intruder on the mountain.

Was that all up for grabs now? Wade had entered a boulder field amid a deep-trough canyon with little cover. Long shadows gathered. He pulled out his binoculars and scanned along scrub and grasslands and over heaps of boulders. He glassed back and forth across the terrain, watching for movement through dimming light, anything to catch his eye. He raised his view to the boulder tops and froze on one tall weirdly shaped boulder, what the natives called hoodoos—tall, narrow columns of oddly eroded rocks. He zoomed in on a form, a life shape. Whether it was a strange hoodoo or something alive, it wasn't moving.

He gave it a wary stare until it stirred—a miracle come to life atop the boulder! Pointy snout and ears, four long legs, and a bushy tail. *Shóódé*, moving steadily and showing no limp. She perched on another hoodoo, facing him, like an ancient Pharaoh's prize animal companion atop an Egyptian monolith. Was she aware of him, keeping an eye on his every move? Was she ever not aware of him, from the start?

Where is he, Shóódé? Lead me to him—show me Buck!

The first night on the trail, Wade had to admit it was all about getting Buck off his hands. Then a sea change and his need to protect the dog, the need not to lose him, all the while trying to shake off that one-of-a-kind coyote. When Buck went missing the first time, it was: Take a walk, Shóódé. He's not yours. We're not for you! But then the whole story shifted after the bridge collapse. He needed her to find Buck. Maybe they'd needed her all along—he and Buck. Now with great care and respect, he must follow this curious creature through the boulder field. She would be his scout and guiding spirit.

Where's Buck? Lead me, Shóódé ... lead the way.

Near the first cluster of boulders, he spotted Shóódé darting left and right, all the while appearing to keep sight of him. He moved closer, concerned that any boldness might spook her. Would she vanish and would he lose his only link? He slowed to a cautious walk, struggling to show a soothing presence, trying to keep a proper bearing to interact with this being, all the while running out of time and light.

There she lay on another boulder, sprawled out on her belly, watching his approach. He eased up, catching his breath, a man about to fall apart, attempting composure. He willed himself to slow his every action; he found a flat rock to sit on. From some fifty yards away, Shóódé eyed him carefully, while he kept his focus on her alone. However improbable, he found himself sitting in an awkward position, cross-legged, lotus-like, the way Katy sat at times. He placed his fingertips on his temples and struggled to clear his mind.

Shóódé must become his map, a lifeline for Buck and a man's own future.

Lead on, friend, I will follow. You're my only way, Shóódé.

Ranger and coyote stayed immobile until, at last, she turned her head. Her slim muzzle pointed toward another rock cluster farther south. She got up and ambled along the boulders, jumping from one giant rock to the next while cautiously eyeing her way ahead.

Wade got up and struggled to climb among smaller boulders, anxious to keep her in sight. Was it to be follow-the-leader? It seemed he'd been following her since they first spotted her. So be it! Shóódé moved along boulders into scrub and back up among more jagged rocks. Beyond all doubt, Wade would place his trust in this coyote, willing Shóódé to show him the right path, wherever it led.

As he got nearer, he watched her make a staggering jump to a high boulder. There she stopped, and after another glance south, she voiced a single low *whup.* He searched the soft light to the south to see where she signaled. Through failing amber light, he glassed a larger figure, a vision that sucked the breath right out of him. A very different, four-legged creature stood upon dun-colored, rugged granite rocks, surrounded by pale-green brush.

Wade turned to Shóódé and raised an open palm. When he looked back, on high he beheld a predator, its head held unnaturally upright with the shape of something hanging from its jaws, a pale form he did not want to make out.

41

No need to glass in for proof, no need for close, gory evidence. Wade felt his chest cave, his breath stop. He took a long, raw look with a naked eye.

Buck … a dull, white form hanging below Mirage's large head in those awful jaws … Wade's senses blurred from crushing pain. Buck! So, this is how it ends, Little Fella. He stepped toward them but realized she would only move farther south—deeper into the pine-oak woodlands among the massive boulders.

She did move, through sycamores and cottonwoods, climbing and leaping atop one huge perilous boulder after another, all the while clutching her catch securely. The ranger's senses seemed to blur from a heavy hurt. Still, he followed, not knowing why or for what purpose. Where was she heading? A secluded den? On toward the border? Quite likely she would break across the boundary and head back into the rugged, remote interior miles of Mexico. No matter, she has her prey and that's the end.

Yet it wasn't. Something pulled him on. He tracked her slow, uneasy progress over boulders through a never-ending canyon. She moved across rolling hills and grasslands, and he followed.

Where is she going? What is she doing? Why keep to open ground, so exposed, instead of hunkering down under cover of brush and thickets?

He held his distance, but just barely, without a care of risk. Many times, he had entered the danger zone, different encounters that might have turned deadly. This was the zenith, he knew, but he had no option but to stick it out to the finish. He made Buck a promise. How could he ever turn back?

He would find peace in the fury. But how? What could be done? Buck was gone ....

42

Jesse tried to keep an even pace, taking random crossovers and listening for more yip-yips to keep him going. After a brief sighting of Shóódé, he hiked a switchback from one side of the gap to the other, trying to locate and keep contact with her. She pulled him deeper into a shadowy canyon, but he no longer worried about where it led. Reaching the trailhead without Mr. Wade and Buck would never do. It would haunt him forever if he didn't find them.

He wondered if he might be having one of those out-of-body experiences his parents used to go on about. They even talked about tripping on drugs in the old days. He'd never had one that he knew of, though many times he wished to be in another body in another place, whenever he was seized by the trauma.

Now he definitely felt like he was out of his body, in a different state of being but a weirdly calming effect. He was drifting without a care in the world, gliding by a whole variety of pine trees, their pointy needles brushing against his skin, gently stroking him. He swooped through evergreens and leafy oaks like the ones back home, until he hovered like a drone at the bottom of the canyon, a desert of cactus, mesquite, and trees he couldn't identify.

A vision came of a pouncing predator that devoured him but having no effect on his calm. Maybe more like what people mean when they say 'He didn't know what hit him.'

But the vision snapped him out of his out-of-body experience. Maybe as close as he would ever come to one—unless he had just died. No, he felt himself still moving under his own power, and in a great floating calm of quiet.

He crossed a field of rocks, and faint calls from Shóódé interrupted the gliding sensation. He landed among some truly awesome boulders. Was this some strange life transformation? Whatever was going on, he stood in a huge field of grassland with humungous boulders bigger than he had ever imagined.

Hearing Shóódé's clear cries, he sensed an ever-stronger link with this strange creature. And there she was, perched atop a boulder some forty yards away, waiting for something, alert, watchful. Was she calling him, leading him on? Signaling? She must have a reason for wandering through this gigantic pile of rocks. It hit him that he and Shóódé might have a connection after all. Like Mr. Wade felt with animals.

That big cat had to be out there somewhere, because she'd been all over his case for days. She was near—he was sure she was very near. Will we meet again? Like a struggle for survival in a story book, except this was no story. Will this big cat finally get me?

Jesse tiptoed among the boulders, losing sight of Shóódé, but hoping for her help. Overcome with weakness, he dropped down on a big rock in a strange field full of them. He grew very still. Had he used up all his choices, even his favorite—running away? He felt so tired and drained. Yet, as sure as he still breathed, if Shóódé was hanging around, crazy as it seemed, Mr. Wade must be close by.

He took comfort from Shóódé, like a hiker hoping to find the warmth of a campfire on a cold night.

43

"[Mexico's] Sierra Madre jaguar population thrives in an area of relatively continuous and unfragmented habitat, including a mix of ranchlands and protected reserves. It is the northernmost known breeding population of jaguars." — Sonorensis: Arizona – Sonora Desert Museum

Wade focused on the largest and highest boulder he'd ever seen, in a field of megatons of eroded bedrock from ice ages eons ago. Dusk gave only faint light to Mirage standing atop that tallest boulder.

Even though his binoculars hung from his neck, he had refused to look close-up at the limp prey hanging from those massive jaws. His insides a knot of pain and heartache, he lifted the binoculars. At last, he took an unsteady, dreaded look.

Movement. A small, white body moving ... Buck alive? Dangling from her mouth?

Could he believe his own eyes? That she actually held him by the mended harness? Her head still positioned unnaturally high to keep from dragging his tail end along the ground?

Wade steadied himself, holding his binoculars on a miracle—Mirage, her frozen image atop the flattest, biggest boulder. Buck, his paws wiggling, body squirming, hanging helplessly below the fearsome bulk of her head.

His mind raced through Rachel's speculations, and the one she feared the worst: The grisly prospect of Mirage holding Buck as fresh, live prey for her cubs; a gruesome act of nature. Rachel's words hammered in his head ... Adult female wild cats with yearlings often kill for sport to teach their young how to get food. This was the natural world of feral cats.

The ranger made a tentative approach. Mirage remained curiously composed, taking her stand on the highest point. Wade felt a fleeting presence of Shóódé, but he figured she would stay clear— maybe beat a hasty retreat, downwind. He yearned for her shrewd-loco presence.

Anyway, who am I to call her loco? Who's jumping from rock to boulder toward the greatest predator of these lands. A half-crazed ranger!

Crazy or not, he needed a way to distract this mighty cat's attention. For certain, his life depended on how he executed his next move. Climb up that giant rock and find a way to take Buck from her clutches.

Somehow, someway, I am going to save Buck.

All the while, Buck dangled below those mighty jaws.

44

"Jaguars in both Arizona and Sonora have stood their
ground to the point that they have reportedly been killed
with rocks." —David E. Brown and Carlos A. Lopez Gonzalez

Before Jesse's very eyes, Shóódé vanished. He struggled to a higher spot to try to see her. He fumbled and stumbled back and forth between the large rocks. The boulders took on a monstrous life of their own, ghosts of the long-dead, haunting the surrounding pine trees. He looked for the slightest movement in the bush and smaller rocks.

At last, he caught sight of a set of pointy ears and the profile of her sharp nose. Crouched, still, and absorbed, he studied her and she seemed to measure him. It was a brief exchange. She turned her attention to something else.

He followed her gaze and was flooded with relief and joy. Mr. Wade!

The ranger stood next to what had to be the biggest monster-boulder in the world. He was propped up against it, with an eye on Jesse. When Jesse moved toward him, a determined ranger motioned him to stay put. When Jesse started to call out, the ranger cut him off, slicing his arm through the air. Then he raised his hand, pointing a finger some forty-feet high to the top of the immense boulder he stood against.

Jesse looked up and saw a long black-ringed tail of a cat, gracefully swishing in the air. His viscera heaved and his legs wobbled. He slid down the face of a rock, folding and collapsing on the ground.

He huddled, struggling to get hold of himself. Then a pulse of strength and resolve enveloped him, the same as he'd felt during creative protests. He got to his feet and with quick breaths, he searched for the ranger. He no longer saw him.

Forcing himself to move, willing himself to climb, Jesse carefully hugged his way across smaller boulders until he found some footing on a larger one. Thinking only of Mr. Wade, he boosted himself to climb higher. Upward and around he went, scaling and mounting ever bigger boulders.

He was seized by a familiar, contented rush, a surge of curious excitement. He tried not to think of what to expect as he mounted a boulder upon which the big cat might be standing. Mr. Wade was somewhere close.

He stopped at a high boulder and pulled out his GoPro. He ripped off the bandana still wrapped around his wound, then switched on the camera, and fastened it around his head.

45

"So strong was the feline's cultural aura that it continues to resonate in the [Maya] region today … [Travelers] in the Guatemala district of Chamula may witness during the annual Fiesta of San Sebastian the age-old ritual of the balam tun—"jaguar rock"—whereupon a Maya boy feigns sacrificial death on a large stone slab." —Writer Richard Mahler

From a high perch on the mountain, Rachel couldn't believe the startling scene some five-hundred feet below. Mirage, amid a vast boulder field, moved with remarkable deftness from rock to rock along her way. Rachel had her binoculars focused on the unidentified prey dangling from the jaguar's awesome jaws, Mirage keeping her head gracefully high to avoid dragging it over the rocks.

Still no sign of the ranger.

After one final, grueling hike, Rachel and her two colleagues had reached an incredible field of giant boulders. She knew those slopes and canyons better than anybody. But she had never run into so many enormous granite boulders, a terminal deposit of debris left over from the Southwest's last Ice Age.

She and her colleagues were now proud witness to the first live spotting of Mirage. A free animal in the wild, no longer a mirage to Rachel, but a wonder of nature. Her every move and action a marvel, from her massive swaying head to her undulating feline gait. As she clutched her prey, she sprang with ease and grace from one boulder to the next, thick paws on powerful legs, flicking her tail all the while.

Would an inner compass be leading her south into these stone fields?

In soft voices, the biologists traded theories, posing issues the cat faced if instinct led her toward the border, and the higher risks of searching for a path to cross.

Rachel glassed in search of the ranger, while Ben took pictures and monitored the jaguar's path. Like a beacon in the dying light, she skimmed and sprang along the biggest boulders.

"It's ideal terrain, isn't it?" Rachel said.

"A perfect wildlife corridor each way," Erica offered. "Except for that frickin' wall of shame."

While the Mexican reserve was only a three hours' drive away, would Mirage ever find her way back to a Sonoran reserve with that grotesque barricade still a threat across the vast desert borderlands? How would a jaguar ever leap over that monolithic misfortune?

"Well, she's found an awesome corridor," Ben said. "She must feel right at home, like the habitat in her own birthplace."

"She's got everything she'll want here," Rachel replied. "Ponderosa and piñon pine. Oak and sycamore farther down. No matter where she wanders, lots of cactus and mesquite trees along her way. All the comforts of her Sonoran habitat, with plenty of water."

"Great cover and camouflage for surprising prey," Erica observed.

"I only hope it's not a last viable habitat for her," Rachel suggested. "What a game changer, if she's able to find a mate."

"If she stays and establishes territory," Ben said.

"And if her mate shows up when she's ready, before wandering off on his merry way," Erica quipped.

"He'll show up, for sure," Ben added.

"Can you see a bump?" Erica asked.

"Difficult to tell how close she is to birthing." Rachel tried to glass in and check for a bulge around the jaguar's midsection.

"Wow, just imagine her becoming part of a breeding pair." Erica added.

"Oh, my God!" Rachel now recognized what Mirage was holding in her jaws. "She's got Buck, the dog the ranger rescued." Rachel pulled the binoculars away and shook her head, saddened and sure of Mirage's prey.

"Hey, who's that?" Erica was glassing in on another boulder opposite Mirage.

Rachel found the spot.

A human—male—and not Wade, but a young man sprawled on a rock opposite the boulder on which Mirage stood. He had something attached to his head, and he was positioning himself in a curious pose on the rock.

Rachel studied him closely, his submissive prostrate pose appearing as a stylized position of surrender. For her, it evoked an age-old sacrificial ritual from Maya legend. How strange that today a young boy would adopt such an ancient custom, she wondered.

When she glassed back to Mirage on the higher rock, another person caught her eye. A familiar figure, crawling up the cliff face of the boulder where Mirage clutched Buck.

"Oh, Mr. Park Ranger," she whispered, "you are crazy."

46

"I do not want to be a lonely species set adrift from all the
rest." —Author Craig Childs

By the time Wade managed to finger-grip his sore and cramped hands to the highest boulder, the light above the canyon had colored the rock a deep orange.

He crawled up, no longer thinking of Jesse and how the devil he ever found his way to that remote spot. The ranger couldn't begin to imagine it, and he had no time to consider it. As he neared the crest, the wind stirred, bringing a strange, wild odor he'd sensed nowhere on that mountain until two days ago. He reached the top of the rectangular rock and he peered above the granite face.

There she sat at the far side, like a living hoodoo atop the boulder. One big paw rested on Buck, sprawled just below her. Buck squirmed slightly as Wade ever so carefully inched himself over the top. She pressed her paw more firmly on Buck. He stopped squirming.

On his stomach, Wade took a deep, quiet breath, and raised his head—but froze when he spotted Jesse, laid out on a lower boulder some twenty feet to the right. The ranger's eyes darted back and forth between the kid and the cat. Jesse stayed flat on his belly, lying oddly still, except for his raised head.

Wade struggled to keep control ... What the hell is he up to? Should have left that boy stuck in the tunnel! Is that his camera on his head?

He tried to wipe Jesse from the scene, to stay focused on Mirage and Buck.

He peered at the cat, and she turned toward Jesse. She lifted her paw off Buck, and abruptly got up to take a good look at the boy. Did she feel threatened by his presence? Would she jump to the next boulder and pounce on him?

Wade moved an inch and the jaguar instantly turned back to him.

With one knee on the ground, he remained still. Two sets of mammal eyes waited for the slightest movement. Never lose eye contact with a wild predator. Her eyes were so intense and alluring, it was hard not to blink, or look away. What an exotic creature to behold. He felt compelled to pay homage to this queen of the feral world, decked out in her colorful, magnificent coat.

Focus! But on what? Poor Buck, looking bone-tired and half alive? Jesse, still in the same submissive pose? Mirage, alert to each flank, to every angle?

He knew she was aware of everything. Bowed and still, he agonized over what to do, what not to do. What could he do? How would he connect with this natural ruler? How to reach this wild, fearsome creature?

He seemed to watch himself from above as he gently slipped his backpack strap off one shoulder, then let the other slide off. The pack fell softly on the rock.

On all fours, he tried to mirror her moves, struggling to hold her gaze. Though he outweighed her by seventy-five pounds, he sensed her elemental power and felt weak in her presence.

Was there ever a more beguiling cat?

She stood her ground while he hugged the boulder, frail and fragile in this eerie, uneven standoff.

Wade, ever so carefully, inched in her direction.

She lowered her head, and snapped Buck up by the harness. Wade stopped his crawl and lifted his head slightly. Buck swayed from her jaws, while she seemed to study this strange two-legged mammal crawling toward her on four limbs.

Wade edged forward only a few paces, then froze and waited for her to make the next move.

Her tail flicked back and forth, the furry coat of butterflies floating to life. A white strip ran the length along the bottom of her tail, which had black rings and a black tip. Her head moved side to side, Buck a pendulum swaying in the harness. She was agitated, starting to pace like a caged cat, except she wasn't caged.

Wade stopped breathing, waiting for her next move, unsure of his own.

Still and quiet, she pierced him with huge, red yellow, fiery eyes.

Let him go ... he's not even wild ... let him be.

She bowed her head. Stunned, Wade recorded every micro-movement as she let the harness drop softly on the boulder and Buck lay on the rock.

Then came a fierce growl, the resonant rumble cutting right through him; her breath so pungent, he went lightheaded from its odor. She went silent, head bent toward Buck, cowering beneath her.

Is this it, Buck, when we got this far?

Mirage opened her massive mouth, stuck out a huge fleshy tongue—and gave Buck a lick that covered his whole face.

And a gentle nudge that pushed him away.

Wade had no time to react as she leapt and landed on the boulder next to Jesse. Wade was breathless with shock, but the boy remained quite passive, except for his eyes following her. She bent and inhaled him curiously, starting with the GoPro covering the gash across his forehead, his stringy head of hair, then sniffing along his neck, shoulder, arm, and down his back—covering the whole smelly torso.

In agony, unable to stop the unbearable moment to come, the ranger watched for her next move.

Wuh-whup ... came the call from the canyon.

Mirage heard her, too. After another look up at Wade and Buck, she circled and jumped lightly to a smaller rock beyond Jesse, and down to several others.

Back on the ground, she strutted south and vanished—like a true mirage among the dark flora canopy of Jaguar Canyon.

Wade was on his knees, weak and disoriented, as if waking from a coma. He tried to get up, to watch her amble through the sepia light, but he could hardly move. He looked to Jesse, now on his knees, the GoPro still strapped to his head. He appeared as deeply confused as the ranger.

Buck was alive!

Wade motioned him. Buck was hesitant to move.

"Come on, Buck," he called outright. The dog turned toward Mirage, but she was truly gone, south into the canyon.

He turned back to the ranger.

Come on, Buck, he willed silently and motioned again.

At first Buck came forward slowly, stiff and tentative. Within a few steps, he found his normal bouncy Westie strut. Wade, on knees, unsteady and shaking with emotion, pulled him up and held him firmly in his arms, soft to the touch—but smelling wild.

47

"One brave deed is worth a hundred books, a thousand theories, a million words. Now—as always—we need heroes. And heroines!" —Author Edward Abbey

Rachel chortled to herself in the back seat of the silver SUV bearing their logo—*Jag Lab*. Wade sat next to her in silence. Buck, having groomed himself until falling asleep, snuggled between them.

"Puck," she whispered and smiled.

Wade squirmed a bit but stayed quiet. On their arrival at Bedrock Springs trailhead before dawn, Erica and Ben had found a notice on the bulletin board stating "LOST—a West Highland White Terrier, 2-year-old male, answers to the name of *Puck*."

When they passed it to Wade, he'd repeated it aloud several times to himself (and the dog)—Puck … Puck? … Puck!? Each time frowning as he looked askance at the Westie. "You've been messin' with me, Buck," he chided, shaking his head. "So, they call you Puck, eh?" He raised an eyebrow, "Like a little hockey puck?"

In the dark under the glare of the ranger's headlight, Buck's ears had wiggled, a pair of pointy, miniature antennae, his head tilting left and right, a waggle from the tail.

Once the humans regrouped after Mirage's departure, the trip back to the trailhead proved a stroll in a dog park by comparison—Wade and Ben tag teaming it, slinging the exhausted Westie over their shoulders.

Their odyssey in the wild over, Rachel enjoyed a few laughs over the name confusion. As for the ranger, the frantic search for the dog, and the surreal encounter with the jaguar had been exhausting.

Wade reached out and gently stroked Buck/Puck on his soft back. He vaguely remembered a "Puck" from English class, a Shakespeare play about a sprite-like character. That made more sense—maybe that was where he got his name.

No matter, he reflected, he's just tuckered-out Buck—not much more than a spent pup.

Rachel opened her window a bit, an odor of wildness lingering on Buck, pungent in the vehicle. She stayed quiet about the ranger's crazy, desperate, ultimate act to save the dog. In the end, it was more like a miracle rescue. How would one account for such outrageous, counterintuitive behavior? Had Wade actually saved Buck? Well, duh, Rachel!

And Jesse too, she had to admit, came through with flying colors, having been sniffed up close (and rejected) by a jaguar—Mirage, no less—and lived to tell the story.

"Interspecies relationships are tricky," she said, thinking aloud. "We know many wild animals develop a bond with other species—an elephant with a goat, a cheetah with a dog, lions and tigers even with their prey—the list is long. But in all the cases I know of, they are captive animals brought up together from birth. In their natural habitat, they would nearly always be natural enemies—predator and prey."

"Well, I reckon Buck and Mirage got to know each other, off and on, for about three days," Wade replied.

"And when you tie the coyote into the mix—"

"Yup, Shóódé could be the biggest mystery of all," the ranger added.

"Mostly alien territory for an animal biologist," she confessed. Rachel, and no doubt the others, knew the ranger was on very shaky ground out there in that boulder field, but she knew that was something he didn't have to be told.

That Mirage had released Buck on some baffling, wild, mysterious instinct, Wade was certain. An animal instinct he would never understand or explain.

For Rachel, the prospect of Mirage and other jaguars breeding in Southeastern Arizona was both exciting and challenging, considering the ordeals they'd just gone through and the many more to come. Yet she couldn't help ticking off a list of priorities—estimating how many jaguars might end up roaming the region; confirming if Mirage was part of a breeding pair; and how to make it vividly plain to the public that Jaguar Canyon and the mountain region surrounding it were a viable, critical habitat for jaguars—and off limits for hunters. And that was just the start.

"What do you figure Mirage and her cubs' chances," she mused, "breeding in these mountains?"

"There are alternative interventions to consider," Ben said, cracking his window open. "We know it would be a mistake to attempt to tranquilize her, before or after the birth of her cubs, in order to move the family back to the Mexican Reserve. Their long-term prospects might be better there, but the risks are too high."

Rachel agreed, of course. Many conservation plans and various trial resettlement ideas had been proposed, including relocating a few jaguars from the Sonoran reserve to the range north of the border. All these proposals were seriously flawed, and besides, politically, they knew the U.S. and Mexico would never reach an agreement.

"I believe our data leave only one viable alternative," Rachel continued.

"And what's that?" Erica asked.

"Better to let a wandering male take his chances of finding Mirage on his own."

Erica, from the driver's side, cracked her window as well.

"Buck's brought a wild scent along with him," Wade announced.

"I'm betting it's not all Buck." Erica pointed a thumb toward the rear where Jesse lay curled up asleep with the cargo, hugging his bike and worldly possessions retrieved by a National Forest volunteer. He reeked of the wild—and weeks without a good shower.

Smirks all round before more silence.

Wade settled back, rested his head, and closed his eyes, keeping a hand on Buck. His fingers touched the gouges on the nape of the dog's neck. Erica suggested Buck get a tetanus shot.

In the end, for Wade it was more than enough that Mirage released Buck. Yet he did wonder how much, if any, the ultimate showdown and rescue had to do with any special affinity he might possess with animals, tame or wild—which he would never admit out loud. And the last thing he'd ever choose to be known by was "wildlife whisperer" or some other crazy tag. If he had any so-called gift for animal communication—with Buck, Mirage, a few coyotes, and others he met along the way—he would keep it between him and the wild ones.

And what about that friendly coyote? After they gained the trailhead and were loading up, Wade couldn't believe what he heard: the familiar yip-yip in the early dawn. As he looked around, there was Shóódé peering from the cover of the bulletin board. She moved right near and sat down to watch them load. Just as they were all ready to pile into the SUV, Wade handed Buck's lead to Ben.

They all watched as the ranger moved slowly toward Shóódé, still sitting perfectly motionless. He gradually came to within a few feet and still she kept her ground. He squatted down, and after a moment, he carefully reached out with his right hand and held it loose in front of her. Curious, she tentatively leaned in and gave his scarred fingers a delicate sniff.

"Wild," Jesse whispered, awestruck by the close contact.

Back at the vehicle, Wade watched her amble off with her slight limp. Would she be heading north, away from Mirage and in the same direction as so many animals these days?

For sure, he knew Shóódé had a big hand—a mysterious paw—in the outcome and the good fortune of a teen adrift, an unsettled ranger, and a lost dog he called Buck.

If only Westies could talk, once and for all, Buck would sort it all out for them.

48

"Many breeds are known for their attitude. Westies are known for their indomitable Westitude! The Westie is possessed of no small amount of self-esteem, and the Westie will not tolerate being ignored." —Deb Duncan, Westie owner and dog trainer

Back in his pickup, Wade still replayed the rough path to a boulder field and the final surreal encounter with a great predator. A ranger who seemed a lot like himself had rampaged through the wild, tangled up in situations he never imagined. It seemed more a chaotic dream, with a final, fearsome showdown tossed in, before, at last, waking.

For Buck, who knows? Maybe it was no more than a brief romp on the wild side. Curled up asleep beside him for the last time, "Puck" was on his way back home, back to decent dog food, baths, and long naps on a soft bed, for sure.

In his rear-view mirror, Wade checked on Jesse in the bed of the pickup. His head of dirty-blond hair was blowing in the breeze, his grimy body tucked close against his bike and duffel bag. He'd long finished the last of four peanut-butter-and-jelly sandwiches Ben and Erica had passed his way during the hike to the trailhead.

When the ranger agreed to take him to the bus station in Tucson, Jesse, well aware of the odor jokes, volunteered to ride in the back. Reason enough, but mostly he wanted a break from Jesse's thank-you's—for "Mr. Wade, the best ranger in the West"—not to mention those heartfelt confessions about his life being changed forever, having survived Mirage and his demons head-on, literally.

At a stop in town, south of the university campus, Jesse labored out of the pickup while the ranger unloaded his duffel and bike.

"Where's the station, Mr. Wade?" Jesse, his destination Phoenix, looked up and down the street for a bus.

"Oh, it's only a couple blocks from here." The kid looked confused. "There's another thing to take care of before you catch that bus."

"Oh, I see, you want me to clean up first." He was looking at the clinic in front of them.

"Well, that'd be good. But this is for urgent medical care. You need that gash stitched up before any more prefrontal brain matter falls out."

Jesse flashed an open smile across a guileless face, but then he hesitated before heading toward the front door.

"Don't worry, I've already called. They'll charge it to me—they know me here."

He shied away for a moment, and then faced the ranger.

"Thank you, Mr. Wade ... I mean for everything."

"OK, kid … Jesse." Wade handed him a piece of paper folded around a couple of twenty-dollar bills.

When he spotted the bills, his face did a flip-flop in wonder. "Gee, Mr. Wade, you're the best."

"That's my cell number in case of a real emergency, OK? No calls just for yakking. Don't much like talking on the phone at all."

"Oh, I don't either. Thanks again, Mr. Wade."

Wade watched him trail off with his gear toward the clinic. What a pungent experience awaited those inside, and nothing compared to the people on the bus trip.

At the entrance Jesse turned back. "Don't worry, Mr. Wade, they got OK bathrooms at the station. I'll do a real decent wash-up before I board the bus." Hell, now the kid's a mind reader.

With a huge grin, Jesse waved a final goodbye, and hauled his gear into the clinic.

Wade shook his head. It had to be about the first time he'd actually noticed Jesse's smile. After he cleaned himself up, he might even look more human than feral boy. The ranger waited a minute to make sure the lad didn't change his mind and duck out, then Wade got back in the pickup with Buck.

49

> "We need big wilderness, big national habitat, not more technological information about big wilderness. Why not work to set aside vast areas where we limit all forms of human influence? Let wilderness again become a blank on our maps." —Naturalist and writer Jack Turner

Buck's owner lived east of town, but Wade wanted to stop at Tractor Supply for some dog treats. There, the trail-hardened pair paraded forth, Buck in full bouncy strut. They got some double-takes, people even stopping to stare at the seemingly mismatched duo. In separate encounters women stopped to fawn over Buck, using the same expression—"Oh, isn't he adorable!"—in spite of Buck's odor, his gray and dusty coat, and grimy paws. Back on the street, a young fellow in a muscle car slowed down to take a long, gawky look. The ranger gave him a withering, What're-you-lookin'-at glance. And an old local sitting on a bench asked, "Whose furry white cat you walkin'?"

They met some curious, friendly folk. Even the town dogs seemed to sense or smell something special about Buck, an aura they wouldn't mind rubbing or licking off on themselves. Buck had a different bearing, more flair than his usual, innate

Westie charm, which hinted at a mighty ordeal overcome out in the wild on the Arizona Trail.

Back in the pickup, Buck sat up straight in the passenger seat eyeing the foot traffic. Wade pulled out a dog treat. "OK, Buck, here's the real stuff."

He was awarded a whole biscuit. Oh, how he worked that treat, his head bobbing about as he chewed and devoured it. Naturally, he waited for another, alert and attentive, the perky, antenna ears like animated eyebrows, the head tilting and hunting for familiar signals, watching for every subtle expression or sound.

"Well, Buck," Wade took a deep breath and lifted Buck against his chest. "Looks like we got one more stop together." Facing him straight on, nose to nose, he rubbed one of his pointy ears. After a gap of silence, he set him back down, pulled the pendant from his pocket, and pinned it back on his harness.

"OK, champ, don't ever lose it again." He tried to sound upbeat, but when his eyes got dewy, he quickly wiped them dry with the back of his hand.

50

"They say when you die and go to heaven, all the dogs and cats you've ever had in your life come running to meet you."
—Writer Kinky Friedman

When the road turned twisty at the eastern edge of town, Buck got all alert and restless. Hell, Wade ruminated, he's picked up on all my bad habits. As soon as the road straightened out, Buck took to whining, bobbing about, and straining at the window. By the time they pulled up to a big iron gate, Buck was at full throttle, barking and whining and scratching at the door.

Let me out!

At the front gate, Buck stood on hind legs, his head pushed through steely bars and barking his head off. Peering through the locked gate, Wade viewed a stylish circular driveway leading a couple of hundred yards to an elegant flag-stoned entrance. It fronted a fancy new "starter castle," with a stunning view of the Rincon Mountains in the background.

That Buck lived on the right side of the tracks, Wade was relieved to see. Not unlucky or feckless folks crowded in a dilapidated doublewide. Castle or doublewide, he knew the house was no matter to a dog, but the souls living there and how they treated their animals mattered. With all their obvious comforts and resources, Wade wondered why his owners failed to keep their wee Westie safe.

Wade inspected the gate for the security button. Buck barked incessantly, focused on the castle he knew as home.

Gotta get on with it. Finish it off—get closure, Katy would say. He found the button and a speaker next to the gate.

"Yes?" A woman's voice came on the line, causing Buck to bark louder.

Wade asked if this was the Garber residence. It was, she answered.

"I've got a delivery for you, ma'am," the ranger managed over the noisy terrier.

"I don't believe I ordered anything," she said, a bit wary.

"How about a small white Westie?"

For a second she was silent—then "Puck?!"

Wade could hardly hear her words, what with her excitement and Buck's barking. Next came shouting and yelling, voices crying out, "They found Puck! It's Puck! Puck's home!"

A lock clicked and the iron gate swung open, followed by a great clamor coming from the big house. Barefoot children in shorts and pajamas streamed onto a wide front terrace, as Wade restrained Buck, who tugged at his lead, still barking furiously.

"You made it, Buck." He gave him a last stroke on his soft back. "You're home, champ—you're Puck now." Four children of varying sizes ran toward them, with Puck barking, whining, and straining at his leash.

"Go for it, Puck," Wade cried, releasing him.

The Westie pulled away toward the kids, but then he slowed and stopped. He charged back to the ranger.

"What is it, champ?" He knelt and Puck jumped and bumped at him, whining and nosing him.

"OK—it's OK," he soothed, starting to choke up. He pointed the dog in the direction of the kids, and the grimy gray bundle of a dog was gone in a flash.

Wade watched him run off, his ears streaming back in the wind, his short legs churning as fast as when they chased after rabbits and a crazy coyote along the trail. The flock of children came flying forward, falling, colliding, and hugging Puck.

The ranger felt he would hand over his one good hand to know why that Westie turned back for him. But he would keep his hand and believe what his heart told him: The caring, the instant attachment ... their kind of love. He felt overwhelmed, in a panic to leave, but Mrs. Garber, a middle-aged, very fit and attractive woman, caught up to him.

"We were leaving the trailhead," she explained in a warm voice. "We often hike part of the trail there. Our youngest was taking Puck's collar off while getting him back in the car. Puck always rides without his collar. That was when Puck heard, smelled, or saw something, and ... well, he was off and running back up the trail."

Mrs. Garber got a little teary, though all the while she held his gaze without a blink. Her story was so affecting in the moment that Wade had to lean against his truck cab.

"We searched and called for him for hours, moving along the trail until it got too dark." She paused to enjoy the kids and Puck at play. "After a sleepless night of tears, we were all out the next morning, searching the slopes, but the few people we met never spotted him."

Wade turned away. Puck cavorting with the kids, running and chasing them around and around the elegant front driveway. Judging where he found him, he estimated their champ had covered a whole lot of trail through a number of campsites in less than a day—or night.

At last, Puck came racing back up the gravel path, circling them, a wild Westie romping about. That was when Mrs. Garber caught sight of the pendant on Puck's harness.

"Well, it's kind of a long story," Wade said. "It's said to be a good-luck piece."

"He'll never be without it, because now he's surely blessed with the best of luck." Without a blink, Mrs. Garber beamed at him and then at Puck.

Wade urged her to have their vet check Puck out and give him a tetanus shot. She and the children thanked him again and again. She insisted he come back, meet her husband, and visit Puck and the family. Wade thanked her kindly and said he might be out that way one day soon. He felt a deep sense of serenity at Puck's fortune and good home. But he felt out of place and knew he wouldn't return to the Garber's.

His brief bond with the Westie, Buck to him, had come to an end. They met up and sort of rescued each other at the perfect moment. That's how he saw it anyway.

Epilogue

"The right of all forms to live is a universal right, which cannot be quantified. No single species of living being has more of this particular right to live and unfold than any other species." —Norwegian philosopher Arne Naess

Southeast into the foothills, down the gravel road home, Wade was shrouded in a stillness, feeling empty and downcast.

He tried not to dwell on his unusual, extraordinary behavior in confronting Mirage, an encounter so fresh he would need some distance to understand it. Yet the dangerous face-off kept coming back, leaving him somehow half-haunted and half-restored. Was this an end to one life and the beginning of another? Always the animals had come first, in keeping with a string of natural commandments he patched together. Then Buck and Shóódé, and maybe even Mirage, conspired to guide him along a different path, one that turned into a miracle of sorts, one in which a ranger and a dog were each given a new start.

When he pulled up, Katy stood on the porch, the one he built for her—a wraparound about the same size as the tiny old ranch house itself. As he got out of his pickup, he heard a familiar bark. When the screen door behind Katy pushed open, a golden jewel nudged up against her.

Wade caught his breath and blinked several times.

Abby!

The jolt of surprise drove him to his knees in the dirt driveway. His eyes were shut when her furry body pummeled him, pushing and pawing and licking.

Abby!

Miracles in the wild, sure, but on your own front steps? He opened his eyes to make sure he wasn't hallucinating. There she is, my beautiful Goldie, my woolly pot of gold.

Abby, a second miracle in three days!

Wade reached in his pocket and pulled out the morsel of a treat he'd been saving for the last month. Abby delicately took it from his fingers and had it swallowed after one bite. Wade wrapped her in his arms, staggered to his feet, and proudly carried her toward the porch.

"She's been back for two days," Katy said. "If you'd checked in, ya' big dummy, you'd have known."

Wade stood on the steps holding and hugging Abby. She made a quiet whine, same as whenever he got home from work—but this time without a bark.

They sat on the porch steps while Katy explained how she found her. She and Marie from the animal clinic decided to give it another try. They would stake out around Abby's favorite haunts. Sure enough, Abby showed up not far from the ranch house, Katy coaxing her into her waiting arms.

"Why would she do something like that?" Wade wondered.

"We had a long talk about it."

"What—you and Abby?"

"No! Well, actually, yes, but I'm talking about the human-animal chat at the clinic. We all agreed—including Doc Ruth—pets sometimes need to go off on their own. Not always due to trauma or injury—they just sometimes do. Probably not that unusual. It happens. Like going on a walkabout?"

He hugged Abby. "Yup. You know all about that. You knew we wouldn't give up on you, girl," he said softly.

Later, they worked their way around to the back porch, and then over dinner Wade gave Katy the broad outlines of his encounters on and off the trail.

"So how do you feel about what happened?" she asked.

Wade hesitated. After double miracles, he felt it high time for an honest response, which they both deserved.

"I think the experience changed me," he said. "Out on that mountain on my own—finding, losing, then searching again for that crazy terrier, and a crazier coyote popping up—I realized I've been sorta crazy myself. Ya' can't live a life only for animals, as much as I tried to believe it—or needed it. Times out on that path I felt ... despair, I guess ... like before I found the pendant and—"

"Pendant?"

"A good-luck charm the biologist gave us, the one I had attached to Buck, which I later spotted on the ground—a small medallion. Guess it played a part in the whole mess, at least it triggered something bigger for me. By then, I was down about as far as ever ... when I found the pendant that dropped off Buck's harness ..."

"And?"

"Well, I got to the point when all the fear and anger and losing Abby and then Buck—well, I was feeling buried by the whole mess." Wade paused and stroked Abby, snuggled up tight against his feet. "Anyway, I came to realize a few truths, you might say, and I had to face up to some things ..."

"What kind of things?"

"Well, you know, living with more ... than one species. If I started, well, with a certain one of my own species."

"One of your own species?"

Wade hesitated. "You!" he exclaimed.

"Oh, Wade, that's so sweet ... if I understand what you're trying to say."

"Darn it, I mean I want you more in my life." He gave Abby a rough stroke. "*We* want it—don't we, Abby?"

Katy put an arm around his shoulder and hugged him.

"Abby might never go walkabout again," he added lamely, "if we're all a tighter unit?"

"Maybe so. You know, Wade, I'd never be uncomfortable playing second fiddle to Abby—never have."

Wade looked defensive. "Well, if things got reversed, and you went on a walkabout, Abby and I would be out looking for you day and night, twenty-four seven."

"That's good enough for me." She beamed.

Teary-eyed, he gazed at her for a time, until they fell into a long slow kiss.

Forty-eight hours later, Wade returned from a short hike with Katy and Abby near the ranch house when he found a message on his cell.

"Uh, Mr. Wade, I wanted you to know that my GoPro recording of you on the boulder with Mirage is truly awesome. I hope you don't mind that I sent it to Rachel, but I said it's only to be used for her research, with her being a cat biologist and all. So, don't worry—you won't show up starring on YouTube."

Jesse included a selfie of himself, standing out front of a gate next to a sign that read 'Phoenix Regional Office—U.S. Department of Agriculture.'

Katy looked at the photo. "This is the boy you met on the trail? He looks as old as you."

"Life on the street is hard, whether you're a bum, young drifter, or a creative protestor. He's not wasting any time—he's already stirring things up again."

Later, Wade was on the back porch with Abby, when Katy rushed out with her cell phone.

"I was catching up on local news—listen to this!" she said, reading "'Phoenix: A lone bicyclist was taken into custody after chaining himself to a steel gate in front of the motor pool at a regional office for the U.S. Department of Agriculture. Jesse Hayduke, age 19, address unknown, said he was protesting the department's Wildlife Services division and its policy of killing wild animals, in particular, the yearly wholesale slaughter of coyotes.'"

She handed Wade her cell with a photo.

There was Jesse, idling on the ground with a huge chain wrapped snakelike around his scraggy body, locked to the gate of the motor pool. Wade shook his head, pondering the photo. "I could be wrong about this kid. He might end up with a future, maybe evolve from just protesting. Who knows, maybe he'll end up nurturing wild beings or become a naturalist."

"Or a natural, wonderful man like you—that would do." Katy smiled and gave him a hug.

He felt a rush of renewal in her simple touch, like the rush of truths he had faced on that big mountain. Was it hope, even redemption, he had tried to explain to her—and to himself? Maybe it takes time to understand new truths. For now, it was enough to accept a few of his own kind in his life.

"I'd better come up with some change in case I need to post bail for him."

About the Author

From Washington State, Robert had an early career in the theatre that took him far afield. On an acting fellowship in classic repertory theatre, he earned a Ph.D. in communication arts. He taught performance of literature at City University of New York.

He directed two plays Off-Broadway; a comedy about George Bernard Shaw and a concert docudrama on Albert Einstein at Lincoln Center. Theatre study lured him to London, where he lived off and on for several years. His writing has appeared in academic as well as popular publications, including *Channels in Communications*, *Scene4 Magazine*, *Quarterly Journal of Speech*, and locally in Tucson's *Desert Leaf* Magazine. Drawn to activist literature, he pivoted to write about wildlife and conservation. He considers his proudest achievements rescuing and assisting the rescue of lost dogs. Robert and his wife Kathleen Alden live in Tucson, where he has taught writing. He has the good fortune to summer in a cabin in Arizona's White Mountains, just a daily dog walk to the Sitgreaves National Forest, where coyotes, bears, wild horses, and other creatures are often spotted. He considers himself a recovering golfer, now an avid Pickleball player who likes to unwind with a crossword puzzle.

Acknowledgments

Writing a readable book might not take a whole village, but it takes a pack of people. Thanks to Jodi Venning who shows by example how important dogs are in our lives. Thanks to Erin Wilcox and her bare-bones story evaluation and Kim Vacariu for an early manuscript critique. And credit to Wynne Brown's mid-stage edits to put flesh on the bare bones.

To Becky Masterman for her writer wisdom, the simple kind that sticks with you along the way. I much appreciated early feedback from Tom Thompson, Jean Roqueni, Victor King, Brad Fiero, Bhaj Townsend and Gordon Currie, Greg and Cheryl McConnell, Sue and Dave Pope. And many thanks to Vicki and Larry Stein for years of best-buddy e-mails on topics far and wide.

Cheers to generous Tucson-based hiking groups, including Rincon Group Sierra Club Adventures. Credits to Tony Davis, Arizona Star's environmental reporter, for his tenacious coverage of jaguar activity in the Santa Rita Mountains and the fight to oppose digging a mile-wide copper mine in this beautiful region.

To Pima County Library, a provider of prompt material with a staff that answers obvious and obscure questions. And how do I recognize the many naturalists and animal biologists I've read over the last ten years when those in the Southwest alone would take up a whole page? Perhaps my chapter epigraphs will serve as a token tribute to so many inspiring souls.

Thank you to Sebastien Gabriel for use of your Unsplash photo on the front cover; thank you to P. J. Bickell for designing the cover; and to Brad Peterson, Unique Design & Web Services, for adding the hiking figure to it.

Many thanks to Arizona Authors' Kathleen Cook for her counsel at crucial moments.

Huge thanks to Jessica Groenendijk for her excellent manuscript critique and recommending it to Donna Mulvenna at Stormbird Press. Thanks for Donna's adept guidance and Sabrina Davis's line edits. And special recognition to Margi Prideaux, publisher at Stormbird Press on Kangaroo Island, her staff and volunteers who suspended operations to battle bushfires at their doors and to manage a remarkable recovery.

And for a force equal to a huge fan club of one, my gratitude to Pam Bickell, sensitive editor and all-around enthusiast, for her guidance from early in the project to the very end.

Deepest thank you to my wife and pack leader, Kathleen Alden, for spousal patience and a gift for showing interest and empathy in a project that must have seemed interminable.

Epigraph Credits

Chapter 1 epigraph: Writer Ann Patchett's comments can be found on journalist Richard Grant's website http://www.richardgrant.us/ taken from his original interview which appeared in the U. K.'s Telegraph, 7 November 2013.

Chapter 2 epigraph: Kathy Kirsh quoted by writer Eliza Murphy, *Caught in the Headlights,* High Country News, 7 February 2005.

Chapter 3 epigraph: Matthew J. Nelson and the Arizona Trail Association. *Arizona National Scenic Trail*, Wilderness Press, 2014, p. 75.

Chapter 4 epigraph: Wildlife biologist William Newmark on a simple evolutionary fact: how large predators survived in Africa when many were driven extinct in the Americas after the arrival of Homo sapiens. Quoted in *Rewilding the World,* Dispatches from the Conservation Revolution, by Caroline Fraser, Metropolitan Books, 2014.

Chapter 5 epigraph: Peter Alagona, Associate Professor of History, Geography, and Environmental Studies at U.C. California, Santa Barbara: *Concrete jungle: cities adapt to growing ranks of coyotes, cougars and other urban wildlife,* 1 July 2015. Professor Alagona is also author of *The Accidental Ecosystem: People and Wildlife in*

American Cities, University of California Press, 2022.

Chapter 6 epigraph: Elizabeth Marshall Thomas, *The Hidden Life of Dogs*, Mariner Books, 2010.

Chapter 7 epigraph: Philosopher and animal rights advocate Peter Singer, *Animal Liberation*, New York, HarperCollins, 1975, p. 150. The writer also acknowledges the use of a short passage from Peter Singer's *Animal Liberation*, quoted by Jesse in Chapter 5, p. 41-42.

Chapter 8 epigraph: Poet Richard Shelton, *Going Back to Bisbee*, University of Arizona Press, 1992.

Chapter 9 epigraph: Kierán Suckling, Executive Director, Center for Biological Diversity, e-mail to the author, 30 January 2019.

Chapter 10 epigraph: Deb Duncan, Westie owner and trainer, *Popular Dogs Series Magazine*, Vol. 36, 2004, p. 20. Her website: "Come, Sit, Stay … Canine Etiquette Behavior & Training Consultations," www.thedogspeaks.com

Chapter 11 epigraph: Anne Sanders, past president of the West Highland White Terrier Club of America. *Popular Dogs Series Magazine,* Vol. 36, 2004, p. 14. Quoted by Deb Duncan who noted that Anne Sanders has bred, shown, and trained her Westies in all areas of competition for 30 years.

Chapter 12 epigraph: World Wildlife Fund, 29 October   2018.

https://www.worldwildlife.org/press-releases/wwf-reportreveals-staggering-extent-of-human-impact-on-planet

Chapter 13 epigraph: From the book *The Emotional Lives of Animals*. Copyright © 2007 by Marc Bekoff. Reprinted with permission of New World Library, Novato, CA. www.newworldlibrary.com, Preface xxi. Emeritus professor Marc Bekoff's main fields are animal behavior and cognitive ethology.

Chapter 14 epigraph: Deb Duncan, *Popular Dogs Series Magazine,* Vol. 36, 2004, p. 15. Her website: "Come, Sit, Stay ... Canine Etiquette Behavior & Training Consultations," www.thedogspeaks.com Also, in chapter 14, p. 102, the writer acknowledges the use of a short quote from John Steinbeck's *Travels with Charlie,* New York, Penguin Books, 1980.

Chapter 15 epigraph: U.S. National Park Service park ranger motto, quoted by Jerry Smith, Snohomish County (Washington State) Park Ranger, e-mail to the author, 18 May 2019. Quote from https://www.rd.com/advice/travel/park-rangers/.

Chapter 16 epigraph: Author/Essayist Edward Abbey, *Desert Solitaire*, p. 162-63, New York; Random House, 1968.

Chapter 17 epigraph: U.S. National Parks Service Junior park ranger motto. "The Junior Ranger motto is recited by children around the country; each taking an oath of their own to

protect parks, continue to learn about parks, and share their own ranger story with friends and family."
https://www.nps.gov/kids/jrrangers.cfm.

Chapter 18 epigraph: Jack London, *The Call of the Wild*, 1903, end of chapter 2. http://www.classicreader.com/book/73/2/.

Chapter 19 epigraph: Rich Landers, *Trail cams, GPS a big boost for wildlife research,* The Spokesman-Review, 26 July 2015.

Chapter 20 epigraph: Center for Biological Diversity, e-mail to the author, 15 April 2019. Arizona only recently banned organized contests where hunters try to kill the most coyotes or other wildlife predators for prizes such as cash or hunting equipment. The ban took effect in November 2019. Washington State has joined to ban wildlife-killing contests, making it the seventh state to enact such a measure.

Chapter 21 epigraph: Pro-tracker Susan Morse, quoted in *Sonorensis: Jaguar, Arizona*—Sonora Desert Museum, Winter 2008, p. 41.

Chapter 22 epigraph: Biologist Sergio Avila-Villegas, *The Jaguar and the Ph.D.,* https://doi.org/10.1371/journal.pbio.2004152. Published: 7 February 2018. The actual quote has been separated into two parts. Chapter 22 is part one.

Chapter 23 epigraph: Biologist Sergio Avila-Villegas, *The Jaguar and the Ph.D.,* https://doi.org/10.1371/journal.pbio.2004152.

Published: 7 February 2018. This is the second part of the quote from Chapter 22.

Chapter 24 epigraph: Mark Twain, *New Acquaintances—The Coyote, Roughing It,* Signet Classic, 1962, Chapter V, p. 50.

Chapter 25 epigraph: Shipherd Reed, Flandrau Science Center, University of Arizona, Shipherd Reed, Marketing & Communications, shipherd@email.arizona.edu.

Chapter 26 epigraph: Author/Essayist Edward Abbey, *Ed Abbey to Earth First!, The Earth First! Reader: Ten Years of Radical Environmentalism,* edited by John Davis (Gibbs Smith Publisher, Peregrine Smith Books, Salt Lake City, 1991), p. 248.

Chapter 27 epigraph: Michael Robinson at the Center for Biological Diversity, e-mail to author, 2 May 2019.

Chapter 28 epigraph: The Endangered Species Act of 1973, Department of the Interior, U.S. Fish & Wildlife Service, Washington, D.C. Definitions, Sec. 3 (19). The federal Endangered Species Act defines *take* as "to harass, harm, pursue, hunt, shoot, wound, kill, trap, capture or collect, or to attempt to engage in such conduct." https://www.fws.gov/endangered/esa-library/pdf/ESAall.pdf.

Chapter 29 epigraph: Excerpted from *Seeking Enlightenment ... Hat by Hat* by Nevada Barr. Copyright © 2003 by Nevada Barr. Published by G. P. Putnam's Sons.

Chapter 30 epigraph: Deb Duncan, Westie owner and dog trainer, *Popular Dogs Magazine*, Vol. 36, 2004, p.16. Deb Duncan, a dog behaviorist, has owned several different breeds, including Westies. Her website: "Come, Sit, Stay … Canine Etiquette Behavior & Training Consultations," www.thedogspeaks.com.

Chapter 31 epigraph: Biologist Sergio Avila-Villegas, *Northern Jaguars: View from the Field*, Desert Leaf Magazine, May 2017, p. 18.

Chapter 32 epigraph: Wildlife writer Jack Turner, *The Abstract Wild*, University of Arizona Press, 1996, p. 85.

Chapter 33 epigraph: Richard Mahler, *The Jaguar's Shadow: Searching for a Mythic Cat*, Yale University Press, 2009, p. 32.

Chapter 34 epigraph: Kieran Suckling, Executive Director, Center for Biological Diversity, e-mail to the author, 9 August 2016.

Chapter 35 epigraph: Sergio Avila-Villegas, *Northern Jaguars: View from the Field*, Desert Leaf Magazine, May 2017 p. 19.

Chapter 36 epigraph: Doug Peacock's oft-cited quote appears in *Beyond the Wall: Essays from the Outside*, Henry Holt and Co., 1971, p. 167. Doug Peacock's latest work, *Was It Worth It?: A Wilderness Warrior's Long Trail Home*, published by Patagonia, 2022.

Chapter 37 epigraph: Ecologist Bob Crabtree began studying coyotes in Yellowstone in the

1980s. Quoted in Ben Goldfarb's *The Forever War,* High Country News, 25 January 2016.

Chapter 38 epigraph: Environmental reporter Tony Davis, Arizona Daily Star, 13 January 2013.

Chapter 39 epigraph: Reporter Tony Davis, Arizona Daily Star, 13 January 2013.

Chapter 40 epigraph: Writer Edwin Dobb, *Still here: Can humans help other species defy extinction?* High Country News, 18 December 2000.

Chapter 41 epigraph: Walt Anderson quoted from a presentation the naturalist/artist delivered at the Prescott Public Library for the Regional Urban Wildlife Symposium, 20 October 2011, entitled *The Call of the Wild: Are We Listening?* See Anderson's *Borderlands Musings* and his website/blog:
http://www.geolobo.com/?page_id=34.

Chapter 42 epigraph: Camilla Fox, executive director of Project Coyote. Quoted in *The killing agency: Wildlife Services' brutal methods leave a trail of animal death,* by Tom Knudson, published in Sacramento Bee, 29 April 2012 http://www.projectcoyote.org/about/contact-us/e-m: info@projectcoyote.org. The fuller context of Fox's quote reads: "This is an ineffective, wasteful program that is largely unaccountable, lacks transparency and continues to rely on cruel and indiscriminate methods."

Chapter 43 epigraph: Melanie Culver, PhD, Lisa Haynes, PhD, and Kirk Emerson, PhD, authors of

University of Arizona's Jaguar Survey Project, Sonorensis, Winter 2013, p. 18.

Chapter 44 epigraph: David E Brown and Carlos A. Lopez Gonzalez, *Jaguars and People,* from *Borderland Jaguars*, University of Utah Press, 2001, p. 111.

Chapter 45 epigraph: Richard Mahler, *The Jaguar's Shadow: Searching for a Mythic Cat,* Yale University Press, 2009, p. 104, 108.

Chapter 46 epigraph: Writer and Naturalist Craig Childs, *The Animal Dialogues, Uncommon Encounters in the Wild*, "Raven," Little, Brown and Co., 1997/2007, p. 138.

Chapter 47 epigraph: Author/Essayist Edward Abbey, *Abbey on Books—And Gurus*, Samhain 1982, *The Earth First! Reader, Ten Years of Radical Environmentalism*, edited by John Davis, Gibbs Smith Publisher, Peregrine Smith Books, Salt Lake City, 1991, p. 157.

Chapter 48 epigraph: Deb Duncan, Westie owner and trainer, *Popular Dogs Series Magazine,* Vol. 36, 2004, p. 12. Duncan's website: "Come, Sit, Stay ... Canine Etiquette Behavior & Training Consultations," https://www.thedogspeaks.com/index.html. For years, Westies were introduced at the Westminster Kennel Club dog show as follows: "The Westie is possessed of no small amount of self-esteem, and the Westie will not tolerate being ignored."

Chapter 49 epigraph: Writer and Naturalist Jack Turner, *The Abstract Wild*, University of Arizona Press, 1996, p. 120.

Chapter 50 epigraph: Writer Kinky Friedman's Epilogue in *Elvis, Jesus & Coca-Cola,* as well as *Kinky's Celebrity Pet Files,* with the essay *Kinky and Cuddles* (p. 53-54), which concludes with the quote. https://kinkyfriedman.com.

Epilogue epigraph: Norwegian philosopher Arne Naess, *Ecology, community and lifestyle.* Cambridge University Press, 1989, pp. 164-65.